*The rat began to gnaw the rope
the rope began to hang the butcher
the butcher began to kill the ox
the ox began to drink the water...*

—MOTHER GOOSE

THE RAT BEGAN TO GNAW THE ROPE

C. W. GRAFTON

Edited, with an introduction and notes,
by Leslie S. Klinger

LIBRARY OF CONGRESS

Poisoned Pen PRESS

Copyright © 1943, 2020 by C. W. Grafton
Introduction and notes © 2020 by Leslie S. Klinger
Cover and internal design © 2020 by Sourcebooks and Library of Congress
Cover design by Heather Morris/Sourcebooks

Sourcebooks, Poisoned Pen Press, and the colophon
are registered trademarks of Sourcebooks.

Cover image: *Eliminate Crime in the Slums Through Housing.* Federal Art
Project, 1936. Works Projects Administration Poster Collection, Prints &
Photographs Division, Library of Congress, LC-DIG-ppmsca-52154.

Published by Poisoned Pen Press, an imprint of Sourcebooks,
in association with the Library of Congress
P.O. Box 4410, Naperville, Illinois 60567-4410
(630) 961-3900
sourcebooks.com

The Rat Began to Gnaw the Rope was first published in 1943 by Farrar & Rinehart.
A notation in the Library of Congress's first edition copy states it is a "war edition,"
meaning the novel's complete text appears at reduced size to comply with paper
conservation orders of the War Production Board during World War II.

Library of Congress Cataloging-in-Publication Data is on file with the publisher.

Printed and bound in the United States of America.
SB 10 9 8 7 6 5 4 3 2 1

This book is for Viv, Ann, and Sue for reasons which they will understand.

CONTENTS

FOREWORD

Crime writing as we know it first appeared in 1841, with the publication of *The Murders in the Rue Morgue*. Written by American author Edgar Allan Poe, the short story introduced C. Auguste Dupin, the world's first wholly fictional detective. Other American and British authors had begun working in the genre by the 1860s, and by the 1920s, we had officially entered the Golden Age of Detective Fiction.

Throughout this short history, many authors who paved the way have been lost or forgotten. Library of Congress Crime Classics bring back into print some of the finest American crime writing from the 1860s to the 1960s, showcasing rare and lesser-known titles that represent a range of genres, from "cozies" to police procedurals. With cover designs inspired by images from the Library's collections, each book in this series includes the original text, as well as a contextual introduction, brief biography of the author, notes, recommendations for further reading, and suggested discussion questions. Our hope is for these books to start conversations, inspire further research, and bring obscure works to a new generation of readers.

The Rat Began to Gnaw the Rope chronicles a young lawyer's dogged pursuit of the truth. Like so many other hard-boiled and noir stories, the action begins when a beautiful young woman saunters into a man's office with a request for help. As Gil Henry's investigation of possible stock fraud begins to unravel a wealthy family's scandalous secrets, it quickly becomes clear that his intrusions are not welcome. The car he is driving is sabotaged, and the resulting accident leaves him bloodied, bruised, and needing a new suit. The battered lawyer presses his investigation in a variety of ill-fitting pants and, in the process, manages to antagonize nearly everyone he meets, including his client. Cornelius Warren Grafton's amusing mix of noir and hard-boiled detective fiction earned him the 1943 Mary Roberts Rinehart Award.

Early American crime fiction is not only entertaining to read, it also sheds light on the culture of its time. While many of the titles in this series include outmoded language and stereotypes now considered offensive—Gil Henry's decision to smack his female client in the face, grab her hands, and address her as "little Bopeep" seems unthinkable today—it's fascinating to read these books and reflect on the evolution of our society's perceptions of race, gender, ethnicity, and social standing.

The "War Note" Grafton appended to the novel is another reflection of its time. Although World War II does not figure into the plot of the novel—which was published in 1943—it was clearly at the forefront of the mind of the author, who served as a military deception officer in the India-Burma Theater.

More dark secrets and bloody deeds lurk in the massive collections of the Library of Congress. I encourage you to explore these works for yourself, here in Washington, D.C., or online at www.loc.gov.

—Carla D. Hayden, Librarian of Congress

INTRODUCTION

As a writer, Cornelius Warren "Chip" Grafton may be fairly described as overlooked, underappreciated, or even forgotten. If he is remembered at all today, it is as the father of Sue Grafton, best-selling author of 25 mystery novels about her detective Kinsey Millhone and who was named a Grand Master by the Mystery Writers of America in 2009. Only four of his books were published, three of them mysteries. Yet his first book, *The Rat Began to Gnaw the Rope,*[*] can be seen as the first of many to infuse American crime writing with humor.

Sue Grafton testifies that her father loved reading mysteries, and inevitably his library must have included the popular fiction of the day. By the late 1920s, when Chip Grafton was a teen, authors such as Earl Derr Biggers, Ellery Queen, S. S. Van Dine, W. R. Burnett, and Dashiell Hammett had revitalized American crime writing, and police detectives and private investigators appeared regularly in best-sellers. Though the work of Biggers, Queen, and Van Dine was very much in the tradition of the so-called "fair play" mysteries that pervaded British crime writing, writers like Burnett and Hammett pioneered realism in crime

---

[*]Grafton apparently intended an eight-book series, all with titles from the old English nursery rhyme reproduced elsewhere in this volume, though only two were completed; a partial manuscript of the third volume is owned by his family.

fiction, creating stories about average men and women caught up in crimes.

The 1930s saw American crime writing continue to thrive, with the appearance of new talents like Earl Stanley Gardner, creator of the tough-minded lawyer-protagonist Perry Mason; Rex Stout, author of the Nero Wolfe series; and Zenith Jones Brown, who wrote (as David Frome) English-style murder mysteries for her protagonist Colonel Pinkerton and (as Leslie Ford) American-based crime fiction. Yet the tone of the work of all of these fine writers of the "hard-boiled" mystery school and early noir films like *The Maltese Falcon* was *serious*—comedy need not apply.

Grafton had a different idea. His protagonist is not a professional investigator—Gilmore "Gil" Henry is a young lawyer, probably around the same age as Grafton.* He has no desire to be a detective. Instead, a young female client hires him to look into the value of shares of stock of the Harper Products Company that dominates the nearby town of Harpersville. Dubious that he can help her, only when he finds himself to be a target of violence does he resolve to pursue the investigation.

Henry is in many ways an anti-hero—physically soft, short, "pudgy," "no great shakes at drinking," and admittedly unattractive to women. He's not especially educated in any technical areas—he doesn't understand accounting or taxes—but he is smart and self-deprecating. And Henry is funny, responding to tense situations with wisecracks and joking references. Above all, he is relentless. Nothing—not bullets, not beatings, not warnings, not even removal from the scene of the crimes—stops him from coming back to the case.

The sins involved in the case are all too common: sex-related scandals, harmful cover-ups, and above all, crimes committed

---

*The publication of the book in 1943 suggests that it must have been written either just before Grafton left for military service in 1942 or completed during his service. Grafton was thirty-three in 1942. Henry is the youngest name partner in his small firm, only recently joining the partnership, likely making him around thirty.

out of hunger for power and greed. Here, in early 1941, the Depression era is clearly over—there are no poor or unemployed in the tale—and Gil Henry moves comfortably among the working-class, the college-educated, and the wealthy. There are also a number of professionals in the case, a class Grafton himself knew well—accountants, stock brokers, doctors, and lawyers—and while a few are trustworthy, several have strayed far from their expected roles as reliable advisers.

The story, set at the dawn of America's involvement in World War II, depicts an insular world. This is small-town America, with unsophisticated law enforcement, a town dominated by a wealthy family, an abundance of secrets, and an absence of people of color (except for "Negro boys" at the grocery store and hotel, and a "colored waiter" at the hospital). Yet Gil Henry is more urbane than the reader might expect. He reminds us of the larger world of culture and sports with offhand references to popular figures. As an outsider to Harpersville, he is clear-eyed about things that residents have simply taken for granted, whether it is egg-farming or how the McClure family came by its money.

The characterization of women in the tale is emblematic of this time, just before women played such an important role in the war. The principal women are all educated: Ruth McClure and Janet Harper are college graduates, and the other key women characters are a schoolteacher and a nurse. Yet women are largely passive in the story: Mrs. Harper is an invalid, Ruth McClure is helpless to find out the truth, Janet Harper spends her time on sports, the enigmatic Miss Katie takes action only in response to a direct threat, and the others simply watch. The male protagonists have little use for these women other than as objects or means to an end, and even Gil Henry impulsively kisses and later slaps Ruth McClure and kisses Janet Harper without invitation.

The book merits our attention on several levels. First, as

in the case of all of the books we've selected for inclusion as a Library of Congress Crime Classic, it is a valuable picture of American life at a specific date in our country's history, with an accurate portrayal of the attitudes and behaviors of the time. Second, it helped shape the future of crime writing, as books like *The Rat Began...* lightened the mood of crime fiction and enhanced the pleasure of the regular reader. Third, it is a cracking good mystery, with secrets, murders and violence aplenty, a town full of suspects, and a dramatic denouement. So drive on down the road to Harpersville and enjoy the ride!

—Leslie S. Klinger

1

My secretary said that there was a Miss Ruth McClure to see me and I said that she could come on in. The girl who stood in the doorway a moment later was small and lovely but she was obviously very unhappy and looked as if she were not sure she wanted to come in after all.

I stood up because it seemed to be the right thing to do, and then I waited. When my secretary had closed the door, she came over to the desk but before I could offer her a seat, she said without any preliminaries:

"I want you to find out for me how much some stock is worth."

Ordinarily people tell me who they are and ask me who I am before starting right in to business but she didn't, so I didn't. I tried to look interested and said:

"Corporate stock?"

"Yes."

"Is it listed on an exchange?"

"Yes."

"Well," I said, "there oughtn't to be any trouble about that. Sit down and we'll find out in ten minutes."

I reached for the telephone but she made a gesture as if to stop me.

"You don't understand. I don't want to know what you can get for it. I want to know what it is worth."

I was a little puzzled. I sat down and then stood up and held a chair for her. Then I walked around back of the desk again and played with the paperweight. We eyed each other for a moment and then I said:

"Start from the beginning."

"That is all there is to it. I just wanted to know what some stock is worth."

I pulled a scratch pad toward me.

"What's the name of the corporation?"

"Harper Products Company."

"That's at Harpersville, isn't it?"

"Yes."

"What makes you think the value differs from the trading price? It's a big company and the stock is bought and sold every day. It publishes financial statements and people know about these things."

She put her pocketbook on the desk.

"My father was killed in an automobile accident ten days ago. He was one of the foremen for Harper Products Company. He had some of the stock and all I know is that he told me several times if anything happened to him I was to hold tight. Once I remember we were driving past the main plant and he pointed up to the big sign and said: 'Remember this. There is more here than you can see from the outside.' That's all I know. I want you to find out what the stock is worth."

I said: "Any more ideas?"

She picked up her pocketbook again and put it in her lap and snapped the fastening two or three times.

"Only that somebody wants to pay me more than the market quotation."

"Who?"

"Mr. William Jasper Harper."

"William Jasper Harper himself?"

"Yes, the old man himself."

"Why?"

"He says he wants to help me out."

"You think he's really got another reason?"

"I don't know. I just want to find out."

"He and your father great friends or something?"

"They knew each other. Possibly better than Mr. Harper knew most in the plant, but then my father had worked there a long time. Nothing unusual as far as I know."

"Why didn't you take it?"

"I don't think William Jasper Harper is a philanthropist and I don't understand what is going on. I think I ought to know what the stock is worth."

I started to say: "Yeah, you said that before," but didn't. What I said was: "If you aren't willing to accept the financial statements, there isn't much you can do unless you want to spend some money and maybe raise some hell if you have to. If you just go asking for information, they will simply hand you the annual statement and there you are."

She opened her handbag and brought out a checkbook.

"There are a hundred shares and at the time my father first got them I understand they were worth something over a hundred dollars a share. Now it seems the company is not making much with raw materials being pretty high and the stock is quoted at about twenty-three dollars a share. I can't spend a great deal but I think I could pay you to go to Harpersville and spend a day or two finding out whatever you can. Would that cost very much?"

"Whatever I charged you would probably be more than the results are worth. I'll be glad to go if you want and do the best I can but my guess is that if the stock is selling for twenty-three dollars, it's worth just twenty-three dollars. Put away your checkbook. We can decide about a fee later. How much did you say he is offering you for the stock?"

"I didn't say."

"Well, how much *is* he offering you?"

"One hundred and ten dollars a share."

I don't know whether my mouth physically dropped open but it certainly did so mentally. I didn't say anything because I couldn't think of anything to say. She didn't say anything either. She got up as if the interview were at an end and said:

"Then you will come down. I hope you will come as soon as possible. I'll write down my address and telephone number in Harpersville and you can get in touch with me if you need me. Shouldn't I leave you something for expenses?"

"No, it isn't but twenty-five miles and I'll drive down. The expenses won't be a big item."

She handed me the slip of paper with the address and phone number and went to the door. With her hand on the knob she stopped and looked thoughtful a moment.

"There's something else that may be important. There is a condition."

I waited.

"He says he wants to help me straighten out my father's affairs. He says I'm to turn over everything to him and he and his lawyers will handle everything."

She went out and closed the door. If there were a couple of puzzled wrinkles between my eyebrows at that moment, they were certainly in their proper place.

I went out into the reception room and jerked my thumb at Mr. Mead's door inquiringly. Myrtle contrived a combination of shaking her head and shrugging her shoulders which I took to mean that there was no reason why I shouldn't go in, so I knocked on the glass panel and walked in without waiting for an answer.

Mr. James Mead is the senior partner of the law firm which trickles out to practically nothing by the time it gets to me. He is six feet tall which lets him look over the top of my head without a great deal of difficulty and he has a ruddy complexion and a bristling mustache cut close and neat at all times, just beginning to be gray in spots. Mr. Mead is probably forty-five years old. I said:

"Is there any reason why I shouldn't be hired to look into the affairs of Harper Products Company?"

I knew that he had been seeing a lot of Janet Harper and I wanted to make sure that I was not getting into something that would displease the boss. He said:

"Who wants you to look into them and for what?"

"A young lady. She has inherited some stock and wants to know what it is worth. She won't accept market quotations. Wants to pay me to go down and see what I can find out."

"Better get paid in advance. The odds are you won't find anything and then she won't want to pay you."

"I'm sorry. She wanted to pay in advance and I wouldn't let her."

He lit a cigar and blew out the smoke slowly.

"Well, it wouldn't amount to much anyway."

"No reason why I shouldn't do it?"

He seemed a little annoyed. He knew perfectly well that I was asking because he had been showing a great deal of interest in William Jasper Harper's daughter and I am not sure that he liked it. He said: "Of course not," rather shortly and that was the end of that.

2

Being unmarried and with no family connections, I live demurely at the YMCA. I came in from a picture show around 9:30 that evening and found a message that I was to call Operator Two in Harpersville.* I recognized Miss McClure's voice immediately. She was a little excited.

"Is this Mr. Henry?"

I admitted that it was.

"I forgot to tell you. Mr. Harper wanted an answer yesterday and I didn't give it to him."

I didn't think the information was of great importance and was about to say so but she went on:

"I have been trying to get you ever since I got home. Someone broke into the house today and apparently made a thorough search."

"Why didn't you call the police?"

"There's nothing missing that I can see. I want you to come down."

"Now?"

---

*It was not uncommon, even in the 1940s, for a caller to ask an operator working for the telephone company to relay a message to a recipient who failed to answer a call (in this case, "Operator Two" in Harpersville). This seems a bit unusual, however, for a caller to a law firm, who would have had a receptionist to take messages.

"Just as soon as you can get here."

"Car's being repaired. Tomorrow OK?"

"Can't you come tonight? Get a U-Drive-It.* I'll wait up for you."

I didn't want to go and the whole thing sounded absurd but I couldn't sit and talk all night so I said noncommittally:

"I'll see what I can do."

She said: "Thanks. Don't think I'm silly. I'll wait for you," and hung up.

Mr. Mead has two or three cars and in a pinch we can always get one of them for firm business. I called his residence and when he came to the phone I said:

"This is Gil."

"All right."

"The lady in Harpersville is all excited and insists that I drive down right now. My car is in the garage. Could I take the Ford?"

He did not answer me for a long moment.

"Sure you're not getting into something?"

"I don't know."

"All right. The car will be parked in front of the house. You can pick it up whenever you like."

That was all there was to say but he held the receiver so I held on at my end. It must have been ten seconds before the click came.

---

*That is to say, a rental car. Rent-a-Car, Inc. (later Hertz) was founded in 1916 and was sold to John Hertz in 1923. Hertz in turn sold the company to General Motors, which owned it until the 1950s. Another early competitor was Saunders Drive-It-Yourself System, founded in 1915, which had expanded to eighty-five cities by 1927. The "U-Drive-It Corporation" is known to have issued stock as early as 1925, but whether the name simply became generic or the company continued to conduct business in various localities is unclear.

3

Hawthorne Place is wide and curving with magnificent trees on both sides and it is really one of the snazzy places to live. I paid my cab driver in front of the Mead residence and found the Ford parked in the shadows with the keys wedged up on the top of the sun visor as usual. I checked to see that the oil and gas were in good shape and then made a U-turn contrary to the statutes in such cases made and provided. As I reached the city limits I turned on the radio and caught a hot swing band with one of these women crooners who sounds as if she has gallstones. It was starting to rain a little and the black-top road was shiny like seals in the circus. This was before Pearl Harbor* and no one was thinking about a rubber shortage, so I stepped right along at probably sixty miles an hour as is my custom when uninhibited. The run to Harpersville took no time at all and presently I came over a rise and could see the lights of the town a mile or so away. I was about halfway down the steep hill when there was a sharp explosion and the car jumped and twisted under me like a hula dancer. I went down that hill in a wild zigzag, keeping to the

---

*The surprise attack by Imperial Japanese military forces on the U.S. naval base at Pearl Harbor in Honolulu occurred on December 7, 1941. While the United States was assembling its armory preparatory to entering World War II and for much of the war, rubber was in short supply for civilian uses (such as automobile tires).

road for fifty or seventy-five yards by pressing my hundred and eighty pounds against the wheel and trying to anticipate each move. Then I went into a spin and the last thing I heard was the high whine of the tires skidding sidewise.

I ought to be dead. How many times the car turned over I don't know but when I came to, I was hanging halfway out of the door by the driver's seat and the car was upright some thirty feet off the road down a slight incline. I felt terrible and on top of the bruises and knots, I was soaked to the skin as far down as my hips.

I crawled out with considerable effort, got the flashlight out of the glove compartment, and saw that the left rear tire was not only flat but chewed to ribbons, as I thought. I crawled up the bank on my hands and knees and started walking toward Harpersville and pretty soon the headlights of a car picked me up and I got a ride with a farmer and his wife. Just as I started to get into the car I thought of something, begged their pardon, closed the door and started back up the hill. I could see they thought I was crazy and I guess I thought so myself, but I suddenly wanted to know something and decided it couldn't wait.

I went back to the wreck, propped the flashlight against a rock, took off what was left of that left rear tire and went over it as carefully as if I had been looking for fleas. I didn't know what I was looking for and I didn't find it at first. Then I went over the rim with my fingertips and suddenly felt something that made me stop and take a glance with the flashlight. I looked inside the casing and then looked around in the weeds but I knew that was hopeless. On an off-chance I picked up the tube and shook it. Something was inside. I split open the tube with a piece of broken glass and put what I found in my pocket. Then I walked on in to Harpersville.

4

I guess it was nearly midnight when I got to the square in Harpersville. Everything was closed down for the night and I went into the Hotel Harper where the desk clerk was dozing in a chair behind the counter. He jumped up and glared at the way I was dripping on his rug but I was in no mood to make explanations. I asked for the telephone and he nodded toward a booth in the back corner of the lobby. I entered the booth and then went back and got two or three dollars in change and it was apparent that the desk clerk still wished that I wouldn't drip on his rug although I guess I looked so tough he hesitated to complain about it.

I put through a call to the Mead home back in the city and shifted my weight impatiently until I heard Mr. James Mead's sleepy voice at the other end. I said:

"This is Gil Henry. I'm in Harpersville. Does anyone want you to be dead?"

I could almost hear him wake up.

"What do you mean?"

"Just that. Who would want to kill you?"

He said cautiously: "Are you drunk?"

"No, but I don't know why I'm not dead. I had a wreck in the

Ford. I've got in my pocket something that looks like a soft nose .38 slug that was not put in my tire by the manufacturer. Who knew I was coming to Harpersville?"

"There was a party going on here when you called and I didn't make any secret of it. I couldn't just walk out of the house without explaining to my guests so I told them that my junior partner had a hurry call to Harpersville and was coming by for one of the cars. Are you sure about what you said?"

"The explosion didn't sound like a blowout. When I got to thinking about it, I thought it came from a distance. You can't tell anything from the tire but there's a big dent in the rim and I have the slug in my pocket. I didn't tell anyone I was coming. Who were your guests? Never mind, I'll talk to you about it later. Better write out a list before you forget and we'll look over it some other time."

He said: "Are you badly hurt? Have you seen a doctor?"

I told him I hadn't but I would if I needed one. Then I hung up and called Ruth McClure. I told her what had happened and that I had better get a room at the hotel and get these wet clothes off. She pointed out very sensibly that I would have to have some dry clothes and I told her that was not the half of it, I would have to have some new ones. One leg of my trousers was split open and there was a gash down the back of my coat. She insisted that I come out to her place, but remembering my YMCA connections I took the precaution of asking did she think that would be proper and what would the neighbors think. She was very emphatic about the neighbors and, hell, I'm no puritan, so the next thing I walked right past the desk clerk without saying a word and strolled out into the rain again. I looked back and saw that he was still brooding about where I had dripped on the rug.

I have a bad habit of thinking of things at the wrong time. I doubled back into the lobby and dripped on the rug again while I asked the desk clerk if by any chance he had back numbers of the local newspapers—back to, say, two weeks ago. He said he didn't so I went out again.

5

I would be a lot better off if I didn't think so much. I found Ruth McClure's house, a small cottage that could have used a coat of paint. She was in the door with the light behind her and I should have noticed how pretty she was, but instead, because I think too damn much, I stood and dripped on the door mat and said:

"Where did your father get ten thousand dollars?"

It took her about two seconds to follow me and then she frowned and said:

"I never thought of that. He never had that much money in his life. Come in and get out of those wet clothes. The water heater is on and you can have a hot bath. You will probably want some whiskey too. Tim's clothes will fit you like a circus tent but you can roll up anything you trip on."

I said: "Who's Tim?"

"Tim McClure."

"Who's he?"

"He lives here."

That didn't answer my question and I said so. She took my shoulders and pushed me into the living room without caring whether I dripped or not.

"Don't be silly. You can find out some other time."

Then she pushed me toward an open door and I saw dry clothes and a pint bottle and I could hear hot water running in the bathroom. I suddenly realized again how I felt and without bothering to do anything else first, I drank out of that bottle until I choked and sputtered. I am no great shakes at drinking and I thought the lining of my throat and a good part of the alimentary canal, as a matter of fact, would never be the same again. It did feel good though and almost instantly a big lump of warmth radiated through me.

I am no ladies' man and girls have never thought much of my short pudgy figure and I do not know why I do things like this. But as a matter of fact, with that whiskey inside of me and hot water running in the next room I felt so much better I took Miss Ruth McClure by the shoulders and kissed her on the cheek with astonishing warmth before I pushed her out and closed the door. In the moving pictures it seems that people do this every day and think nothing of it, but I was rather appalled at the thought of what I had done and wondered again who Tim McClure might be and how big.

6

I tell you, I never think of things at logical times. I got out of the bath tub with soap all over me and wrapped a towel around my middle and peered into the living room from behind the door. I said:

"Don't look now but who knew I was coming down here?"

"Nobody. I didn't tell a soul. Of course, Tim. He was here. But nobody else."

"You didn't tell me who Tim is."

"Never mind, I'll tell you later. You get some clothes on."

"Tell me now."

"All right. My father adopted him. That was years ago. He has been Tim McClure as long as I can remember."

Well, that was that. I got back into the tub and almost immediately stuck my head around the door again and said:

"How old were you when Tim was adopted?"

She thought a minute.

"I don't remember. I am told I was about two."

"How long ago was that?"

She looked at me and made a face:

"Rather a roundabout way of getting at it, but I am twenty-eight."

"I'm thirty myself."

I went back and finished my bath but I was not through with what I was thinking about and made a mental note to ask another question in my inimitable way.

7

I began to get a pretty good idea of what Tim McClure might look like when I tried to put on the suit I found on the bed. It may not have been a zoot suit* but the way I wore it, it certainly had a drape shape. I rolled up probably eight inches around my ankles and the overlap at my waistline was something to look at. The shoulders of the coat hung down almost to my elbows and, of course, my hands were clear out of sight up the sleeves. No wonder Miss Ruth McClure laughed when she saw me. I was a dead ringer for the smallest of the seven dwarfs and sure enough she called me Dopey.

I asked her where the stock certificates were and she got a black tin box off of the mantelpiece. It was an ordinary cheap tin box, rather flimsy, with a built-in lock of the type that is just the next thing to being no lock at all. The top was badly twisted where someone had pried it open with something like a screwdriver. Before I looked inside I said:

"This was part of the search, I see."

"Yes."

"Anything missing?"

---

*Popular with young men in Latino, African American, Italian American, and Filipino American communities in the 1940s, the zoot suit featured high-waisted trousers and a long coat with wide lapels and wide padded shoulders. Wearing a suit much too large for himself could have made Gil Henry look like he was wearing a zoot suit. A "drape shape" was a slang description of the jacket style.

"I don't think so but I can't be sure. There was nothing of value in it except the stock certificate and it's still there."

The stock certificate was the top thing. It was a single certificate for one hundred shares of the common capital stock of Harper Products Company. It was made out in the name of John H. McClure and was dated in May, 1915. I turned it over in my hands once or twice while I was thinking of something else.

"Is this the only stock he had in Harper Products Company?"

"I think that's all the stock he had in any company. I never heard him mention any other."

"How much did he make at the company?"

She looked down at her hands and said:

"Not very much. The wages at Harper have never been very high."

"How much?"

"Thirty-five dollars a week. It used to be less."*

I thought that over for a moment.

"You went to college."

It was not a question. She nodded.

"Where?"

"Sweetwater."†

"Tim?"

"Princeton."

I got up and walked around the room until one trouser leg came unwound and I tripped on it, nearly pulling my pants off. She said:

"Now that you put it that way, it does seem odd. I wonder why it never occurred to me before."

"What kind of car did you have?"

---

*For perspective, the U.S. minimum wage in 1941 was $0.30 per hour, or $12.00 per week. The relative wage for a production worker like Mr. McClure earning $35 per week in 1941 is $1,878 per week in 2019. Using the relative price index, $10,000 would be the equivalent of over $135,000 in 2019. Samuel H. Williamson, "Purchasing Power Today of a US Dollar Transaction in the Past," MeasuringWorth, 2019, https://www.measuringworth.com/calculators/ppowerus/.

†Presumably Sweetwater College, in Sweetwater, TN, now defunct.

"A Buick."

"New?"

She was thinking too. She said:

"He traded nearly every year."

She did not like what I was thinking about and I didn't like it myself either. Something else began to gnaw around in the back of my mind and I got up to walk around some more but remembered the trouser legs and sat down again. The big coat hung around me like a horse blanket. I tried to be gentle with my next question: "You say he was killed in an accident?"

She nodded.

"Where?"

"On the long hill north…" She broke off with her eyes wide open and I found that I was standing up. She was on her feet at the same time and her hands were clasped tight in front of her.

"Was he alone?"

"Yes."

"Night?"

"Yes."

"Where is the car now?"

"I don't know. I guess it was brought in with a wrecker or something. It was not there the next day."

The coat was of rough material and I didn't have anything on under it except a cotton undershirt. My shoulders began to itch and I scratched first one and then the other by squirming around inside.

"I guess there is someone at the police station all night, isn't there?"

She said: "I suppose so."

I looked around and saw the telephone on a table by the door to what I assumed was the kitchen. I jerked my head toward it and said: "Call 'em. Tell them who you are and you want to know where your father's car is."

"Now?"

"Right now."

"Won't it look funny at this time of night?"

"What I'm thinking isn't funny at all."

Without another word she went over and picked up the phone. She had some difficulty getting what she wanted but she finally came back and stood in front of me. "He was taking a nap and was slightly profane but the car was taken, he thinks, to the lot outside of Harbison's Garage. He said it was beyond repair."

I went to the door and looked out. The rain had practically stopped but there was a faint misty drizzle and the damp air made me shiver. Someone was coming up the walk and I waited to see who it was. Before he came into the light, I thought it might be Primo Carnera.* He was enormous and he was looking at me intently with an expression I could have done without. I wasn't afraid, you understand, but the damp air was quite chilly and I thought it best to back into the room so I wouldn't catch pneumonia. I had been exposed once before that evening and I didn't want to get sick. I was glad that Miss McClure went to the door so Gargantua† could see I was not a housebreaker.

I could almost swear that he had to turn sideways to come in the door but maybe that was an optical illusion. He took his eyes off of me and said to Ruth: "Who's Dopey?"

I drew myself up to my full five feet seven inches, but I cannot truthfully say that I did so with dignity because after all who can be dignified in the kind of getup I had on?

Even at odd moments I am not unobservant and I saw an expression in the eyes of Miss McClure that did not look to me like the way a sister looks at a brother.

She said: "Tim, this is Mr. Henry, a lawyer I asked to come down from the city. Someone searched the house and you weren't here and I didn't know what to do."

He didn't change expression and if even his eyelids moved

---

*Primo Carnera (1906–1967) was 6'6" tall and weighed nearly 300 pounds; he was the World Heavyweight Boxing Champion from 1933 to 1934.

†A giant, the subject of François Rabelais's sixteenth-century comic novels *Gargantua and Pantagruel*.

I didn't see it and I was watching. He looked at me and his face did not change but he was laughing inside himself. You could tell that. "What do you want with a lawyer?" I gathered lawyers did not rate very high with him. He might have been referring to Pekingese dogs. "My suit?"

I thought it was about time for me to assert myself although I had to clear my throat after the first start and try again. I finally managed: "I was in a wreck and got rained on. You can bet I didn't pick this outfit at Marshall Field's."* Then I said: "Where's your gun?"

He looked from me to Ruth. "What's his angle?"

"He's here because I asked him and he nearly got killed. Someone shot out a tire. He's got more curiosity than an old maid and his mind is so sharp it's about to cut his ears off."

He looked at me with new interest but rather skeptically if I may say so. The description of my mind was a new idea to me and I think I put my hand up and touched one ear with nothing particular in mind of course. I said: "You are Tim McClure. I think you had better take me on credit for the time being. Right now I am in a hurry and you can get your explanation later. I want to go to Harbison's Garage and I would rather not get wet again. What would you suggest?"

He shifted his mental gears right in front of my eyes and I could see that the questioning was temporarily postponed. "Car's outside. You can tell me about it on the way." He looked at Ruth: "You coming?"

She looked at me. I said no one would be likely to search the house twice in the same evening and the next thing she and I were crowded into what was left of the front seat. Mr. Tim McClure either changed his mind or expected me to start talking which I didn't do. I had the flashlight with me and we had no trouble finding the remains of the Buick on the lot behind Harbison's. Someone had jacked up the rear axle and the left rear wheel was gone, tire, tube and all.

---

*A popular Chicago-based chain of department stores.

8

I said: "Come on," and started back toward Tim's car on the run. They didn't ask me any questions but were close behind me. I tripped on a pants leg again but I never hit the ground because a tremendous paw got me by the back of the neck just in time. I was practically paralyzed and would much rather have fallen on my face in the mud. He swung me up with that grip on the back of my neck like a mother dog carries a pup and when I found that there were no bones broken, I was wedged between them and the motor was running. I did not feel in any mood to talk and I am not sure I was physically able to do so, but I managed to point and we went through the dark streets taking corners on two wheels. In about five minutes I indicated he was to slow down and presently I could see the place where my car had left the road. I scrambled down the bank with the flashlight feeling its way in front of me and when I saw the front cushion out on the ground I knew exactly what I was going to find. The jack was under the rear axle and the wheel with the flat tire was missing.

I looked up and found that Tim was watching me intently. How he kept from breaking out in a rash of questions I don't know but when I started back up the bank toward the road he and Ruth were right with me. This time I held up the trouser legs at the knees so I wouldn't fall. I crawled in under the wheel and we put Ruth between us. As we started slowly up the hill I told Tim to keep a watch on his side for tracks where a car might have turned off the road. There wasn't a thing all the way to the top, but about fifty yards farther there was a gravel road on my side and I turned into it. Almost at once I could see tracks that turned off down the hill parallel to the highway behind the thick underbrush.

There was no doubt about it. This was the place. A car had been in there and then back again. Up in the fringe of bushes by the road, someone had knelt on one knee. We looked around with the flashlight and found a footprint and in the middle of it an indentation where someone had stepped on an empty cartridge. The cartridge was not there but we found a couple of gouge marks where a finger and thumb had evidently dug it out.

I went back to the tire marks and it was clear that either two cars had been in ahead of us or one car had been in and had come back again.

We walked back to Tim's car and I walked around it, turning the flashlight on each wheel in turn, then looking back at the tracks in the mud. He was watching me with his hands on his hips and Ruth McClure had the back of her hand against her mouth and she was as tense as I was.

"Satisfied?" said Tim.

I shrugged my shoulders and we got back into the car again. I was tired and sore and I didn't want to think for awhile. I heard Ruth start explaining and then I guess I went to sleep because I didn't hear any more of it. Tim shook me when we pulled up in front of the house again. He looked pretty grim. It was four o'clock in the morning.

9

As soon as we were back in the living room I went straight to the black box and dumped the contents out on the table. There was nothing much to look at. Bill of sale for an automobile, cancelled checks, bank statements, and a little batch of papers surrounded by a rubber band that came to pieces when I touched it. The batch of papers consisted of a deed which evidently related to the home itself, a cancelled mortgage note and a mortgage with a notation that it had been released. Birth certificate of one Ruth Ellington McClure showing that she was born June 21, 1913, adoption proceedings showing that a foundling, true name unknown, parents unknown, was adopted by John H. McClure and Ruth McClure, his wife, in May, 1915, in Louisville, Kentucky. The child had been in the custody of a Mrs. Phoebe Murdoch and had been called Timothy Washington for lack of any other name. The child's birthday was given as August 7, 1909. There was nothing to explain how this date could be known if nothing else was known.

I put this paper beside the stock certificate and pointed to the two dates which were less than a week apart. Timothy McClure was watching over my shoulder and he didn't say anything at all.

I picked up the bank deposit book with considerable interest but there were no unusual entries—nothing except periodic deposits of $35.00 each for a few years back, then $30.00 a week for a while and then $27.50.

I leafed through a few packages of cancelled checks but there was nothing unusual there either. Checks to tradespeople, small checks marked cash. Nothing else.

The bill of sale was for a '41 Buick in February, 1941, but there was no check to the automobile dealer.

I faced the two of them. "How did you get your money when you were off at school?" I asked.

Tim said: "Postal money order." I looked inquiringly at Ruth and she nodded.

"Always?"

"That's right."

"Remember what post office?"

They looked at each other blankly.

Ruth said: "That was years ago. I don't know that I ever noticed. It didn't seem important. We got the money and that was all there was to it."

Tim was thinking with a puckered frown on his face but he shook his head slowly.

10

I guess I jumped four inches when the telephone rang. Six eyes looked at it and it rang again. Ruth went over and picked up the receiver, and after a minute she came back and looked at me and said, "For you."

There was no doubt that she meant me, but it was so hard to believe that I said, "Me?" even while I was on the way.

The voice sounded like it might be talking through a sea shell.

"Mr. Gilmore Henry?"

I wished it was not me but it was and I said so.

"A little nosey, aren't you?"

It was beginning to be fairly evident, but I said, "Think so?" and tried to concentrate on discovering something that would let me recognize the speaker if I ever heard him again, sea shell or no.

The voice went on, "Why don't you take a little vacation or something and mind your own damn business?"

"Maybe I will. Any suggestions?"

"Only that you take a little vacation or something and mind your own damn business. Should I draw you a picture?"

I said, "Who is this?"

There was no answer to that one and the receiver went on the hook at the other end of the line.

I hung up and scratched my shoulders inside the coat again by squirming around. Then I picked up the receiver and jingled the hook, and when the operator said "What number, please?" I said: "This is 1872. I want to talk again to the party I was just talking to. Can you tell me what number that call came from?"

"You mean just now?"

"Not over one minute ago."

"That call was from the hotel."

"Will you give me the hotel, please?"

When I got the hotel operator, I said again: "This is 1872. I want to talk to the party I was just talking to."

"The call was made from a booth."

"If the man's still around, take a good look at him and remember everything you see."

"He just walked out. Hung up the receiver and walked right on out without saying a word."

"Big? Little? Dark? Light? Or what?"

"Who is this talking?"

"Never mind, sweetheart, I'm in a hurry and this is important. Did you notice anything about that man?"

She was silent for a minute, thinking it over, and then she said, "There wasn't much to notice. Just medium and nothing peculiar."

"Clothes?"

"Just plain clothes."

"Big nose? Squint eyes? Scars or anything?"

"Just a plain man. You see them every day. Personally I got a good home life and I don't care if they are Clark Gable."

I wasn't getting anywhere so I said, "Oh yeah," and hung up. I turned around to Tim and Ruth and said, "Just a medium guy that doesn't look like anything wants me to take a vacation somewhere else and mind my own business. I'm all happy to know that the hotel operator has no sex troubles at home."

11

I took the room formerly occupied by the late John H. McClure, Ruth took the living room, and the big ox took the basement. Between us we searched those rooms and then the rest of the house down to everything except the backside of the wall paper. In the dresser drawer I found the only thing that looked interesting at all—a flat key, down in the bottom of a plush-lined box full of collar buttons, paper clips, old theater stubs and other trash. It was not a bright new key, but it was brass looking and hadn't turned green and wasn't dusty, so I judged it had not remained as neglected as the surroundings would indicate.

I found Ruth and held the thing out to her.

"What does that open?"

"It doesn't look like any lock we have around the house. Maybe Tim knows."

Tim turned it over once or twice and shook his head. "Never saw it before."

I turned it over and over myself, while something revolved in the back of my head very slowly. I said: "Could be a lockbox. Know if he had one?"

They looked at each other and Tim said: "Never mentioned it if he did."

"Did he leave a will?"

"Just a short thing, made years ago, leaving everything to Tim and me in equal shares."

"Probated yet?"

"No. We planned to probate it day after tomorrow."

"Name an executor?"

Tim said: "Ruth."

I thought that over for a while. "Look," I said, "as soon as the will is probated we are going to qualify you in an awful hurry, and then you as executor are going to start looking for lock-boxes. Maybe with this key we'll find what somebody wanted awfully bad to find here tonight."

We had wasted a good deal of time and it was nearly six o'clock. Ruth said didn't we think we ought to eat, and suddenly I thought about how hungry I was and sat down with a faint feeling and little red flecks in front of my eyes. I said I thought it was a swell idea.

12

I shaved while breakfast was cooking. On my way to the kitchen to see how things were getting along I passed through the living room and happened to glance at the front door. I stopped in my tracks. The most hideous face I have ever seen was up close to the glass and one bright eye was looking at me. I thought at first the face was disfigured by a giant birthmark, but almost at once I realized that I was looking at scar tissue which covered roughly one whole side of the face which sagged downward, pulling the lower eyelid with it so that the red lining showed. That side of the mouth was also pulled down and partially open, with the lip permanently twisted out. The eye on that side of the face was milky.

I heard Ruth moving around in the kitchen and I said:

"What am I looking at?"

She appeared in the doorway and immediately saw the ghastly thing at the door. To my surprise she did not bat an eye, but sang out with:

"Tim! Where's Tim? Let Katie in. She's at the front door?"

Tim came in from his room and opened the door and said:

"Hello, Miss Katie. Up early this morning, aren't you?"

It was a woman. She wore a bonnet that was almost as tight

around her skull as a skull cap would be, and from the way the scar tissue ran out of sight under it, I guessed the burn or whatever it was must have taken all of her hair off with it. She had a basket on her arm and the good half of her face looked at big Tim McClure with a tenderness that would have been appealing if I could have separated that side from the other, where the permanent leering mask did not change. I do not know what I expected her voice to be like, but I suppose I was waiting for a cackle like witches have in books you read when you're a kid. There was nothing wrong with her voice at all. She looked down and took a cloth from over the basket with a hand that was as horribly misshapen as her face:

"I brought you some eggs again, Mr. Tim. I saw the light in the kitchen, and I thought you and Ruthie might like something fresh right out of my own chicken yard."

She appeared to notice me for the first time and said:

"Who is this young man?"

Tim took the basket and said:

"Thanks, Katie. I don't know what we would do without you to look after us. This is a lawyer Ruth brought down from the city to help with Dad's affairs."

The eye looked at me and got bright again, and she stared at me longer than I thought was necessary. I put in:

"Everything seems to be in order. Just routine stuff."

Katie kept on looking at me, but she said to Tim:

"Doesn't look like much. Why do you want to mess with lawyers? What's wrong with what you can get in Harpersville? I thought Mr. Harper was going to take all that off your hands and do something right nice about the stock, too."

Tim did not seem to be surprised at how much she knew, nor at the air of assurance with which she spoke.

"Just an idea of Ruth's, Miss Katie. Happened to be up in the city, I guess, and got to talking about something else and next thing she knew she had a lawyer."

"Better let Mr. Harper handle it," said Miss Katie sourly, but with an insistence that I did not miss. "If you don't look out Mr. Harper won't pay you a good price for your stock."

"Don't you worry about us, Miss Katie. Thanks a lot for the eggs. We just finished the last ones you brought us, and they are always nice."

Miss Katie transferred her attention to him, and that soft look came over her face again. She patted the hand that was holding the basket and then turned around and left without another word.

When she was gone Tim evidently had no inclination to explain away my obvious perplexity, but Ruth was more accommodating:

"She lives across the street and about two houses down. Keeps a few chickens and is over here every day or two with eggs or with something she has cooked, or something from the garden. I don't know why she takes such a shine to us, but we have always been nice to her, especially Dad and Tim."

I said: "What happened to her?"

"She has never mentioned it, and no one has ever had the heart to ask. Most people think she is tough as nails, and from some of the stories we've heard, I guess maybe she is, although she's certainly never been that way toward us."

13

It was seven-thirty when we finished breakfast. I asked about when the stores would be open, and Ruth said there was a men's store on the main street that opened pretty early. Tim had an office job at Harper Products Company. When Ruth had cleared the table, she took him to work and then ran me downtown in his car. We parked in front of Silverstein's, waiting for someone to show up. Several doors away, behind us, a grocery store was already open and a Negro boy was washing the window with a rubber squeegee while the clerk was arranging oranges and stacks of cans in the window. I watched them idly in the rear-vision mirror, and then noticed Miss Katie coming down the walk with another basket on her arm. She turned into the grocery store. Ruth and I sat and smoked a cigarette and after a while I looked in the mirror again and saw Miss Katie come out with the basket looking rather heavy. Something sticking up out of the basket caught my attention. It was just a glimpse, and I guess it was five or ten seconds before it registered. I did not explain anything to Ruth, but just asked her to wait a minute. I climbed out and went back into the grocery store. There was only one clerk at that time of the morning, and he was straightening cans on the shelf and dusting officiously. Now that I was there I didn't know how to go about it.

I said: "I just saw Miss Katie. If you have any of her eggs, I'll take them all."

He evidently didn't have the foggiest notion what I was talking about.

"I haven't got her eggs. She took them with her. A regular carton. A dozen of them. I remember distinctly—they were right on top of the basket when she paid the bill."

I turned away and said:

"Do you carry Camels? Give me two packs. You mean she didn't forget the eggs she bought?"

He handed me the cigarettes, made change noisily, and said:

"Tell her to look right on top of the basket. She couldn't miss them, unless she dropped them somewhere."

I wished to hell I was just simply lost in the woods in a blizzard or something else simple I could understand.

14

Every person has some cross to bear. Mine is that I am not shaped like people who are intended to get their clothes in ready-to-wear shops. If clothes are to fit me in the middle, they have to be too long at the ends and if they are to fit me at the ends, they hurt me in the middle.

This dilemma confronted me, as usual, in Silverstein's Men's Shop. I didn't want to take the time to wait while alterations were made so I took a suit which hurt when I buttoned it at the waist. Mr. Silverstein had on a black skull cap and a measuring tape hung around his neck. He patted and smoothed and pulled at things to make them hang right and appeared to approve in every particular although he finally said that maybe it was a little snug. I thought *snug* was hardly the appropriate word since my belt was almost out of sight and I could tell that I would not want to sit down very often.

He did not much want to take my check but I brought Ruth in from the car and after she endorsed the check he took it with obvious misgivings. He kept insisting that all transactions in his establishment were "positively kesh" but he would not have missed a sale if his grandmother had been dying of convulsions in the next room.[*]

[*]The anti-Semitism of this paragraph is subtle but includes all the stereotypes of the era as regards a "Silverstein."

I regretted my decision when I crawled in under the wheel of the car. They say when you cut earthworms in two, the halves go about their own business and supply whatever it takes to carry on, but I am no earthworm and I had no faith in my ability to do the same.

Ruth said: "Where now?" I took my mind off my anatomical difficulties and asked if she knew what time of day Mr. William Jasper Harper presented himself at the offices of Harper Products Company. She said about nine o'clock so I took her home, borrowed the car, and drove out there.

Mr. Harper's secretary looked as if she might have personally laid the cornerstone in 1863, and who was I and what did I want. I handed her a card of Mead, Opdyke, Smallwood, Garrison & Henry and she said: "Oh, I see you are from Mr. Mead's office. Wait a minute and I'll see if Mr. Harper will talk to you." She did and he did. It was a big office paneled in dark wood with one side all windows that overlooked a decorative piece of lawn between the office and the factory itself that had ivy growing over it. Mr. Harper sat behind an immense desk with his back to the windows. Even sitting down you could tell he was a very big man and although his hair was practically white, his face was not a very old face and I judged he was not over sixty. He did not get up but waved toward a chair and said heartily: "Well, well, I see you are from Jim Mead's office."

I said I was and that I was here to see him on behalf of Miss Ruth McClure.

He didn't know whether he liked that or not and was a little less hearty. I could see him drawing in his horns and making up his mind what he ought to say. He looked at the card again and said: "Mr. Henry, isn't it?" He knew very well it was Mr. Henry because the card said so. I didn't see any reason to stall around so I said: "Why do you want to pay her four and one-half times what her stock is supposed to be worth?"

I could see him putting himself at ease and his smile was almost genial. "Very cautious girl, Mr. Henry. Very intelligent. Quite right that she should wonder. But I can assure you my motives are purely charitable and I can be plainer to you than I would care to be with her. Her father, Mr. Henry, was one of our oldest employees. I try to look after my own. I don't imagine he left very much, and his son and daughter seem to have been accustomed to live rather comfortably. I couldn't offer to give them anything but I thought it would look natural enough for me to buy my company's stock and the price would be my own business. Sort of family affair, you know. The stock was worth more when McClure bought it and I didn't like to see them take the loss."

"Very interesting, Mr. Harper. How much did you say Mr. McClure paid for his stock?"

He smiled again. "Really, Mr. Henry. I don't know that I could say. The stock always sold for par or better until well into the depression and I assume he bought it at the market."

I could see that he did not think it was any of my business and he did not know where we were going. I said: "Thirty-five dollars a week does not seem awfully liberal to me."

A big vein began to throb in his neck and his face began to get a little red: "Really, Mr. Henry! Just what have you got on your mind?"

I went over and put my hands on the desk: "I don't think, Mr. Harper, that John McClure bought any stock for ten thousand dollars when he never made over thirty-five dollars a week in his life. I don't think Tim went to Princeton on thirty-five dollars a week. I don't think that Ruth McClure went to Sweetwater on thirty-five dollars a week. I don't think John McClure bought a new automobile every year on thirty-five dollars a week. What do you think?"

He did not let himself get any madder. He said: "You're doing the thinking. Suppose you tell me."

"Give me time and I will tell you before I get through finding out some things. Right now I would like to have your permission to go through the books of Harper Products Company and all the records of stock transfers and your personal bank statements. What do you say we begin about 1915?" The blood was coming back up in his neck again and he half rose out of his chair.

"You what?" He fairly shouted it at me.

I said: "All right, so you refuse?"

"I certainly do. I never heard such poppycock in my life. You little pip-squeak, you've got a nerve about you, haven't you? We'll see what Jim Mead has to say about this."

"Mr. Mead," I said evenly, "won't have anything to say about this. I am employed by Ruth McClure and so far this is between me and my client—and you. It can be between us and anybody else you say. There is the telephone. The number in the city is Main 8247."

He was almost beside himself. There was a gurgling sort of roar and he snatched the phone and then suddenly put it down again. "Jim Mead can wait," he said, "you and I can start by you getting out of here. Now!"

"I think I will, Mr. Harper. I think I will go out and look for some very interesting facts. I think I will start at about the month of May, 1915, and I think I will keep in mind that Timothy McClure is not the son of John H. McClure. I think I will recommend to Miss Ruth McClure that she decline your charitable offer which happens to be coupled with a condition that you are to take over all of her father's affairs and shall we say—records, if any. Do you think that would be a good idea, Mr. Harper?"

His face was about as soft as Stone Mountain, Georgia, and his voice was brittle and cold: "What's your game?" he asked, "Are you trying to blackmail me?"

"Should I?"

"Blackmail is a serious business, Mr. Henry, even in Harpersville. How would you like to be slapped in jail in about thirty minutes?"

I got up and put my hat on my head. "Suit yourself, Mr. William Jasper Harper. I assume you know what you're doing."

The buzzer on the interoffice communicating system went off at that point and he pressed the lever without taking his eyes off me. A hollow distorted voice which I could dimly recognize as the ancient secretary outside said: "Miss Katie is here, Mr. Harper."

"Tell her to wait. I am just getting through. If Mr. Henry ever comes back, I will not see him. He is just leaving." He was all smiles again. "Another of my charities, Mr. Henry. I am really a very kindhearted man, Mr. Henry. You will find evidences of it all over this town. A most unfortunate woman, Miss Katie. Very excellent eggs she brings me once a week, and cheaper than the ones you get in the store. But she has had a hard time, Mr. Henry, hideously disfigured and no way to make a living. I have a little envelope for her every week and it has nothing to do with the price of eggs. I suppose your distorted mind will want to make something of that too. Now get out of my sight and if Jim can divert your imagination from the realm of the absurd into more productive channels, perhaps it will not be necessary for me to have you arrested for attempted blackmail."

I said: "I may have some thoughts about the price of eggs at that. You'll remember that I haven't asked you for a cent. If you have an impulse to make childish threats, I hope you will be resourceful enough to make them stick."

15

I stopped at a drugstore and looked in the telephone directory to see if there was a phone listed in the name of Miss Katie Byrnes. There was, and I made a note of the street and number just to make sure I was going to the right place.

I parked the car in front of her house, rang the doorbell once or twice, and then knocked several times. At first I thought there might have been a slight movement discernible somewhere in the shadows, but nothing happened, and I came to the conclusion that there was nobody at home.

I went down the steps, around the corner, and along the cement walk to the back yard. There was a fence there and an unhappy hen who looked up with an air of hope almost as if there was just an outside chance I might be the worm she was looking for. I closed the wire gate behind me and looked around. The yard was small and over in one corner behind a ragged chicken-wire fence there was what might have been called a garden, about the size of a tablecloth. In the other corner was a shed with the door ajar, and I walked over and looked in to see where the rest of the chickens were. I did not see but two. There was a small packing box on its side with the opening nearest the wall, and I strolled over and looked in, on the theory that there might be another hen or two loafing around somewhere. I didn't see anything, but a voice said:

"What do you think you're doing?"

I whirled around, startled, and there was Miss Katie with a gun in her hand. I said:

"Oh, hello there. I was hungry and thought maybe you would sell me an egg."

"I'll just bet you did. I suppose one of the hens was going to make change for you. Talk fast."

"Well, as a matter of fact, Miss Katie, I wasn't hungry, but I got to wondering all about your eggs and everything."

The gun was wavering about as much as if it had been set in concrete. She said coldly:

"You've got a lot more curiosity than you are entitled to. I could shoot you as a chicken thief and never see the inside of a jail, but I would have to clean the gun afterward, and I'm not sure it's worth it. A boy called me from the grocery store a while ago and wanted to know if I had found my eggs. He said a nutty little guy with a bruise on his face, wearing clothes about ten sizes too big for him, was asking about it. Maybe cleaning the gun wouldn't be too much of a job after all."

It didn't seem to me that cleaning a gun would be such a hard job, and I wished she wouldn't talk like that. There wasn't any place I could go, and taking a chance she would miss me wasn't my idea of what you would want to do on your afternoon off.

"Look here, Miss Katie," I said, standing just exactly where I was and not moving even the toes inside my shoes, "you do the damnedest things until the questions come over me like pimples when it's cold. You give away eggs and then you buy eggs, and you sell eggs for less than they cost you. You give away vegetables that you grow in your garden, but you don't grow enough vegetables in your garden to make the chickens even bother to jump the fence. You don't make any money, and yet you have a home and a telephone and everything. How much does Mr. Harper give you?"

The hand with the gun began to tremble, but it was from anger and not from fear.

"What makes it any of your business?" she asked bitterly. "If you've got a job to do for Ruthie, why don't you do it instead of wondering what kind of charity I live on?"

"I think you're right. In fact, I know it. I think I'll just go and do that job right now." I walked past her so close our clothes brushed together. I walked right on through the back yard without hurrying, opened the gate, stepped through it, and turned around to hook it behind me. Miss Katie was looking after me and the gun was still in her hand. I walked on around to the front of the house, got in the car, and drove away. I went right past the McClure home and then pulled over to the curb a couple of blocks beyond and wiped my face to keep the sweat from running down into my eyes. By and by I turned around and went back to the McClures' again. I had not thought about how tight my pants were and how much they hurt my stomach since I walked into Harper's office a long time ago.

16

Ruth was washing the breakfast dishes, and the morning was half gone. She looked up and said:

"Long distance has been trying to get you. It's your office. Mr. Mead is in an awful hotbox to talk to you, but he couldn't wait. Left a message for you to call his secretary and that he was on his way down here."

I had a cold, heavy feeling down in me somewhere. I called the operator and pretty soon Myrtle was on the other end of the wire. I said:

"Gil. Mr. Mead want me?"

"I'll say he does."

"What's up?"

"Does it take much imagination?"

I didn't think it did, so I said something and hung up. I asked Ruth how long it had been since the call first came in, and she said around thirty minutes, which would be just about right from the time I left the office of Harper Products Company. I must have looked nervous, because Ruth was watching me closely.

"Anything the matter?" she asked.

"No more than if I were sitting on a time bomb listening to it tick."

"Cold feet?"

"About up to here," I said, pointing to my knees.

"Quitting?"

I didn't look at her. I said:

"Could be. It all depends."

She was rattling pans without really doing anything with them, and although I was close enough to touch her she might have been in the Smithsonian Institute, she was so far away.

"Better run along home," she said between her teeth. "Might get your little tail spanked."

"Maybe so. I'm allergic to spankings."

The dishes got noisier and noisier, and one of them fell on the floor and broke with a deafening crash. She had another one in her hand, and she suddenly threw it on the floor with another crash and ran blindly out through the living-room door, and I could hear the door of her bedroom shut with a bang. I walked the same way but stopped with my hand almost on the knob of the door, and spent the next five or ten minutes walking around the living room and sitting down and getting up and walking around some more.

The telephone sounded like the crack of doom, and I knew that was just exactly what it was. I went over and sat in front of it while it rang two more times, and then I forced myself to take the receiver off the hook, and to my surprise it didn't hurt a bit.

There was no mistaking the voice of Mr. Jim Mead in one of its more formidable moments.

"Henry."

"Yes, sir."

"I'm at Harper Products Company. Have you got a car there?"

"Yes, sir."

"Get out here right away."

"Yes, sir."

The receiver went up with a bang at the other end of the line, and after a while I remembered I still had something in my hand and I hung it up too. I went over and knocked on Ruth's door and then tried it, but it was locked, so I found my hat and drove on out to the company's office.

Mr. William Jasper Harper was enthroned behind his big desk as pleased as an umpire who has just said, "Strike three!" Mr. James Mead was very erect and he kept me under observation as if he were trying to pick out the best place for the knife to go in. Another man with a big shiny star on his coat was smoking a cigar and, of all things in the world, I had to wonder whether he was going to let the ashes drop on the floor.

There was a great big silence, slightly bluish in color, and I stood as still as the Tropic of Capricorn, which is just a line on the map and very still indeed.

The man with the star crossed his legs and two inches of ash fell right smack on the rug. He said:

"Should I arrest him now?"

Mr. William Jasper Harper spread his hands contentedly on the big desk in front of him, and the light glinted off his polished fingernails.

"Perhaps it won't be necessary, Mr. Sheriff," he said, and cleared his throat significantly, "I think if you will just wait in the outer office, perhaps Mr. Mead and I had better have a little talk with the young man."

The sheriff shrugged his shoulders and went out, and I wondered what would happen if I walked out behind him, but I thought it would probably be better if I didn't do it.

It was Mr. James Mead's turn to clear his throat, and he did it magnificently.

"I think, Gilmore, you have probably been reading too many books. Just what sort of insanity is this?"

"Oh, come now, Jim," said William Jasper Harper in his best after-dinner manner. "Perhaps I have been a bit precipitous and hot-tempered. If he realizes the absurdity of his conduct, perhaps a little trip somewhere would take his mind off of fantastic things and make him, shall we say, a useful servant of the law once more."

Mr. James Mead looked at me severely.

"What do you say to that, Gilmore?"

Well, I really had to say something, so I said:

"Yes, sir," pretty meekly, and then I said, "I'm sure I can't be all bad, Mr. Mead."

"Then it's settled," said Mr. Harper. He swooped up the French phone[*] from its cradle, and then put it back and pressed a lever on his talk box, and said loudly:

"When is the next train, Miss Spindle?" The box croaked something that must have been, "Where to, Mr. Harper?" because he looked up and said, "Oh yes, where would you like to go?"

I knew just where he wanted me to go, but I didn't think it would be dignified to put it in words. I was standing in front of the desk, and when I glanced down I saw an audit report marked, "Harper Products Company—Report of Audit as of December 31, 1940." It was pretty nifty looking, all bound up with a fancy cover, and down at the bottom I saw "Yoland & Jolley, Certified Public Accountants, Louisville, Kentucky." I said:

"Any place will do. I think Louisville, Kentucky, would be nice."

There was considerable croaking over the little brown box and there was every evidence of Harperian displeasure like a thunder cloud on Mt. Olympus.

"It's too late for the morning train to Louisville. You'll have to go somewhere else."

I tried to look crestfallen. "I'm very fond of Louisville, sir," I said respectfully. "If I've got to go some place, that's where I'd like to go. Isn't there a later train?"

"Not till ten or eleven o'clock tonight," said James Mead. There was nothing friendly about the way he was looking at me. He looked like Life with Father.[†]

---

[*]A telephone with a long straight handle, with a pipe-bowl-shaped speaking-tube at one end and a round earpiece at the other, common in the earliest phone models.

[†]The 1935 novel by Clarence Day about a benevolent curmudgeon, made into a very successful stage play in 1939 by Howard Lindsay and Russel Crouse (and a classic film in 1947, starring William Powell and Irene Dunne).

Harper consulted the little box on his desk again. "There's a train going south around 12:30. You can take that and go as far as you please. The farther the better. Or you can be arrested on suspicion and released from the County jail in time to catch the evening train for Louisville. Take your choice."

I wished I were like these movie actresses who can turn their tears on and off like a radio. I looked down at my feet and did my best to squeeze out at least one little tear but I didn't have any luck and had to fall back on a very poor imitation of a sniffle, followed by a heavy blow of the nose. When I looked up at Harper again he didn't look quite so much like the president of the Flint National Bank refusing to make a $10.00 loan. He looked more like the vice president refusing to make a $5.00 loan. There wasn't much change but I was slightly encouraged and said, "Please, sir, I really would like to go to Louisville, but if my poor old mother should hear that I had been in jail like a common criminal she could never hold up her head again at the Tuesday Afternoon Book Club and would probably have to resign as Chairwoman of Circle Number Six of the Women's Auxiliary." I damn near overdid the thing but I lowered my eyes at the proper time and blew my nose loudly again and the pompous old ass swallowed it. Out of the corner of my eye I got a glimpse of Mead opening his mouth with considerable indignation, but he evidently thought better of it and set his lips in a stern, straight line. If he had told Harper that my mother had been dead for fifteen years, I probably would have been put in solitary confinement without any more preliminaries.

William Jasper Harper was visibly weakening. He said: "Of course I don't want to be unduly severe now that we have an agreement in principle. Perhaps we could leave out the arrest and jail part of it if you have had a sincere change of heart and will promise to behave yourself. For example, Mr. Henry, don't you think that the affairs of the McClures would be better off under the supervision of a, shall we say, more mature mind?"

I said, "Yes, sir."

He swooped up the phone again and then put it down and there was more conference with the little box and Miss Spindle. They eyed me and I eyed the ashes on the rug, and in almost no time at all a buzzer went off and Mr. Harper picked up the phone and said, "Hello," almost musically, and then, "Miss McClure," and then, "Just a moment, please. Mr. Henry would like to speak to you." He held the thing out at me, and then there was still some talk coming through it, so he put it back to his ear again and said, "What?" and then after a moment, "Well, perhaps it is just as well. He just wanted you to get the message that he is leaving on the ten-forty train and is sorry that the pressure of other business makes it necessary for him to ask that you seek other counsel."

The noise of the receiver being replaced in the living room of the McClure home reverberated clearly through the office of Mr. William Jasper Harper. He looked up at me.

"Wouldn't talk to you, she said. It would seem that your usefulness here is definitely at an end, no matter how you look at it." He went to the door, summoned the sheriff, took a paper out of his pocket, tore it up, and deposited it in the wastebasket. I picked up my hat without looking at Mr. James Mead and walked out into a very unfriendly world.

17

I walked slowly and did not walk very far. When I had given Harper enough time to go back into his office and close the door I turned around and went back into the building and told ancient Miss Spindle that I wanted to see Tim McClure. She made no secret of the fact that I was a trifle less welcome than something you would scrape off the bottom of your shoe, but she informed me that I should go back to the plant itself and look in the first door to the right of the main entrance.

I found Tim with his big frame hunched over a desk covered with a collection of metallic objects and gadgets which he was measuring with a set of calipers. There could be no doubt that these were the products from which the Harper Company got its name.

The reception I got could hardly be called a reception at all. As a persona I was clearly non grata. If Dale Carnegie had spent the morning with me in Harpersville, Kentucky,[*] he would never have picked up any pointers on How to Win Friends and Influence People.[†]

"All right," Tim growled at me, "what now?"

---

[*]This is the first mention that Harpersville is in Kentucky.

[†]Dale Carnegie (1888–1955) was the author and lecturer behind a very popular series of self-help courses that continue today. His most famous book, *How to Win Friends and Influence People*, was first published in 1936 and remains a steady seller.

Even as disagreeable as he was, there could be no doubt that he had not heard from Ruth in the last hour or so, for in that event I was sure he would have been downright vicious. Instead of answering him, I stuck my head out of the door of his office and looked back into the plant. Except for a couple of small offices near the entrance, the whole first floor was one big room full of complicated machines that chopped things up and punched holes in them and made things round or flat. There wasn't an idle man or machine in sight and from the way the building rumbled and trembled, it was apparent that the floors above were equally as active. I looked back at Tim and said, "Seems busy enough to me."

"What's it to you?"

"Nothing," I said innocently, "nothing at all. Just passing the time of day."

"Who says it *isn't* busy?"

"Nobody. Nobody at all. It just doesn't look like a corporation whose stock is selling for twenty-three dollars a share."

Tim walked to the door and took a look for himself as if he had never seen it before. He ran his hand through his hair and said, "No, it doesn't, for a fact."

I let that soak for a while. "If you're losing money, you're doing it more energetically than anybody I ever saw." I pointed to the gadgets on the table. "War stuff?"

Instead of giving me a direct answer, he looked hostile and said: "I don't like messy little birds who shoot off their mouths all the time. Every time you say a word you insinuate something and it's always trouble. We're getting along all right. Now scram out of here and if you have any more questions, ask yourself and see what bright answers you get. Our contracts with the Government are at a fixed price but the cost of the materials is giving us the pinch and taxes just about take the rest. To hear you talk, you'd think everybody is a crook and the whole world is a nasty place. Now scram. Beat it."

The telephone on his desk rang and he picked it up. I heard him say in a very different kind of voice, "Oh, hello, Ruth," and I walked away quickly. I wasn't retreating, of course, but left because I had other things to do.

18

I still had Tim's car. I drove around town until I found the office of the newspaper. The place of business of the *Harpersville Gazette* did not remind me of the *New York Times* or the *Chicago Tribune*. The windows were dirty. In the front room there were some cases with samples of stationery displayed in them, together with cards for every occasion, including exhortations to get well quick, thank you for the wedding presents and coy ways to announce the birth of a child. There was a railing over at one side and behind that was a safe, a potbellied iron stove and a couple of desks covered with galley proofs, paste pots and stuff. A newspaper from the city was spread out on one of the desks and a man with a green eyeshade was clipping items out of it which could be reprinted in *Harpersville* without giving credit.

I asked if it would be all right for me to see some back numbers and he seemed to think it would not hurt anything. He pointed through a door and I went back into a big gloomy room where there was a medium-size press that the local sheet was evidently printed on and several small job presses that were being fed by hand. Over in the corner a shaded light bulb hung down on a long cord from the ceiling and under it a man sat before a linotype machine with a cigarette drooping from his lips.

Getting the issue that carried the story on John McClure's death was easy and when I had read the thing I didn't know any more than I knew before. He just had an automobile accident and died and was buried like other people and there was a picture and he was a Deacon in the Crescent Avenue Presbyterian Church and a member of the Kiwanis Club. He was the oldest employee of Harper Products Company in point of continuous service and William Jasper Harper himself was quoted as saying that it would be difficult to replace him. I thought about $35.00 a week and was pretty skeptical.

I then suggested that I would like to see the back numbers for a month or two around August, 1909, and the man at the linotype machine said that anybody who would want to read the *Harpersville Gazette* that far back was a fool, but I could go upstairs and look if it would make me happier.

They didn't have much system about keeping their back numbers and I spent a couple of hours fooling with bundles of the dirtiest paper I have even seen in my life. I finally found what I was looking for but I would have been better off if I had never thought about it. There wasn't one line in any of the papers that had any bearing on what I was interested in. When I was through, I looked like a chimneysweep and I was not sure that my new suit would ever be the same.

19

I went down to the men's washroom at the Hotel Harper and scrubbed all visible parts of my anatomy with soap and water that was practically boiling. Then I got the Negro boy and gave him a quarter to brush me off. You would have thought he was beating a rug and so did I, but he got plenty of dust out of me and it was worth it. When he had finished I had to wash all over again but I was more or less respectable.

I had a good deal of curiosity about this Murdoch woman who was mentioned in the adoption papers, and I couldn't escape the feeling that she must have had her origin in Harpersville or somewhere close by. I spent the largest part of the afternoon trying to find a trace of her but twenty-five or twenty-six years is a long time whether you are absent, in jail, or simply trying to make enough to pay your taxes. I went into the post office, both banks, and a flock of grocery stores and drug stores but if Phoebe Murdoch ever lived in the town of Harpersville she had been a most inconspicuous little rabbit or had learned the secret of invisibility.

About 5:30 I gave up. I had been pounding the pavements and was pretty tired but I thought of one more blind alley I could walk into before knocking off for the day. I called the police station without saying who I was and got the information that Mr. Mead's car had been taken to Harbison's Garage. Apparently there was a deal between the garage and the police because they knew where the car had been taken without even looking it up.

As you might suspect, Harbison's Garage was operated by a Mr. Harbison, a garrulous man with a scrawny neck who wore a celluloid collar much too big for him.* His neck looked like an electric wire with a porcelain insulator around it. I told him I represented an insurance company and he let me see the car without any argument. Like John McClure's buggy, it was junk and a very low grade of junk at that. I told him who owned the thing, borrowed a piece of paper and scribbled a note to Jim Mead reminding him to report the accident in a formal way so that he could recover on his collision insurance. I gave Harbison the idea that possibly his testimony as to the value of the car after the accident might be material and he pricked up his ears. You could tell that he could smell a counterfeit penny edgeways at a hundred paces.

While I was there, I maneuvered him over to the McClure car and we almost got into a discussion of what could have happened to the left rear wheel but about that time I had a prickly sensation in the back of my head and when I looked up there was a bright nickel-plated star and the sheriff was wearing it. He looked at me with a high degree of disapproval and said: "I thought you were going to behave yourself. Mr. Harper won't like it."

I opened my eyes wide and looked injured. "What am I doing?" I asked plaintively.

"I don't know as I can say," said the sheriff, "but if it was good you wouldn't be doing it."

"Everybody's got me wrong in this town—" I started to

---

*Men's shirts originally were made with detachable collars, usually made of celluloid. Collars could be purchased in a variety of styles.

say but he interrupted me with an impatient gesture and said: "Yeah, I know. The penitentiary is full of innocent people but all they can do is write letters to the parole board. I tell you what I'll do. I'm going to follow you downtown in my car and watch you buy a ticket to a good double feature and I don't care if you have to see it twice. You can come out in time to buy a ticket and get on the train. Until then I don't want to see you obstructing traffic and if you even ask the usher what time it is I'm going to get a report at home and you'll wish you hadn't."

"I came down here without any baggage," I protested. "Can't I even buy some things so I can make my trip?"

"OK. I'll go with you. Then you can check the stuff at the station and I'll take you to the picture show and Harpersville can do its best to get along without you."

20

We found a parking place on the main street in front of something that looked like a department store and I bought an overnight bag, some pajamas, toothbrush, toothpaste, a cheap razor, underwear, a shirt, a tie, socks and a half-dozen handkerchiefs. I still had $18.75 left and since I was not going back to the office I could see I would either have to get a check cashed in Louisville or call off my trip in a very short time. The Sheriff let me put the car in a parking lot near the station. I ran up the windows, locked the doors and went in and bought my ticket. A glance at the time table showed that I would get to Louisville the next morning. I got to thinking and went back to the ticket window and changed my reservation and paid for a drawing room, which left me very little leeway after allowing for tips and what I hoped would be a big meal on the train.

The sheriff gave me a choice between lousy programs at the Bijou and the Rex. Both had double features and they looked equally bad, but I had seen both of the pictures showing at the Rex and only one picture at the Bijou, so I chose the latter. The sheriff followed me with grim persistence, watched me buy my ticket, escorted me inside and wouldn't leave until I had found a seat. After ten minutes of the picture I had not seen before, I regretted my choice and would have gone over and given my valuable patronage to the Rex Theater except that a very formidable usher in a red sweater with a white *H* on the front of it waggled his finger at me. He looked like a one-man gang. I told him to call me at ten o'clock, found a comfortable seat by myself in a remote corner and tried to sleep, with a notable lack of success.

Afterwards I had time enough to go by the McClure house but in view of what had happened, I thought it would be a mistake.

I walked down to the station and left the car key with instructions to deliver it to Ruth after the train had pulled out.

There were still twenty minutes to wait so I went out and found a liquor store and bought a pint of whiskey which meant the rest of my figuring would have to be pretty close.

When I got back to the waiting room at the station, Tim and Ruth McClure were standing by the magazine counter. Tim nodded his head toward the door that led out to the platform and I followed him out. It was 10:35 and it would have suited me if it had been 10:42 and if the train had been on time.

Ruth said: "Here." Pretty short. She stuck out an envelope at me and I took it and looked inside. I found fifteen new ten dollar bills.

I looked up and said: "What's this?"

"That's to pay you for services rendered. Is it enough?" Before that I had only felt pretty bad. Now I felt awful. Stinking. I did not look at her but nodded and stuffed the envelope in my pocket.

The train whistled and I wanted it to hurry up.

Tim said: "Are we all quits?" I nodded and wondered if the train would ever get there.

"Well," said Tim with a note of satisfaction in his voice, "then if we're all quits I came down here to hit you and I guess I can go ahead and do it."

I drew in a deep breath and looked up at him. Next time I would rather have Joe Louis hit me. It came right in my mouth and my head bounced on the platform pretty hard. I just lay there for a second and then rolled slowly over on my hands and knees and climbed to my feet with my knees feeling very uncertain and things revolving a little around me. The train came in with a rush and a roar and when it stopped I picked up my bag and walked over and climbed on.

I went into my drawing room and locked the door and then rang for the porter and when he came in as the train got under way I told him to call me an hour before the train was due in Louisville. I told the porter to pound good and hard on the door and keep pounding until I opened it. When he was gone I went into the can and looked at my face in the mirror. My lower lip had a swelling on it about the size of a ripe lime and my best tooth right in front in the lower jaw was gone. I looked like hell and felt worse. I got out the pint of whiskey and drank all of it in about thirty minutes and then I was as sick as a bitch and then I went to bed.

21

When I bought that bottle of whiskey, I thought I was buying a pint of sodden dreamless sleep but I guess I pitched most of it when I got sick because the night was a boiling, surging turmoil and my head was full of tumbling messed-up fantasies that brought me up with a jerk every few minutes. The wheels of the train were square and the track had the hiccups. The drawing room was hot and my mouth was dry and my lip was swollen and throbbing and my head hurt. Thoughts bounced around inside my skull and snapped and snarled at each other.

Finally I gave it up as a bad business and sat on the edge of the berth holding my head in my hands. I was thirsty and went into the can and drank three or four glasses of ice water that did better. About that time the train jerked to a stop and I was thrown against the wall right on the spot where my head had bounced off of the concrete platform in Harpersville. For a moment I thought it had split open like a watermelon when you drop it. I went back into the drawing room, crawled into bed again and then raised the shade and tried to see where we were, but I might as well have been looking into the inside of a cow. Somewhere the conductor said "Board," obviously not caring whether anyone heard him or not and then I heard feet pounding down the station platform and a breathless voice said: "Telegram for Mr. Jolley." There was some muttering that I couldn't catch but it didn't last long because the train was already under way, with the square wheels and the hiccups gradually beginning to give each other hell at my expense.

I pulled down the shade and lay back wearily and then suddenly I was standing near the door and something went *click* in my head loud enough for the porter to have heard it. I could hear the feet of the conductor shuffling down the passage outside of my room and I very gently pulled back the catch on my door without making a sound. When the conductor went by, passing down the aisle between the green curtains, I cautiously opened the door a crack and watched him.

About halfway down the length of the car he consulted something in his hand, reached modestly through the crack of the curtains of a lower berth and shook something. There was a sleepy kind of groan and then a pair of pajama legs stuck out into the aisle and a sleepy face yawned out big enough for a doctor to have looked clear down at his liver.

The conductor said: "Telegram for you, Mr. Jolley. When they try to catch you in the middle of a trip, I thought you would want to be waked up."

Mr. Jolley was quite young and blond—probably about my age. Even with his hair tumbled around his face he was good-looking and I could imagine him a heart throb all dressed up. He was sleepier than a country village at midnight and when he said something to the conductor the words were garbled in the middle of a yawn. He took the telegram and fumbled with it stupidly for awhile and then got it open and rubbed his eyes with the back of his hand and looked at it long enough to have read Ezekiel from beginning to end. Then he gave the conductor something that was green and folded and went back into his hole and the conductor went away.

I closed and latched the door and instead of turning on the

light I got in the berth, struck a match and looked at my watch. It was four o'clock. It would be getting light soon. I went in and shaved, dealing with my bruised cheekbone and my painful lip as gently as possible. The stump where the tooth was broken off was hurting very badly. I dressed in the dark, put everything into my handbag and then listened at the door. There was no sign of life. I went out quietly and tiptoed around into the men's washroom where the porter was asleep on the divan. I did not want him to be pounding on my door in an hour or two so I woke him up, explained that I couldn't sleep and asked him if there was a club car on the train. He said yes, there was a combination diner and club car put on a couple of stops back so I told him not to bother about me and I would sit up the rest of the way. I gave him something that was green and folded and he seemed to like it.

When the train pulled into the Tenth Street Station at Louisville, I was the first one off at the very rear. I walked around the end of the club car, crossed the adjoining track and walked rapidly up to the waiting room, where I checked my bag and stood back out of sight to see what I could see. Mr. Jolley was in no hurry and I guess he was two-thirds of the way back in the crowd. I thought he was looking up and down the platform in a rather interested way but he did not loiter. Instead he came into the waiting room and walked straight to the telephone booths. He took the far one and when he got inside I went to the one next to it, closed the door behind me, turned my back to the door and fiddled with the telephone book while I listened. It was a dial phone and I couldn't tell what number he was calling. I heard him say: "Miss Judson?...Hillman Jolley...Just got in... Yes, I'll get a bite here in the station and come straight up. Be there in maybe forty-five minutes. OK."

He went out and walked straight into the restaurant adjoining the waiting room and I looked up the address of his office in the phone book. I went out and got a cab and gave him the address of the building.

Miss Judson was something to look at but I made a mental note to do the looking later. I asked if Mr. Yoland was in and she wanted to know who wanted to know. I gave her my card and she brightened up and said: "Oh, yes, you're from Mr. Mead's office, aren't you. Mr. Yoland ought to be in any minute. Won't you sit down?" I did not want to wait and I did not want to sit down and I did not like the way the hands on the clock kept moving but she gave me the morning paper and I had to sit down and look calm whether I wanted to or not. It was not warm but I sweat through my underwear in no time at all. The minutes went by awfully fast and I sat there with the same feeling I used to have when I was a kid and watched my father serve out big helpings of mashed potatoes to the guests while I wondered if there would be any left for me. Mr. Yoland came in at last, looked at my card, pumped my hand and took me right into his private office. He looked at the card again. "You're from Mr. Harper?"

"I was in his office yesterday." Well, it was true and could I help it if he wanted to think his own thoughts?

"What can I do for you, Mr. Henry?"

"It must be a tax question or something. I want to get copies of the audit reports as far back as they go or for maybe ten years might do."

He thought a minute and then said: "Well, that ought to be easy. Let's see a minute." He pressed a buzzer under his desk and somebody who was not Miss Judson came in. He said something about some files and she went out and more mashed potatoes got put on more plates and I began to get plenty nervous. Presently she came back and put a stack of things on the table and said: "We took over the account in 1938, Mr. Yoland. Here are all our audits and the last one made by McConnell and McConnell just before we took over."

Mr. Yoland had evidently got some ideas while we were waiting and maybe he had noticed that I was perspiring when I shouldn't have been. He sat looking at me and tapping on the table with the eraser on the end of a pencil. Just then Miss Judson came in and said: "Excuse me, Mr. Yoland. Long distance from Harpersville. I think it is Mr. Harper. Do you want to take it now or shall I tell him you will call back?"

My mouth went dry all of a sudden but I managed to put on what I thought was a nice smile and said: "He probably wants to talk to me too. I have only just got here but you know how impatient he is. Probably wants to know what I have found out already. Maybe you better be in conference or something and we can call back in a few minutes."

It didn't go over so good. There was uncertainty in his face. "Mr. Harper does not like to be put off. I think I had better take the call now, Miss Judson. Wait a minute." He glanced at me out of the corners of his eyes, "I'll take it in Mr. Jolley's office if Mr. Henry will excuse me." I said certainly. What was I supposed to do in a case like that?

He walked out across the hall and through the glass door just opposite and closed it behind him. I waited until I heard him start talking and then I picked up the bundle on the table and walked out past Miss Judson and said: "I'll be studying these in my room at the Brown Hotel. My bag is over there with the notes I took. Mr. Yoland can get me if he likes. Room 719."

She obviously thought it was not right and opened her mouth to say something but I walked on out and down to the elevator. For once my luck was good. An up-car and a down-car flashed their lights at almost the same instant, the down-car stopping a couple of seconds sooner. As I stepped in I could see a blond man with a suitcase pushing to the front of the other car and then I heard running footsteps in the hall and the door closed behind me.

People were all going up at that time of the morning and the down-car moved pretty fast. When we got to the lobby of the building, I made my feet walk although my mind was running. I went quickly around the corner and got into the first taxi I found. The driver said, "Where." I pointed straight ahead and said, "That way," and we got through just as the light was turning to amber and I breathed for the first time in hours.

22

I had no idea where I wanted to go except that it was not room 719 at the Brown Hotel and not even the Brown Hotel. I thought about it for a couple of blocks and the more I thought about it the more I didn't want to go to any hotel at all. I had myself an idea and said: "Have you got a free public library in this town?"

"You want information or you want to go there?"

I said I wanted to go there and we turned at the next corner and went this way and that way and presently stopped on a curving drive in front of a big stone building. I went to the big reading room and got a table by myself where I could watch the door and spread out in front of me the audit reports of Harper Products Company for 1937, 1938, 1939 and 1940. The first one was in a gray cover with the name of *McConnell & McConnell* on it and the others were black from the office of Yoland & Jolley.

Well, here I was and I didn't know what to do any more than if I was sitting down in front of a dish of poi. I picked up the 1937 book and saw there was a letter in front addressed to the company and then more figures than Earl Carroll's *Vanities.**

---

*A series of Broadway musical comedy revues that began in the 1920s and ran for many years. In the mid-1940s, Hollywood began to produce film versions. Of course, the revues featured numerous dancing girls.

First of all there was a balance sheet that unfolded like a road map and then a profit and loss statement and then page after page of breakdowns on this and that.

Except for the color of the cover, the 1938 report was laid out pretty much the same way only in 1937 the company made what looked to me like a fairly sizable chunk of money and in 1938 the earnings were shown as a little less than the dividends paid. In 1939 the profit was a little better than 1938 but the dividend was cut in half. In 1940 the profit didn't look so bad and the rate of dividends was the same as for the previous year. The profit was still under 1937 and since business generally was supposed to be improving all the time, it didn't look like you could say the company was doing so good.

I went back to 1937 and 1938 again and had myself a good look at the balance sheets. There was a pretty sizable drop in surplus and instead of lots of cash on hand and in bank in 1937, the cash business looked pretty tight the following year. Bank loans had been reduced pretty sharply and I began to get a new respect for bankers. It looked an awful lot like they smartened up a jump ahead of everybody else. Inventory at the end of 1938 was pretty low.

I know a figure when I see one but I am no accountant and I was not sure I had the faintest idea what I was doing. I turned back to the letter of transmittal at the beginning of the 1938 report and read it. It was pretty stuffy going and I would have gotten as much out of an hour or two in the middle of Macaulay's *History of England.*[*] I read all the other letters and didn't know any more than when I started. The company just wasn't making a lot of dough and no wonder the stock was going down.

I sat there and wondered whether I had got myself in Dutch[†] with Mr. Mead on a brainstorm after all. Then I got back to Mr.

---

[*]Lord Thomas Babington Macauley's five-volume *History of England from the Accession of James II* (*1848–1861*), a popular if verbose history.

[†]In trouble. The *Oxford English Dictionary* reports this usage as early as 1912, though no lexicographer has suggested the origin of the phrase.

Harper wanting to pay a helluva lot of money for something he could buy cheap and shook my head. I had stumbled on enough about the adoption of Tim McClure and the way the McClure family lived to understand why William Jasper Harper might want to do something handsome for them but I couldn't escape the conviction that $110.00 a share must be a combination of that and something else. The more I thought about it the more I was convinced I had something if I only knew what it was.

I picked up the 1938 report and went through it again and still didn't learn anything so I read the letter of transmittal again and finally put a check mark by each of the two paragraphs which set forth the only changes recommended by Yoland & Jolley in their first year with the account.

The first one said that the inventories of raw materials had always been handled on a "first-in first-out" basis and because of the nature of the business which required a certain minimum inventory to be maintained at all times, it was suggested that the system ought to be changed to the "base stock" basis. There were a flock of reasons given and I didn't know any more than I did before. The terms meant nothing to me.

The second item was about depreciation and said that the company was heading for trouble because it was not setting up depreciation as fast as the equipment was depreciating. The rate ought to be stepped up, it said. The report informed the directors that after conferences with the president the above changes had been made in line with sound and conservative policy and the books had been adjusted accordingly.

I bundled all of the papers together and went out and looked at the names of all the accountants in town in the classified section of the telephone book. I picked out a harmless sounding name that looked like it was just one man all by himself and went out and flagged a cab.

23

The accountant was all by himself sure enough. The office did not look prosperous and I gathered that even the clients left him all by himself. He must have spent his life on the books of little butcher shops and beer joints because he didn't know much about inventories and since I didn't know anything about them at all the conversation was pretty futile. I had picked him because I thought his time would be cheap but I came to the conclusion that anything at all would be an overpayment so after awhile I just thanked him and left.

I found myself a flossy firm with a lot of typewriters going in it and asked for the top name on the door. His secretary did not want to let me in with one tooth missing and looking as rough as I did but I finally talked her into it and the Great Presence consented to let me be in the room with him for awhile. I figured he probably had a meter that started ticking when I went in the door so I didn't waste any time. "When you do an inventory on a first-in first-out basis, what happens?"

I thought for a minute he was going to say nothing happened at all but he took what I said and peeled the skin off and looked for a nice spot to bite into it. "It's a way of looking at cost," he said in measured tones. "Prices fluctuate and you buy from time to time and pretty soon you have a quantity of items, all just alike, except for what they cost. Then you take some of them out and sell them. The question is which ones did you sell and how much did they cost you and how much profit did you make."

"That sounds all right, which ones did I sell?"

"On a first-in first-out basis you sold the first ones you had. Your books show what they cost and that's all of it."

"But what if I didn't sell the first ones? Suppose I sold the last ones?"

"It doesn't make any difference. They are all the same. You have to have some system and you asked me about a particular system and I told you."

I said: "All right, now give out about some other ways."

"Well, it depends upon what kind of a business you're in. Sometimes you have on hand a million little items like a ten-cent store and your stock turns over very fast. You could spend all your profit trying to figure out costs."

I tried to be as appreciative an audience as I could. I felt like Dr. Watson. "So what do you do then?" I asked.

"Usually you have a standard mark-up figure for everything or at least for big classes of items. Whatever it costs, you sell it for half again as much. Then you don't worry about the individual items but just keep track of the retail price, and the cost is automatically two-thirds of that."

"Is that called the base stock method?"

"No, that's something else again."

I told him to keep right on talking.

"Perhaps an illustration would be the best way to explain it," he said. "You run a stationery store. You figure you've got to have a hundred reams of a certain kind of paper on hand all the time in order to stay in business. That is your base. Your base stock. Every time you go below a hundred reams you order some more to bring it back up and if you begin to get down pretty close you put in an order so that by the time the shipment comes in you will be back to your minimum standard stock again. Since you aren't going to fall below that figure you decide to put a value on the hundred reams you have on hand and then pretend you aren't selling those reams at all. When you sell five reams you pretend you are selling the five reams that you have just ordered to keep from falling below your standard. It is just another way of looking at it."

I thought something ought to be dawning on me about this time but something definitely was not dawning at all. I said: "What happens if you do first-in first-out for awhile and then change over to that last way you were talking about?" He got out a pencil and a piece of paper and we assumed some figures and by and by I began to see that if the price of what you are buying is going up when you make your change, the cheap stuff you already have on hand is treated as your base stock with the result that you act like you are selling stuff that cost plenty, and naturally you don't make much dough. The sun began to come up along the back of my neck and I had a feeling that pretty soon the inside of my cranium would be illuminated if I just sat still and waited. I said: "And if you did it when the price of raw materials is going down then, of course, you'd make a big profit, wouldn't you?"

That seemed to be the idea. I was doing fine. I said: "But how in hell can you make any money that way?"

"You really do just the same business as before. It just doesn't look as good."

I thought that over for a long time and then I thought I had better cut it short since the meter was probably ticking.

"Suppose," I said feeling my way along, "suppose there comes a time when you want to make lots and lots of money for awhile. If the price of what you are buying keeps going up and you change back to the other system again, what would happen then?"

"Young man," he said smiling, "you have an imagination that

will either get you in jail or put warts on your fingers from clipping coupons. It would be much simpler to rob a bank and be done with it."

"Is there anything wrong with either system?"

"From an accounting standpoint, no. Not if you know when to use one system and when to use the other. But the federal government does not approve of the base stock method for income tax purposes."

This was getting a little off base and I did not want to go any farther with it. I wanted to pay him for his time but he said it was all right and never mind.

24

I looked at my watch and found I had spent more time at the library than I thought. My head was aching abominably and before I left the building, I stopped at the newsstand and asked the girl if she had any aspirin. While she was looking in the drawer back of the counter, a man brought in the first edition of the *Louisville Times* and put a pile of them right in front of me. He was in a hurry and he put the pile upside down so that an item at the bottom of the front page caught my eye as quickly as if it had winked at me. It was one of these little pieces of spot news that they jam into the front page at the last minute, down in the corner. The heading said SNEAK THIEF GETS RECORDS. The item said:

> A sneak thief entered the offices of Yoland & Jolley, Certified Public Accountants in the Heyburn Building, just as the office was opening for business this morning, talked himself into the private office of Gregory Yoland, senior partner of the firm, and then calmly walked out with a bundle of valuable records while Mr. Yoland was engaged at the telephone in an adjoining room.

Mr. Yoland and Miss Mayberry Judson, secretary, immediately gave the alarm but the culprit had mingled with the crowd in the lobby and was not immediately apprehended. Police officers working on the case said that the thief had been described as a short, heavily built man of about 35, with bruises on his face and a lower front tooth missing. He was dressed in a brown suit, tan shoes and straw hat. It was said that the thief obtained entry by identifying himself as a member of a prominent law firm of another city, but police were working on the theory that this was merely a ruse and would not disclose the name given. George Clay, cab driver giving an address on Catalpa Street, reported that he had taken a man answering the above description to the main branch of the Louisville Free Public Library shortly after 9:00 a.m. An early arrest is expected.

I wondered if there was any way to grow a new tooth, remove bruises, reduce thirty pounds or grow eight inches taller in a few minutes, but decided there wasn't. I thought about buying a new suit and incidentally giving my tortured stomach a rest, but with the other details so accurately reported, I thought it would be a waste of time and money.

There wasn't any water at the newsstand so I took two tablets out of the box and munched them disagreeably as I walked down the street wondering how long it would be before I was on the inside looking out.

A block or so away I went into a shoe repair shop and gave the man at the counter two bits to wrap up my bundle of papers and put a string around it. Then I found a Western Union office and paid out another two bits to have the package delivered to the office of Yoland & Jolley. The girl seemed to have trouble with the name and address and I wondered if she were stalling, but then it occurred to me that the newspaper had just hit the streets and it might be some time before I was in real danger. I borrowed a telephone directory but it didn't list anyone by the name of Phoebe Murdoch. There were three people listed who spelled their names with a *k* instead of an *h*, but no "Murdochs" at all. I tried several other spellings but no results.

Just to be sure, I went over to the Court House, looked up the indexes and got a clerk to dig out the adoption file for me. The name was definitely spelled with an *h* several times and there was the name signed plainly at the end of a notarized statement. I inquired about the company that publishes the city directories and found it was only a few blocks away.

They had back numbers almost to the time of Daniel Boone and wouldn't mind if I took a look.

I found a Phoebe Murdoch listed in 1915 at the address given in the Court records. I followed her through volume after volume until about 1925 and then she disappeared altogether. I noted the last address on the back of an envelope and then on an off-chance I asked the directory people if there was any way to tell whether she moved, died or got married, and they said there wasn't.

I didn't like the idea of doing too much messing around with my description and criminal activities on the front page of every newspaper, but I did want to see Miss Phoebe Murdoch or find out what had happened to her. I walked down Third Street to the State Board of Health office and ordered an attested copy of the death certificate of a Miss Phoebe Murdoch who died a resident of Jefferson County probably in 1925, but they said if she was dead, she must have died some place else. I wanted to check the marriage records, but that meant going back into the Court House right in the teeth of the law and I didn't think it was quite as important as that.

Not being familiar with the town, I didn't have the faintest idea how you got to the last known address of the lady I was looking for, so I muttered a prayer and flagged a cab. I was careful to keep my mouth shut as much as possible.

The neighborhood was modest but respectable enough. I paid the cabdriver, rang the bell, and a woman who looked like Edna Mae Oliver told me in a few well-chosen words that she never heard of anyone by that name and slammed the door.* Then I crossed the street and rang every doorbell for a while and from the character of the reception I was getting I might as well have been selling Bluine,† like if you sell enough of it you get a "Marvo" chemical set packed for shipment in a handsome cardboard case in three colors. It began to look as if Miss Phoebe Murdoch was going to have to be one of the major unsolved crimes of history, but I decided I would ring two more bells, then give it up as a bad job.

It didn't take two more bells. The next one I rung a pretty girl was about to slam the door in my face, as usual, and then said, "Murdoch! Wait a minute." She left the door open and called out something toward the back of the house with a voice that Paul Robeson‡ would trade his in for. A fat woman waddled out of somewhere wiping soap off of her hands and fumbling for her glasses. She peered at me intently and I thought for a moment that she must be checking up on a brown suit, tan shoes, straw hat, missing tooth, etc., until I remembered that I hadn't seen any newspapers on any front porches and probably it was a later edition that was delivered at home. Finally the fat woman said:

---

*Edna Mae Oliver (1883–1942) was a well-known character actor, who described herself as having "a horse's face." In a lovely coincidence, she played the detective Hildegarde Withers in the early 1930s series of Stuart Palmer's mystery novels.

†A popular laundry product for bleaching, bluing, and purifying clothing. The earliest advertisements date to 1907, when it sold for 10 cents for a four-month supply. A 1921 advertisement offered a premium of a school box with a pen, pencils, etc., for selling 10 packages of Bluine, and there were undoubtedly many more sales incentives offered over the years.

‡Robeson (1898–1976) was a renowned African American bass baritone singer and performer who became famous for his activism as well as his artistry.

"Yes, I remember a Miss Murdoch a long time ago. She lived over there."

"I am a lawyer trying to find the heirs of a Dr. Ellis Murdoch of Philadelphia. I think maybe Miss Phoebe Murdoch would come in for a pretty good slice of the estate. Do you know what happened to her?"

The fat woman said to come in and sit down and wanted to know was it a very big estate and she didn't know Miss Murdoch had any relatives in Philadelphia but it was a little world and anything could happen, couldn't it.

I said anything could certainly happen and for example how about what happened to Miss Phoebe Murdoch. Well, she didn't rightly know and would have to think about it and maybe ask her husband and how many other relatives were there and what did he die of. I wondered what she would say if I told her he died of leprosy but I told her cancer because that seemed safe enough. It seems she had an Uncle Tobias who died of cancer in Minneapolis in 1910 and I thought that was pretty interesting and I said it was quite a coincidence and she said yes, wasn't it.

Her husband ran a secondhand store on Market Street. Would she call him and see what he knew about Miss Phoebe Murdoch. Well she didn't know about that. He didn't like for her to call him in the daytime because he might lose a sale sometime, but then maybe he wouldn't mind if it was about lost heirs and things like that like on the radio, and it certainly would be a big help to me if she would do just that very thing and she believed she would. I had to sit there while she went over the whole thing by telephone, including Uncle Tobias and his cancer, but finally she came back and said that Miss Phoebe Murdoch had sold her house and moved out of town, he thought to Cincinnati or New Orleans or some such place. I asked if there was anyone else in the neighborhood who had lived there as long as she had and she said no the place had changed a good deal and a lot of people had got the idea that they were too high-toned and had moved to other parts of town, but come to think of it there was a Mrs. Kilgallen over on the next street whose house backed up to where Miss Murdoch used to live and she had been there a long time. I thanked her and hoped that Mrs. Kilgallen did not have an Uncle Tobias, especially if he had cancer sometime or other. I thought I probably could have saved a lot of time by making it leprosy after all.

Mrs. Kilgallen was a neat little woman who sat with her feet together and her hands in her lap. She remembered Miss Murdoch very well and liked her all right except that they always had a sort of dispute about something she couldn't remember now exactly what it was. She didn't know what had happened to Miss Murdoch but wished she was still living there, even with the dispute and everything, because the people she sold her place to and all the subsequent occupants of the premises were pretty common and one of them had got caught with a still in the attic and was in the papers and everything. I asked if Miss Murdoch had ever gotten over the severe burns she had and Mrs. Kilgallen said that must have been after she left since she didn't have any burns that she knew of, although she herself had once burned her hand pretty bad on the stove.

I said good-bye and was closing the door behind me when the telephone rang and in a minute Mrs. Kilgallen came pattering to the door to tell me to wait a minute. Then she went back to finish her conversation and when she returned it seems that the call was from the fat lady and she said the postman had just been by her house and he had been on that route ever since anyone could remember and maybe he would know something.

I had spent a lot of time already but the postman sounded like he might be a good bet so I walked around the block and caught up with him. He was friendly enough and said I could do all the talking I wanted to if I was willing to walk along with him so he wouldn't lose any time. At that point he blew his whistle and left me on a sidewalk while he went up some steps and stuck something in a mailbox.

He remembered Miss Phoebe Murdoch all right, and then blew his whistle and went up some more steps and I waited for him again. Between that house and the next one I learned that Miss Murdoch was not very friendly, but perfectly respectable, and then there was that whistle again. We completed the block in this fashion and to the best of my recollection every house on both sides of the street got a communication of some sort through the facilities of the post office department on that day. Sometimes he would not get back to the subject at all between two houses but would get off on the subject of people in the neighborhood, or talk to the lady on the porch he had just left or on the porch he was about to get to. He seemed to be about my last chance to make any progress so I put up with this procedure with all the patience I could muster and it was about the end of the block on the far side of the street when I finally got it out of him that Miss Murdoch had indeed left a forwarding address and at that point I asked would he mind very much if we just stood still for a minute and got through what we were talking about and if his time were awfully valuable, I would pay it to him in cash. He wanted to see the cash in advance and he did and so we stopped.

I said: "I know it was a long time ago but I'll bet you just happen to remember what that forwarding address was." I had a five dollar bill rather carelessly in my hands and I wouldn't be surprised if it might have been waving around a little in front of his eyes. He thought a long time and his eyeballs looked pretty hard at the five dollar bill. Finally he said:

"Nope, can't remember."

"Not at all?"

"Well, I remember the name. That was Miss Phoebe Murdoch. I remember that."

"Well, that's something. It would sure be tough if you didn't remember even that."

"But I don't remember the street. No, sir. I've clean forgot the street. That was when did you say? 1925. Hmmmmm. Sixteen years ago. My daughter was seven. She didn't cost me much then but by God she sure does now."

"I'll bet she does. Don't remember the street, huh?"

"Nope, don't remember the number either. Can't even remember whether it was a big number or a little number and can't remember whether it was odd or even. Just don't remember it. Don't remember a thing."

I was definitely discouraged but if I was going to pay him for his time anyway I was certainly going to stay there until the well was dry. I said:

"How about the city?"

"Wasn't a city at all. Seems to me it was some little place somewhere. Do you ever read history?"

I said I had read some history but what did that have to do with it.

"John Brown," he said, shaking his head with a distant expression, "something to do with John Brown or something like that."

"All I know about John Brown is that his body lies mouldering in the grave," I ventured.*

"Well, that might be it. I don't know anything much about him myself. Might be where the body lies mouldering or something."

I said: "Well, let's see. I believe he was killed at Harpers Ferry. That mean anything?"

"Yep. Kinda believe it does. Son of a gun if that ain't where she moved. That's just about it. Yessir. You just about got it. Harpers Ferry sounds just about right. Didn't think I would remember it, did you? Well, as a matter of fact, I didn't think I would either."

I thought I began to see something I hadn't seen before.

"Aren't quite sure, are you?"

"Well I wouldn't say that."

---

*Gil humorously refers to the well-known Civil War marching song about the famous abolitionist who was killed in his daring raid on Harper's Ferry. The tune was subsequently reused for "The Battle Hymn of the Republic."

"How does Harpersville sound?"

"Sounds a lot like Harpers Ferry, don't it?"

He shook his head and muttered, "Harpers Ferry Harpersville-Harpers Ferry-Harpersville," and then he looked up and said:

"Son of a gun, damn if I can tell one from the other. Could be Harpersville. Could be Harpers Ferry."

I could see I wasn't going to get anything more out of him and I thought I knew what I wanted to know anyway so I said thanks a lot and gave him the five dollar bill.

25

I went into a grocery store and borrowed the telephone and called to see when I could get a train out for my own stamping ground. There weren't any more trains until eight o'clock in the evening and that would put me back in my office the next day, which wouldn't do. I called the bus terminal and found that one bus had left a few minutes before and the next one was at 6:30 in the evening, so that wouldn't do either. I had an awful urge to get out of town in the first place, and I wanted to get back to the office and on to Harpersville in the second place.

While I was turning this over in my mind, I put in a call to Yoland & Jolley and asked to speak to Mr. Jolley. I recognized Miss Judson's voice and she said:

"Sorry, Mr. Jolley is out of town. Could I take a message please?"

"He told me he would be back this morning."

"He did come back this morning, but he went out of town again. It may be several days before he is back. Who's calling, please?"

"Did he say where he was going?"

"Who is this speaking, please?"

"Did you get a package from Western Union?"

"Oh! Wait just a minute, please."

"Never mind," I said, "the police haven't got me yet."

I hung up. If Hillman Jolley was out of town, it looked as if he hadn't gone to Harpersville since I didn't think he was the kind who would travel by bus if he could help it, and if he had gone by train, he would have had to catch one about an hour after he got back to the office.

I looked up the airport and called the office about chartering a plane and I was told to get in touch with a flying service, which I did. They didn't have much to offer but there was a Piper Cub I could get and I had enough money left to pay for it. I gave them the first name I could think of just in case the police were checking up, and then told them to have the plane ready and I would be there as fast as a cab would take me.

26

I was back in the city again after it was good and dark and the office was closed. I had to let myself in with my key. I was pretty quiet about it for no particular reason and I was glad of it. There was a light shining through the frosted glass panel of Mr. James Mead's door and I did not much want to talk to Mr. James Mead at that time. I went into my own room on tiptoe but I was afraid I would make a noise if I shut the door, so I just sat down quietly in the dark and didn't even smoke a cigarette. There was nothing to do and I sat there and remembered I hadn't eaten anything since the first World War, and I was so hungry I almost felt dizzy.

Then I heard Mr. Mead's door open and the light went off and someone walked through the outer office in the dark. The door into the hall was the kind you can always open from the inside whether it's locked from the outside or not. From where I was sitting I could not see the door and by the time I got up for a better look the door was closing and all I could see was a shadow against it before Mr. Mead walked away. The only trouble was, it definitely was not the shadow of Mr. James Mead, although shadows are more or less shapeless sorts of things and I could not have told you why. All the same, it was definitely not the shadow of Mr. Mead, and the footsteps that rang on the cement floor of the hall did not sound like Mr. Mead either. The footsteps were very quick and precise, not like when someone is running but like the footsteps of a person who walks rapidly with a very short stride.

I knew there was no chance to follow since my leather heels would raise hell out in the corridor, but I did go as far as the door and opened it softly. Whoever it was had just disappeared around the corner toward the elevators and a moment later I heard the night bell ring. I waited until the elevator door clicked shut and then I went down to the elevator myself and after a decent interval I rang the bell. The elevator operator told me I ought to make up my mind. He said he had just made a trip to the same floor and nobody got on.

27

I told the elevator man to go on down without me and from the expression on his face I didn't doubt that he would stay right where he was the next time the bell rang for the tenth floor. I stood where I was and listened to the elevator until it stopped and then the building was so quiet I could hear my heart beat. I put my back to the elevator door and looked down the hall to the comer I had just come around. There was a dim light over my head and another one at the corner of the corridor, but otherwise the whole floor was dark. There was no light in any of the offices and as far as I could see the doors were shut tight.

I wondered what I would have done if I had rung the elevator bell and disappeared. I could have opened the door to the stairway and gone up or down. I could also have walked into one of the offices and closed the door behind me, and if I had some sort of key that would let me into the office of Mead, Opdyke, Smallwood, Garrison and Henry, it might also be a key that would open other doors in the building like the keys held by the night elevator man and the cleaning women. Since I had seen the man turn the corner toward the elevator, this would mean he was behind one of the doors I was looking at, if he were behind any door at all. Among the doors before me were those of the men's washroom and the ladies' washroom, but these lock like any other doors and you had to have a key to get in, so they didn't belong to any special class. That about covered the possibilities as far as I could see.

I remained there as long as I could stand it, and although it seemed like thirty minutes, it was probably not more than five. Nothing happened and the building was so still I could hear the water dripping from a defective tap in one of the washrooms. I knew I was going back to the office to see what I could find, but it was hard to make up my mind to move because I knew if anyone were listening, the clattering of my heels would tell them exactly what I was doing.

Finally I thought of something and took off my shoes as quietly as I could. I was glad none of our better clients was present because there was a big hole in one of my socks and the floor was cool where my bare toes touched it.

I made so little sound on my way back to the office that I couldn't even hear myself. I got the key in the lock without difficulty even in the gloom and eased the door shut behind me. I went straight into Mr. Mead's office and since there was no way to avoid it, I turned on the light. At first I couldn't see any evidence that anyone had been there at all, but then I remembered that Mr. James Mead was not like me and always kept the top of his desk clear of everything except an appointment book and a pen set. It was not clear now. A file was on one corner of it and the file was marked "Harper Products Company—Income Tax Deficiency—1938."

I wish telephones would not ring so loud and so suddenly. Looking back at the last few days, I realized that I was getting awfully jumpy and telephones had acquired a new significance.

I went out to the switchboard and if I had been smart I guess it would have occurred to me that the phone had no business ringing since no one could be expected to be in the office at that hour.

I answered it just the same. I guess my mind was on the file in the other room and anyway there is practically no one human who can sit and watch a telephone scream its head off without doing something about it. I picked up the operator's headphone and put it to my ear and said, "Hello," into the little horn that she hangs around her neck.

Nothing happened. I said hello again and thought maybe I didn't know how to operate the switches but I tried all of them and said hello several times and still nothing happened. Then I realized that somebody wanted to know whether I was in the office or not, and somebody knew.

You can't stay in an office on the tenth floor of a building the rest of your life, especially when you are as hungry as a mother wolf. However, you can stay there quite a while when you don't want to go out, and I expect even a mother wolf would rather be hungry a little while longer if the alternative is to come out and look a hunter between the eyes. I decided I wasn't so terribly hungry after all and went in and opened the file on Mr. Mead's desk.

There wasn't much to see. The Bureau of Internal Revenue had given notice to Harper Products Company of a deficiency assessment for the year 1938 and there were a lot of figures showing the Bureau's computation of how much profit the Company had actually made. Even allowing for the fact that the government always claims everything in sight so as to be sure not to miss anything, the figure did not look anything like what I remembered seeing in the audit report. I would have been glad to take the difference in the taxes and retire from the practice of law.

There was some correspondence between William Jasper Harper and James Mead as to whether the additional assessment should be paid or contested, with Mr. Mead recommending for various reasons that it be paid and William Jasper Harper insisting that it be fought. The top thing in the file was a letter signed

by William Jasper Harper instructing my partner to file a pro-
test immediately and carry on the battle with all ammunition at
hand. I couldn't see why anyone should break into an office to
read a dull file like that and made a mental note to come back
sometime when I was not starving to death and make a more
thorough investigation of the attractions the office might have
to offer. I picked up my shoes, turned out the light and listened
at the outer door. There was not a sound. I looked out cautiously
and the hall was empty. I made up my mind I was not walking
down ten flights of stairs and if the elevator man didn't want to
come up to the tenth floor, I was going to hold my hand on the
bell until he did.

Once started, there was no use dillydallying. I walked rapidly
down the corridor, turned the corner and proceeded briskly
toward the elevators, watching all the doors like a cat watches
ratholes.

It would have paid me to look behind but I could hear the
elevator coming up and I guess that is what distracted me.
When I heard a sound it was too late. Somebody hit me and I
don't remember going down.

28

I have never had a particularly high regard for women who clean office buildings. I never had anything against them but we had always moved in different social circles and they were just things that were there like running water and light switches.

Now cleaning women have an enviable place in my esteem, especially the shapeless old woman who was bending over me when I opened my eyes. I probably owe my life to the fact that the elevator was bringing her up when a blunt instrument clipped me behind my right ear. It was entirely possible that my assailant did not intend to make me extinct but it did not seem logical that he would hang around waiting for me so that he could practice with his blunt instrument. It seemed obvious enough that he must have heard me when I walked into the office the first time and my subsequent maneuvers must have made him think I knew who he was. If that were the case, it would do no good to have me sleeping for a few minutes in a corridor where I was sure to be found sooner or later. If my knowledge didn't hurt him he would have left me alone. If it was dangerous enough to make him clout me over the head, there could hardly be any doubt of his intention to get rid of me permanently.

The cleaning woman was a sensible soul and instead of

asking a lot of foolish questions, she opened the door to the ladies' washroom and helped me get in where I could put some water on my face and explore the swelling on the back of my head. It was a nasty-looking place and I was pretty tired of having everything north of my neck beaten out of shape.

There wasn't much blood and a handkerchief soaked in cool water stopped what little there was. I explained to old Mother Hubbard that I had slipped in some unaccountable way and I suppose she must have heard all the silly explanations in the world because her expression clearly said that if it was my business, it was my business and to hell with it. I asked her if anyone who might have tripped me had passed her in the hall, but she said the place was as empty as a gourd so I left it at that.

29

My first thought was to get hold of the police and search the building but I remembered that I had given my name to Mr. Yoland and Mr. Yoland had given it to the police in Louisville. The way police departments work together these days I didn't think there was much to commend the idea that I could call the local gendarmes without getting myself involved in something more than explanations. If the price of getting a man put in the Bastille* was getting in there myself along with him, the price was decidedly too high.

I rang for the elevator again, gave the operator a dollar to make him feel better, bought a late edition of the afternoon newspaper and walked down to the YMCA. On the way I chewed some more aspirin tablets and wondered if life would ever reach a lower ebb. In addition to the tooth and the bruises and the lump on the back of my head, I was hungry almost to the point of unconsciousness and my pants were still squeezing my empty middle and there were bloodstains on my collar. I half expected to find a policeman in the lobby waiting for me but I guess the possibility of chartering a plane had not occurred to them and no doubt I was supposed to be still in Louisville. I went up to

*The notorious French fortress, in which many of the prisoners of the French kings were incarcerated—stormed by revolutionaries at the onset of the French Revolution.

my room and found that someone had been there and had scattered my belongings all over the floor. The drawers were out of the dresser and such suits as I had were scattered around with most of the pockets turned wrong side out. Feeling as I was, the sight was almost more than I could stand.

I called the Greek who runs the cafe in the middle of the next block and told him to send me up the best steak he could find and a hatful of French fried potatoes and a whole pot of coffee. After that I called him back again and told him if he loved his mother he was to get some whiskey from somewhere and send it along. He said he couldn't do it but I knew he would. Then I got under a hot shower and stayed there until I was as limp as a piece of spaghetti. I was just drying myself when the boy came up with the food. I felt rather lavish and gave him a five dollar bill and told him to keep the change. George, the Greek, hadn't been able to get me a bottle of whiskey but there was a tumbler half full of it from some supply of his own and I drank it as soon as the door was closed. This time it went down much easier than on the train and it occurred to me that if this kept up, I would be seeing faces on the barroom floor* and spoiling all of the good habits which I had spent a lifetime learning.

I spread the dinner on my desk and the sight of it had me trembling so I could hardly pour the coffee. I opened the newspaper so I could read the headlines while I was eating and the top thing in letters about three inches high stopped me in my tracks. When I got as far as learning that William Jasper Harper was dead I didn't wait for the details but hustled into a suit of clothes and down to the all-night garage where my car was being repaired, in something like a world's record. The car was ready and before the steak was cold I was about halfway to Harpersville.

---

* "The Face Upon the Barroom Floor" is a famous (infamous?) 1872 poem by John Henry Titus about a drunk and his lost love, later adapted to songs, paintings, and movies.

30

There was not much gas in the tank and before I got to Harpersville I had to pull into a filling station. While I was there I saw some of these little packages of sandwiches made out of crackers and stuff and I jammed six or eight of them in my pocket to eat on the road. Then I opened the newspaper to learn what I could while the attendant was working on the car. The paper was not a late afternoon edition at all but was an extra and the ink wasn't even dry on it. William Jasper Harper had been alive about an hour and a half before and I could imagine the pandemonium in the newspaper office when they hustled to get that extra on the streets. There was a lot of stuff about his life, including where he was born and where he was educated and what he owned and what he was a director of and I guess that much of the article had been written up and kept on file for years against such a moment as this, just as if Mr. William Jasper Harper were Adolf Hitler or Mahatma Gandhi or somebody. The part about his death was very short and said practically nothing. The Harper family was big stuff in this part of the state and the news was handled as if it were a venereal disease. It was perfectly plain that the guy was defunct and it was also made pretty clear that he did not die of old age, but as for the rest of it, you could draw your own conclusions and your guess would have been as good as mine. Practically the only fact was that he was not living any more and his body had been found in his study in his home about nine o'clock that evening with a bullet hole in its head. He had dined at 7:00 with the family and shortly afterwards he had gone into the study and closed the door. The study had French doors opening on a paved terrace. The kitchen help had heard something that could have been a chair falling over or could have been a shot, but they were in another part of the house and did not immediately connect the sound with the study. Mrs. Harper, who was an invalid, had a room downstairs near the study and she was the first one to think there must be something wrong. She summoned the servants and that was how he was found.

The newspaper article also said that the sheriff and coroner had been called after the family physician came and said he was dead and the sheriff "was following a number of leads" and expected to make important disclosures soon. If you read the guarded wordings two or three times you could take your choice between suicide and murder and obviously the newspaper was not making any choices of its own.

Harpersville was a good deal wider awake than it was when I drove in two nights before. One car was rolling up to the police station just off the main street and another was roaring away. I decided that it was safe enough to barge on into the town since the sheriff was not likely to worry about small stuff like abandoned charges of attempted blackmail while he was confronted with his big chance to get on half of the front pages of the country.

I did not know where the Harper home was located so I drove around to the McClures' and parked. There was a light on in the living room and Ruth McClure was just coming out of her own room with her hat on and before I even got in the door I could tell that she had been crying and not so long ago at that. Miss Katie was there too and I was about as welcome as Mussolini would have been.

Something had upset Ruth pretty badly but she was not in such condition that she could forget who I was. When she saw me she was as mad in three-fifths of a second as anyone could possibly get and I could see that I was going to be a goat of something I didn't understand. She clinched her fists and when she spoke she was the next thing to strangling she was so mad. She said:

"Of all the nerve! Millions of lawyers in the world and I had to pick you. Get out of this house and if I ever see your shadow again, I'll kill you if I have to do it with a corkscrew."

It was hard to tell whether she was going to kick me or burst out crying. I don't know anything about women and probably never will, but I didn't have time to put up with any foolishness and I had been pushed around about all I could stand, so I smacked her in the face pretty hard and then shook her until my own teeth rattled.

I thought Miss Katie was going to take a bite out of my arm with the good side of her mouth, but I gave her a glare that nearly set fire to her clothes and she didn't do any more than bare her fangs at me and keep her distance. Ruth sat down hard in the nearest chair and burst into tears. I have never been more exasperated in my life and I said with considerable feeling:

"What in hell is going on here?"

Ruth went right on crying but Miss Katie said:

"It was Tim. They think he did it. They've got him down at the police station and he won't say a word."

31

I got down on my knees in front of Ruth McClure and took both her hands and held them firmly although she was trying to jerk them away. She tried to get up but I pushed her back. I was pretty peeved. I said: "Listen little Bopeep, the sheep you are losing aren't the kind that come home wagging their tails behind them. You have to go out and look for them and I may be just the guy who can do it whether you think I'm Hercule Poirot or Alias Jimmy Valentine.* Now get up and wash your face and powder your beak and let's start something."

It didn't go over too big. The look she gave me made it plain that in her bluebook the value of a '41 model Gilmore Henry was lower than net income after taxes.

"You started the whole thing," she said bitterly. "We were stupid and happy and everything was doing fine and then you had to come along and ask a lot of questions so Tim gets to thinking about things and then he slams out of here and goes to see Mr. Harper and now Mr. Harper is dead and Tim's in jail and I hate your damn g-guts."

---

*The exploits of the former detective were recorded at length by Dame Agatha Christie; Jimmy Valentine, a reformed ex-convict, is the protagonist of the 1910 play by Paul Armstrong titled *Alias Jimmy Valentine* based on O. Henry's 1903 short story "A Retrieved Reformation." Three films of the play were made between 1915 and 1928, and a radio drama appeared in the late 1930s.

"All right, if I've got to do it the hard way, I'll do it the hard way. As Tim's lawyer I could get in and talk to him and probably I could get into the Harper house and find out a lot of things. If I'm not Tim's lawyer, I'm just a guy named Joe and the law will push me around like a vacuum cleaner. I didn't start anything that wasn't started long ago and I suppose I came down here two weeks ago and made a bull's eye out of the tire on your father's car just to win the cheap cigar or a baby doll for the kiddies. I didn't get the lump on my head out of a sugar bowl." It was a pretty long speech for me and if I hadn't been wound up as tight as a watch spring, I would have run down before I got it all out. I had forgotten all about Miss Katie but she brought me back to the present tense.

"Kick him out," she said coldly, "he's no good. He asks all the questions in the book but he doesn't supply any answers. Tell him to beat it and good riddance if you ask me."

But I had gotten under Ruth's hide somewhere down the line and she stood up quite steadily and blew her nose.

"No, Miss Katie, I'm not so sure. He's a stinker in a lot of ways and I wouldn't name a child after him but he's probably right when he says he came in for only the second feature, the news reel and the preview of coming attractions."

"What would Tim say?"

"Tim isn't in position to choose and neither am I." She went into her room and Miss Katie glared at me and went out and banged the door shut behind her.

32

At the door of police headquarters we ran into Mr. James Mead and he looked at me and then at Ruth and then at me again with evident surprise.

"What are you doing here?" he asked angrily. "I thought you were going to Louisville and that a certain agreement was made."

"I was going to Louisville and I did go to Louisville, but that was yesterday. I didn't say anything about not coming back."

"Where do you figure in this thing?"

"I happen to be the attorney for Mr. Timothy McClure."

"You can't do that. This is the second time you've gotten off base. You accepted an employment hostile to the interests of a client of the firm and I thought that was all cleaned up. I represent the family of the deceased. You can't represent the murderer."

"I can, will and do. How do you like that?"

"You can't, it's unethical."

I drew in a deep breath and looked straight at him. "I asked permission to represent Miss McClure in the first place and told you what she wanted and you said it was all right. I never knew until this evening that you represented Harper or his family or his company or any part thereof and when I got it, it didn't come from you. I saw a file on your desk. As for the present employment, it might have been improper two minutes ago but it is not improper now."

"What do you mean?"

"A partnership is terminable at will. Ours is terminated now. I hereby terminate the partnership of Mead, Opdyke, Smallwood, Garrison & Henry and you can call in the auditors and figure what's coming to me, if anything."

It is curious the way the human mind sometimes digresses in moments of stress and seizes upon the most absurdly inconsequential aspects of a matter, like people who run out of a burning building and at the moment see nothing illogical in taking a chamber pot with them. What Mr. Mead said, after a long moment of study, was: "We'll have to send out announcements."

I said, "Yes, won't we?" and then I took Ruth by the arm and we walked into headquarters and left him standing there.

33

There was an officer who looked like he might be in charge and we told him we wanted to talk to Tim McClure. He said we couldn't do it, but I told him I was Tim's lawyer and he said that he guessed a man had a right to see a lawyer so he could be sent to the electric chair all legal and proper. This view of the matter did not particularly appeal to me, but I didn't think I would solve any of the world's problems in a conference with this cluck, so I let it go at that. He disappeared down a hall and pretty soon he came back and said:

"Wouldn't see you. Says he hasn't got a lawyer and doesn't want one and if it's a little fat guy bunged up pretty good, it's all right by him if you dissolve in sulfuric acid."

"Never mind him," said Ruth, taking my arm, "I've hired a lawyer for him whether he likes it or not. Let me go in and talk to him and we'll see."

The officer knew Ruth and didn't think it would hurt anything for her to go in, so she went. I sat down and pulled a package of cracker-sandwiches out of my pocket and ate them slowly. They were as dry as a hard boiled egg. I offered one to the police officer and he took it absent-mindedly and popped it into his mouth.

"How come the city's working on this case?" I asked companionably. "The newspaper said the sheriff was called in."

"Don't know. I do what I'm told. I got a job and they pay me to do it and what do I care who's right and who's wrong." Then he relented a little. "Harper place is part in and part out of the city limits. Everytime something comes up around there, it's been little and nasty, and then the county says it's in the city and the city says it's in the county and we wind up doing whatever Mr. Harper says. Now we got something big and just between you and me it's the other way around and everybody wants to get wrote up in the newspaper. Us fellers and the county fellers do the work and the sheriff and the chief will fight about the headlines."

Ruth came to the door about that time and beckoned to me and I went back into the city jail with her. There were just a few cells and the whole place smelled bad. There was a drunk asleep in one of them and Tim was in another and the rest were empty. Tim was defiant and sullen-looking at the same time but evidently Ruth had talked him into seeing me and if he was going to see me at all, he was going through with it the right way just to please her.

They unlocked the door and we went in and they locked it behind us. I wondered uneasily whether they were going to let me out when I was through what I was doing, or whether they were going to charge me with something in the books and let this be my permanent address.

Tim said impatiently: "All right, ask your questions and hurry up and then go away."

I said: "Were you there or weren't you?"

"Yes, I was there."

"What time?"

"I don't know exactly. I think I left the house about ten minutes after eight and stopped at a store in town and bought a coke to see if I would change my mind and I didn't. I would say it's about a ten-minute drive to the Harper place from home and I may have taken five minutes or ten minutes at the store."

"That would make it around half past or a couple minutes one way or the other."

"I guess so. That's about it. I couldn't figure it any closer than that."

"How long did you stay?"

"I don't know. We were having a talk and then we didn't get along so good and time gets away from you when you aren't thinking about it."

"Drove away in your own car, of course?"

"Yes, I drove there in it but I didn't go into the driveway. Left the car out on the street and walked up to the door."

"Who let you in?"

"A man who drives for Mr. Harper and sometimes for Mrs. Harper. He wears a uniform and everything."

"Did he show you out?"

"No. I lost my temper and was feeling pretty upset and went out through the French windows. There is a terrace there and some bushes and then the drive leading back to the rear entrance and the garages."

"See anybody when you left?"

He frowned in concentration and I could see him following himself to the driveway and out to his car, trying to get it all back clearly. He shook his head and said:

"No, I don't remember seeing a soul, either on my way out to the car or on the drive to town. If I had seen anyone I doubt if I would remember it, anyway. I had lots to think about."

"What, for example?"

A clam has never shut up more visibly than he did. He said:

"Because Ruth wants it, you ask all the questions you want about what happened. What I think about is my business."

"All right, you think about it yourself then. When you talk, that's something happening and I can ask about that. What did you talk about?"

"I think we'll just skip that too."

I turned to Ruth and shrugged my shoulders. "I am supposed to be his lawyer for my benefit instead of his. Maybe he's not so far wrong at that. Between wrecks and people slapping me over the head, it's a tossup who's in trouble and who's out of it. We can come back to this later. Right now I think we had better run out to the Harper place and see what we can find."

"You go out by yourself, Gil," said Ruth. "I don't think they would let me in anyway and I want to talk to Tim awhile."

Tim was taking a good look at the lump on the back of my head. "Somebody sock you?"

"You should ask."

"I mean back there."

"Does it look like a fungus growth?"

"Leave out the comedy. I socked you in front but that doesn't give you a goose egg behind. Not like that one, anyway. Maybe you aren't so popular."

"I think that's a very conservative way to put it. I went from here to Louisville and stole some records trying to figure out your puzzle for you and before I got through, I felt as if the whole town was alive with policemen peering at me from behind telephone poles and from under automobiles. I flew back to my office and got knocked cold in the hall and somebody searched my room at the YMCA. I nearly got arrested for attempted blackmail right here in Harpersville and I've quit my law firm. I am rewarded by the undying love and affection of everyone concerned—I don't think. I wouldn't trust myself with a quarter as far as from here out to the water cooler. I'll see you subsequently." It sounded worse when I talked about it than it had seemed before. I walked out madder than a hatter and got my car and drove out to the Harper home.

34

The house was set back maybe 200 feet from the road and there were so many trees and shrubs you could hardly see the place. There were two parallel drives, one for you to use going in and the other for you to use coming out. In front of the impressive portico, there was a circle with a welter of flower beds in the middle so that you could drive in and go round and round and back out again if you wanted to. Another branch of the drive led around the house to a battery of garages with servants' quarters over them. Every flower in the place looked healthy and happy and every shrub had just had a haircut. To one of my plebeian tastes and experience it looked like Buckingham Palace in one of its more palatial moments. There was a big sign where you could see it from the road with a name like Elmhurst or Oakland or Parkbourne and under it the name of William Jasper Harper in gold letters and no abbreviations.

I was stopped when I turned into the entrance and asked a lot of questions. The police wanted to know was I a reporter and didn't I have cameras and flash bulbs and such, and when I said that I didn't, they looked into the car anyway and poked their fingers here and there like the Department of Agriculture looking for Japanese beetles or cow ticks. This seemed to be the sole function of the men at the entrance and when they were finally satisfied that I was not connected with any newspapers, I was allowed to go on up to the front door. There were a lot of cars and it took me quite a while to maneuver into a little crack between a Cadillac about the size of a locomotive and a police car.

A county patrolman and a city police officer were at the big door and each one acted as if the other wasn't there so I had to answer two sets of questions and finally neither one of them could decide whether I could go in or not. One man sent a message to the sheriff and the other sent a message to the chief of police and apparently both had the same idea at once because I was finally escorted down to the basement and into a big playroom where I was told to wait.

I didn't like it very much but there was nothing I could do about it, so I looked around to see what I could see. It was a gorgeous place and it could have been the main room of a country club as far as I was concerned. The house was built on ground that sloped from front to rear so that you could walk up three steps, through a door and out on a big lawn that ended in a pair of tennis courts made of asphalt. There was a big fireplace on one side of the room and plenty of comfortable chairs and a billiard table and a pingpong table and a bar. The space over the mantelpiece was full of a perfectly enormous mounted fish with a revolting expression on its face and on the mantel itself were a flock of trophies, mostly big silver cups with a few shields and other miscellaneous objects symbolic of various kinds of prowesses. No one seemed to be in any hurry to talk to me so I strolled over and started reading the inscriptions. The fish was the unfortunate prey of William Jasper Harper himself and there was an occasional solid silver trifle which he had won yachting and fishing at various play spots on the Eastern coast. The rest of the silverware had been awarded to Janet Harper for everything except throwing the 56 lb. weight. Apparently she was quite a tenniser and golfer and what she couldn't do with a bow and arrow, an Indian wouldn't want to do, but the thing I was particularly interested in was a series of gadgets testifying as to her excellence with pistol, rifle and shotgun.

Maybe you have played gin rummy and you hold a spread of four sixes, plus the eight and nine of diamonds. Then you draw the seven of diamonds right in the hole between the six and eight and so you shift your hand around and make one spread of three sixes and a four-card diamond spread on the side. This business of guns and Janet Harper was the seven of diamonds in my hand and since I did not want to overlook any bets, I shifted my cards accordingly and wondered about one thing and another.

While I was standing there, the door opened and you did not have to tell me that I was looking at Janet Harper. She was fairly tall and her face was inclined to be a little horsey, although not to such a degree that you could say she was unattractive. She was heavily tanned on all visible parts and her figure was good in a muscular sort of way. When she walked across the room, the calves of her legs showed the outlines of hard muscles. In a strangling contest, I would want somebody else for a partner.

She came clear over to the fireplace before she spoke to me and the closer she got the more I was reminded of a sleek panther, although there was nothing feline about her eyes. The air of composure and assurance that she carried around with her was one of a person content with all her assets and undisturbed by the opinions of others. You have seen people like her and you will know what I mean when I say that you did not have to read the racing form to know that she had won her last six starts and would probably win the next one.

She looked me over coolly and objectively and I had the feeling that in her racing stable I was roughly the equivalent of a one-eyed burro with hoof and mouth disease, but I also had the feeling that for the time being she might treat me like Whirlaway.*

---

*Whirlaway was the American thoroughbred horse that won the Triple Crown of racing in 1941.

I waited and presently she said:

"I believe they said the name was Mr. Gilmore Henry."

No argument so far. I thought I might as well wait and see what was coming and anyway if I opened my mouth there would be that tooth business and I already looked disreputable enough.

"My father mentioned you. He didn't like you much."

"I think that's a fair statement of known facts," I contributed cautiously.

"My father was a man who made up his mind quickly and sometimes violently."

"That was my observation."

She kept looking straight at me and my time was not too valuable so I looked straight at her. After a while she said:

"I hope you don't expect us to be too cordial. Especially at a time like this."

"No."

"I believe they said you were a lawyer and that you represent Timothy McClure."

"That's right."

"I suppose you will cause all the trouble you can and will look for anything which will put my father in an unfavorable light."

"That depends."

"I suppose people who are accused of crimes have rights and people are supposed to respect those rights whatever their personal inclinations may be."

"That's what it says in the books."

Something about me had her puzzled but I could not tell whether it was my face, shape, condition or maybe the fact that I was not giving her any sass or argument. She had a direct way of looking at me that made me want to look away, but I didn't do so. Finally she said:

"Exactly what do you want?"

I shrugged my shoulders very slightly.

"I'm a lawyer and I have a client. You want to convict him of killing your father. I didn't ask him, but I'm quite sure he doesn't want to be convicted. I want to look and talk and listen, here and elsewhere, now and whenever it may be necessary."

"And look around for any dirt you can find?"

"If there is dirt, who put it there?"

"That's one way of looking at it," she admitted. "Another way of looking at it might include the thought that if there is anything here, it's strictly the business of the family."

I said: "Do you have some particular dirt in mind?"

She flushed quickly and I thought she was going to flare up, but she didn't.

"That's not fair," she said, with more composure than I expected. "My father was a fine man and his life was as clean as most. But a mind with an evil turn in it can make anything look bad."

"I can see that you think that's the kind of mind I have. Well, you may be right. I already know a lot I was not intended to know and I expect to know more than that before I am through. I could remember a lot of things and maybe if I'm wrong about what I'm thinking—maybe you understand—I could keep them to myself. You don't trust me, do you?"

"When I came in here, I didn't. Maybe I still don't. And then again maybe I don't know. You're funny."

She turned on her heel and walked over to the door and closed it behind her without looking back. I tried to remember whether the rhythm of her footsteps was like the clicking of heels in the corridor outside my office a few hours before, but I couldn't tell for sure. While she was talking to me, I suddenly remembered that although I had unconsciously assumed that the person who hit me was a man, yet I had never seen the person and the shadow on the door had not been conclusive one way or the other. A lot of new avenues were opened up and I could see that I was going to have to do a lot of exploring before I knew where I was.

35

I waited maybe five minutes more expecting either the sheriff or the chief of police to come in for a conference, but there were no signs of anything doing. I could faintly hear people walking around upstairs and doors were opening and shutting every now and then. I didn't see any reason to cool my heels in solitude so I walked up the three steps, opened the glass door that led out to the lawn and looked around. Although it was well after midnight, every light in the house was on and when you say that about a place like the Harper home, it means you could have played night baseball in the back yard.

I walked away from the house and turned and looked up. Immediately above the playroom where I had been was what looked like the dining room and one branch of the law (I couldn't tell which) had taken over that room as headquarters. There seemed to be a butler's pantry next to the dining room and behind that in the corner of the same floor, to my right as I faced the house, was obviously the kitchen. Through the window of the kitchen I could see a heavy-set woman puttering around and I didn't see what she could be doing at that hour unless she was fixing coffee and maybe some food for the law. The idea interested me strangely. There was no door leading from the kitchen into the back yard where I was standing, so I wandered around the corner of the house and there sure enough was a door and some steps discreetly veiled behind heavy bushes so that blue-blooded guests who might gambol on the lawn need not be upset by domestic sights.

I walked on up to the door and went in without knocking. There was a divine odor of coffee that set me to trembling. The heavy-set cook had her broad behind in my direction and was carving slices from a tremendous ham. She turned and glowered at me and she had a faint fuzzy mustache on her upper lip.

"Who're you?" she asked, with more resignation than hostility.

"Another one of the crowd," I said casually and my salivary glands were in full operation. "Investigating crimes always makes me hungry. Particularly for ham and coffee in the middle of the night. Be a sweetheart, will you?"

She did not act very gracious but even so I could see her soften up perceptibly. People who fix things to eat like to see other people eat them, especially when they are hungry and say so, and I was so hungry it must have been shining out of my eyes for anybody to see. She kicked a chair around as if to indicate that was where I could sit and while she stomped around grumbling and muttering about people who wanted to eat at all kinds of filthy hours, she was nevertheless getting me a plate and a cup.

This suited me fine. I wanted to ask plenty of questions but even more than that I wanted to wrap myself around a considerable percentage of that ham and I knew I might have to do it before it was discovered that I was no longer in the playroom like a good little boy.

I went through a big thick sandwich like a snow plow and you could not have gotten rid of a cup of coffee any faster if you had poured it on the floor. The cook looked at me with something akin to admiration and awe but what she said was:

"You keep on eating like that the rest of your life and you'll rot all your insides out. If you want another sandwich get it yourself. I don't want anybody snapping off three fingers if I'm not quick."

I said: "Lady, there is something beautiful about you here in this pastoral setting with a pot of coffee in one hand and life-giving substances at your beck and call. If you would massacre a couple of eggs for me, I would strike a medal for you in honor of the occasion. When they made the original hungry man, they used me as a model."

She snorted: "Eggs! I'm not running a hotel. Ham and coffee are good enough for the others and they're good enough for you too."

Then she got out a frying pan and brought two eggs from the refrigerator and turned up the gas. I went to the refrigerator right behind her and took out two more eggs and tried to look at her like a setter dog about to lick your hand and so I had four scrambled eggs, very good indeed, in almost no time at all. After a while I said:

"Is this where you were when it happened?"

"Do I have to go over all that again?"

"There's no telling what dumb babies you have talked to before. I'm the only smart one in the whole outfit. I expect to have this whole thing figured out in maybe twenty-four hours at the most and I'll probably sleep twelve of them at that."

She really did not expect to get out of answering questions. "Wait until I come back," she said over her shoulder and I hurried after her just in time to hold open the swinging door to the butler's pantry so she could get out with the coffee pot and a big platter of sandwiches. I was careful not to show myself at the other swinging door that led from the butler's pantry into the dining room.

She was back in a moment and I could hear her making a great clatter with the cups and saucers in the butler's pantry and after that she finally came back and sat down, so I started all over again.

"Is this where you were when it happened?"

"Yes, the family finished their dinner sometime before eight and after the table was cleared we had our dinner here in the kitchen. Then I washed the dishes and I was tired and in no particular hurry, so it must have been nearly nine o'clock."

"Who's we?"

"Me and the butler and the chauffeur and the maid. The nurse is too good to eat with us and not good enough to eat with the family so she and Mrs. Harper have their dinner separately on a little table in Mrs. Harper's room."

"The nurse?" I asked.

"Mrs. Harper's nurse. She's been an invalid ever since the Lord knows when. They tell me she had some kind of sickness and it left her heart awfully bad. Just how sick she is I wouldn't know, but the way she's treated looks like somebody thinks she's three-fourths dead."

"All right, so you were washing the dishes. Were the others still here?"

"The maid was still in here talking to me while I did the work, but the butler and Mr. Miles had gone."

"Mr. Miles?"

"He's the chauffeur. He don't talk much. He looks like Humphrey Bogart and he's as cold as an eel."

"So just you and the maid were here. Then what?"

"Then was the noise. Boom. Kinda muffled and far away but we could hear it and it could have been a heavy chair falling over down in the playroom or it could have been a shot off some place else in the house or maybe it could have been a door slamming real hard. Didn't seem like anything to worry about so we listened a minute and didn't hear any yells or screams or anything and I went right on washing dishes."

"I'm listening. Tell it your own way."

"Well after a little while Miss Knight—that's the nurse—came back here and said did we hear a noise and we said that we did and she asked if we knew what it was and we said that we didn't. Then she said she was upstairs herself but Mrs. Harper gave her a buzz and wanted to know what was going on. She said Mrs. Harper was dozing and the noise woke her up and if we couldn't locate what it was we were to ask Mr. Harper in the study since it sounded kind of close to her. So Miss Knight is a pantywaist about investigating noises and the maid had her shoes off so I wiped my hands and tagged along. We knocked on the door of the study and I was feeling pretty silly and we didn't get any answer. We knocked again and then went next door into Mrs. Harper's room to ask should we go on in and she said that we should, so we went and there he was, as dead as a dead mackerel."

"The paper said shot. Whereabouts?"

"In the back of the head. He was sprawled in the middle of the floor on his face."

"The paper says there are French windows. Were they open or shut?"

"Open. We noticed that first thing."

"Gun anywhere around?"

"Didn't look at first. Miss Knight hollered and ran out and I went out too and pretty soon everybody was running from every which direction and when I peeped back in the door again, there was the butler in his shirt sleeves with his pants half unbuttoned and the chauffeur and Miss Janet came running down from upstairs and pushed by me and went in too."

"How did Miss Janet act?"

"She stood and looked but she didn't scream or anything and pretty soon she walked out without saying anything and I could hear her telephoning. Mrs. Harper was raising Cain* and why

---

*This phrase, meaning to cause trouble, has a long history. As early as 1840, a newspaper joked, "Why have we every reason to believe that Adam and Eve were both rowdies? Because…they both raised Cain!"

didn't anybody tell her anything, so I went in and told her. Then they shooed me back to the kitchen and that's all I know."

"You say Mrs. Harper's room is next to the study?"

"Yes, I understand it used to be a downstairs sitting room for the family so they wouldn't have to sit around in the hotel lobby they've got for big occasions, but when Mrs. Harper got sick they made it over into a bedroom for her and built in a private bath and everything."

I got up and walked around the kitchen once or twice and carelessly ate another sandwich. I had not heard anything startling and if there was anything I wanted to be it was startled. I had spent enough time in the kitchen and there were some things I wanted to know before the sheriff started looking for me as I knew he would be doing any minute. I thanked the cook and told her to come see me if she ever happened to be out of a job and then I went back into the yard again.

Exploring around cautiously I found that the driveway took a wide sweep around the far side of the house and looped back behind the tennis courts to the garages and servants' quarters which were set back from the corner where the kitchen was. Inside the loop was the lawn, about the size of a national park, and the tennis courts. Both sides of the drive were lined with thick bushes and when I walked around I could see through them into the French windows of the room on the other back corner of the house which was obviously the study and where I could see a lot of people milling around taking pictures and things. Between my bushes and the French windows there was a terrace paved with big square red tiles ending in a balustrade and a drop of eight or ten feet down to the level of the back lawn. The terrace extended on up toward the front of the house and there was another set of French windows opening out on it. I have a good deal of Peeping Tom blood in me and I walked up a few steps and did some of my best peeping. What I looked into was a room where a scrawny looking woman was sitting in a wheelchair with her head back against a headrest and her eyes closed. She looked very fragile and was as pale as the Hands I Loved Beside the Shalimar.* I wanted very much to have a talk with Mrs. Harper but she had gone through plenty and looked as if she were asleep. The French windows were open and I could not help wondering if they were open about nine o'clock that evening and just how sick Mrs. Harper was. And one of these days I wanted to have a heart to heart talk with Miss Knight.

---

*The popular poem "Kashmiri Song" (1901) by Laurence Hope, the pseudonym of Adela Florence Nicolson, begins with the line "Pale hands I loved beside the Shalimar." The poem was set to music in 1902, and the popularity of the song did not wane until World War II.

36

A couple of cars careened up the drive and Tim McClure got out of one of them, handcuffed to an officer. City and County patrolmen piled out around the two of them, and he was hustled toward the front door. I ran lightly around by the drive to the back of the house, walked through the playroom, and listened at the door. There was no evidence of any movement outside, so I opened the door, found the stairway, walked up to the first floor. At the head of the steps I looked around and located what I thought was the door of the dining room. No guard was stationed there, and I had my hand on the knob before the man inside the front door saw me.

He yelled, "Hey you!" and started after me, but I was in the room and had the door shut behind me in an instant. Tim was standing before the table, still handcuffed and surrounded. Two men were seated on the far side of the table. I walked quickly over, pushed through to Tim's side and said, "Go right ahead. I'm his lawyer."

"Where did you come from?" shouted the sheriff, half rising and knocking over his chair.

The door burst open behind me at this point and the policeman who had started after me in the hall jostled in and grabbed me by the collar. "Come here you!" he shouted energetically, "there don't nobody come in here without permission, see?"

The sheriff made a gesture with his hand, and the cop turned me loose. "I didn't let him by," he explained, panting. "He come up from the basement and busted in before I saw him even."

"OK, OK," said the sheriff in evident disgust. "Get back to the front door. Never mind this," pointing to me, "I'll take care of him."

I pulled my coat straight, and when I adjusted the collar I found that the swelling on the back of my head was bleeding again. I put my handkerchief to it. "Thanks, Sheriff. I'm glad somebody around here realizes my client has some constitutional rights."

The sheriff growled, "Rights hell. You'll stay around as long as you keep your mouth shut, and not a minute longer. Is that straight?"

I said it was. Having constitutional rights outside was not nearly so nice as being inside, with them or without them. A chair was produced for Tim, and I was permitted to find one and sit beside him.

"One question first," I put in as inconspicuously as possible, "who's got jurisdiction? The city or the county. I'm entitled to know who's in charge around here."

The sheriff turned to the man seated beside him, and asked should I be thrown out now or later. It was evidently the chief of police. Instead of answering, he said to me: "You can have all you're entitled to out in the street. One more crack out of you and I'll stick you in the can on suspicion. This investigation is being conducted jointly. Go ahead, Sheriff. One more word out of him and we'll throw him out without even taking a vote."

I didn't say anything more and the questioning started. As I listened, I could tell that this was just a rehash of a previous session and they were hoping to get Tim in a lie somewhere. I didn't learn anything new, and Tim told them over and over again pretty much what he had told me sometime earlier in the night. When it came to the point of the reason for his visit with William Jasper Harper and what was said between them, he wouldn't talk. Then they would go back and start all over again with what time did he leave home and exactly where did he go and how long did it take and when did he leave and why did he park his car out on the road instead of in the drive, and why did he go out by the windows instead of the way he came in.

Finally the chief said, "Hell, this ain't getting us anywhere. Bring in Ruth McClure and we'll check with her again on this time business. She hasn't gone to bed with all this excitement going on. See if she's at home."

"You leave Ruth out of this," said Tim ominously.

"You speak when you're spoken to," said the sheriff. "What say while we're waiting we take him over into the study and go over that part of it again?"

The chief thought that was a good enough idea and we all paraded across the hall and toward the back of the house a little and into a paneled room where a rich blue rug had a dark stain in the middle. I sat over by the French windows, which were still open, and a county patrolman stepped just outside the windows and stood there, blocking that exit. Then they took the cuffs off of Tim and he showed them two or three times where Mr. Harper was when he came in, and where they sat and stood and did. He stuck stubbornly to the story that William Jasper Harper followed him to the windows when he left and was standing there the last time Tim looked back. They came at him from every angle, but they couldn't shake him or catch him in a contradiction anywhere.

I guess this kind of thing went on pretty close to half an hour. Then an officer came in, looking a little flustered, and said, "Miss Ruth is gone. Can't find her anywhere. Lights on at the house. Stuff scattered everywhere. Bed rumpled but not slept in. Thought she might be staying with friends, but I called around several places and can't locate her. Car's gone too."

This was something I wasn't looking for. I was on my feet
with my mouth open to say something when out of the corner
of my eye I saw Tim, and stopped. He had a worried look on his
face, and he was in a half-crouch and as tense as just before the
kickoff. I didn't have to be told what he had on his mind. He
glanced quickly around the room and when he saw I was the
only one watching him, he held my eyes for a second and he
might have been begging for a dog biscuit. He must have found
the answer he wanted, because after that he was out on the terrace with four running strides and the shoulder he put in the
stomach of the policeman standing guard produced a grunt you
could have heard for about four city blocks. Bronko Nagurski
would have stood aside in admiration.*

Someone yelled, "Hey! Look out! Get him!" and all hell
broke loose. I ducked through the French windows as close
behind him as I could, and managed to trip rather realistically
over the policeman, who was groaning and holding his belly.
Two men right on my heels fell over me hard and swore fluently.
I couldn't do anything more, so I rolled over and looked to see
how Tim was doing.

I would say the bushes were maybe four and a half or five
feet high, and they were thick. As I looked up I saw Tim going
over them with all of his two hundred forty-five pounds and six
feet five inches, in as neat and light-footed a Western Roll† as I
ever hope to see. I was afraid he would break an ankle on the
asphalt of the drive, but I heard him land almost as easily as a
cat, and then there were some more short, driving strides and I
thought I saw a shadow loom briefly over the bushes on the far
side. A gun went off about eight inches from my head, and the
sound deafened me for a moment so I couldn't hear what direction Tim had taken after that. The police were crashing through

---

*Nagurski (1908–1990) was a star football player for the NFL's Chicago Bears, active between
1930 and 1943; he was also a professional wrestler with multiple championship titles.

†A high-jumping technique in which the leg farthest from the bar goes over first, followed by the
body. The style first became popular in 1912, when George Horine set the world's record at 6'7".

the bushes and feet were pounding all around, and the sheriff was shouting orders, and from Mrs. Harper's room someone was asking in a shrill voice what was happening, and if someone didn't tell her she would scream.

I did not want to enter into any discussions with constituted authority at that moment. In the confusion, I flattened myself in the gloom, against the wall. Then I walked casually back to the balustrade, took a look to see whether I was noticed, swung over, hung a moment, and dropped to the darkness of the back lawn. I did not want to walk across the brilliantly lighted area outside of the playroom, but there was no choice, so I stepped out of the shadows and did it as casually as I could. I went around the corner by the kitchen door, still without raising any hue and cry, and broke into a dogtrot through the trees and shrubbery toward the road, avoiding the front drive and picking my way as best I could. Once on the road, I dropped back to a walk and legged it toward town.

37

When I got to thinking about it, the road leading straight into town did not seem to be the very best place to walk, so the first chance I had, I turned off and found me a rather gloomy side street and even then I stayed under the trees wherever possible and didn't walk fast enough to attract attention. I had been on this side street about a block and a half when the headlights of a car found me. The car drew up alongside and a voice said:

"Want a ride?"

I couldn't see who it was. If it was a policeman I knew I was going to ride whether I wanted to or not, and if it was not a policeman I could certainly save some time. I opened the door and climbed in by the driver and then I saw it was Tim McClure and I was not sure whether I wanted to ride after all.

I said: "Where did you get the car?"

"Just a little thing I picked up along the road," he said and then looked at me and almost grinned. "I took a loop around in the dark and sure enough they had all stampeded after me and here was a car with keys in it and everything."

I was perspiring freely and I reached into my hip pocket for a handkerchief. In doing so my foot moved on the floor and I felt something gooey. As I bent down and stuck my hand in it to see what it was, I felt his pants leg and it was gooey too. I said:

"Looks like they winged you. Is it bad?"

"What do you mean, winged me? Those dopes couldn't have hit me standing still in broad daylight."

"Then what's this gooey stuff you have all over you? I suppose you had eggs for breakfast and spilled some of it."

"Huh," he said and pulled over and stopped at the curb. I held my hand under the dash light and I am a son of a bitch if it didn't look like egg yolk after all.

I held my hand where he could see it and said:

"Do you see what I see, or have I got astigmatism?"

He stared at it with a frown on his face and then put his own hand down and came up with the same stuff all over it. I wiped my hand off on my handkerchief and then held the handkerchief out to him and he did the same. He started the car up and we drove another block without saying a word. Finally he said:

"I think that must have been it. You saw me jumping those hedges and when I went over the second one my foot lit square in a basket and I fell all over myself. It's lucky I didn't break my leg. The damn thing got tangled around my foot and I thought I had a bear trap for a minute, and believe me I was in a hurry."

"I had an idea you weren't stopping to mail any letters," I observed.

He shut off the lights, pulled the car over to the curb and got out. I said:

"Where are we?"

"In the block right behind our house. They don't think very fast and even at the rate I was driving, we ought to be here with a few minutes to spare. I don't care what they do to me but I couldn't have those stupes locking me up when something has happened to Ruth. Come on, we can cut through here and get into the back yard and the kitchen. Make it quiet."

I followed him through an unpaved alley and when we were

in his backyard we stopped and crouched by the garage and took a look around. While we were there he said, keeping his voice low: "Maybe I had the wrong idea about you. I heard them falling all over something behind me. Did you get hurt?"

I shook my head. We walked up through the back yard and on into the house. Every light in the place was on but there was no one around. Clothes were scattered everywhere, drawers were pulled out on the floor and even the mattresses had been pulled off the beds.

"Looking for something," said Tim. "I wonder what."

I thought I might have a fair idea. I went into Tim's room and found on the top of the dresser the litter of stuff I had taken out of my pockets the first night when I had changed into Tim's clothes. I remembered that before breakfast that morning I had put the key in the pile, thinking that I would pick up all my stuff in due course of time. In the excitement of what had happened, I had forgotten all about it.

I pawed through all the stuff that was there. Wound around in the watch chain I found the key and held it up.

"Maybe I'm wrong," I said, "but I think someone is very anxious to get hold of this key. Like the purloined letter, he or she or whoever it is looked every place but the most obvious ones."

All of a sudden something hit me with a jolt. Not a lick on the head—just a thought. I said:

"Tim!"

He looked at me.

"Eggs," I said, "what do eggs in a basket mean to you around in this town?"

"I don't know. Nothing, unless Miss Katie."

I looked at him and he looked at me. We forgot all about the cops being on our trail and when I ran out and down the steps and across the street he was pounding along right behind.

38

At the foot of Miss Katie's front steps, Tim grabbed me by the arm and pulled up short.

"Listen," he said, "I'm not getting sidetracked until I find out something about Ruth. I may have five minutes and I may have fifteen, but it certainly isn't going to be long before the town is buzzing around my ears and if I'm going to do anything, I'll have to start doing it fast. You find Miss Katie. I'm going back. Where do you suppose Ruth could have gone?"

I said: "Why don't you try to find out if there was a telephone call to the house in the last hour or so. The police have probably been using the telephone a good deal but outside of them I wouldn't think there would be many calls at this hour of the night and there's an off-chance the operator might remember. Maybe the neighbors would know. Looks to me as if someone might have called her away on a wild-goose chase so that the house could be searched. You'll notice that every shade in the house has been drawn so the lights could be used and somebody was in an awful hurry. Whoever it was must have known you were sewed up tight so why would anyone be in a hurry unless Ruth were expected back any minute."

"Maybe you're right but unless the telephone operator

happens to remember, I'm out of luck. Everybody in town probably knows I've been arrested and if I start asking questions in the neighborhood, I'll be right back in jail in short order."

He left me and ran back toward the house. I clumped up to the front door of Miss Katie's place so I wouldn't be mistaken for a burglar and I was about to ring the bell when I saw that there was a light on in the back of the house. The front door was a big glass affair with a lace curtain on the inside and by peering intently I could see at an angle through the door of the room where the light was and it was obviously the kitchen. There was a shadow moving back and forth and at first I thought it was Miss Katie but then I realized that it was just the shadow of the kitchen furniture and that the light was moving. I didn't know why a light should want to move but in a moment I realized that it must be a bulb hung on a cord from the ceiling and it was swinging. That was fine. It meant that Miss Katie was at home and not in bed so I could probably get to talk to her without arousing the neighborhood or getting shot with that big cannon she liked to carry around.

I put my thumb on the bell and gave it a short buzz, and waited. The light went on swinging, slowing down a little, but Miss Katie did not come to the door. I gave it another buzz and still no Miss Katie. I knew she was not deaf and I could hear that the bell was working and I was not in a mood to stand around while she played hide and seek with me so I walked around to the back of the house and up on the back porch and looked in. The kitchen was empty and the light bulb was still swinging. The door was open a crack and I pushed it and it swung wide. I knocked on the door frame and said: "Miss Katie! Can I come in?"

There was no answer and all of a sudden that house seemed as quiet as if it were crouching there waiting for something. I raised my voice and called again and the quiet was so loud you could hear it. The swinging light was beginning to get on my nerves and so I went over and put up my hand and stopped it. The thing was plenty hot and there was no doubt that it had been on for some little time. I walked on into the living room and found a light switch and pushed it. There was nothing to see except just a living room with nobody in it. Beside the living room at the front of the house was a room with glass doors and I walked over and looked in. It was the dining room. Empty. That left the bedroom which I knew had to be behind the dining room because there was no other place for it to be. I went back into the living room and found the door to a little square back hall surrounded by four doors. I was standing in one of them and the door to the kitchen was at my left. The door straight ahead was open and with the light from behind me I could see it was the bathroom. The door to my right was open and the room was dark. I peered into it and there was a shoe out in the middle of the floor, only there was something very funny about the shoe because although it was near the foot of the bed, it was standing up on the back of the heel and I was looking at the sole and the thing was not propped against the bed either.

I knew exactly what I was going to see and when I turned on the light there she was in a queer position on the floor with her throat cut literally from one ear to the other and blood in every direction. It was a ghastly sight and the first thing I did was to duck into the bathroom and vomit. Then I went back and looked and you didn't have to have a medical report to know that she was one of the deadest persons who ever lived.

I took out my handkerchief, wiped the switch carefully and turned the light off. I retraced my steps all over the house trying to remember exactly what I might have touched and wiping every spot I could remember. In the kitchen I wiped off the light bulb and then turned to the door knob. I could have sworn I had left the kitchen door open when I came in. It was not open now.

39

I reached up and turned off the light bulb as quickly as I would turn off the electric chair if I were sitting in it and you gave me the switch. Then I backed quickly into the living room and stood there and listened. I don't suppose it is physically possible for your heart to be actually in your throat but something was in mine and it was beating loud and fast.

There was no breeze blowing through the house and frankly I didn't think that a rat had closed the door. I'm as brave as the next man facing things that I can see and understand, but I was not very enthusiastic about playing games in the dark with somebody fresh from a human barbecuing. I wouldn't kid you. Me and my knee joints were plain scared and I felt clammy all over.

Even in such moments you can do a certain amount of figuring after your mind gets over its first numb paralysis. I had just been in every room of the house with the light on and I was sure that whoever had closed the door was on the outside. The person took form in my mind as a shapeless something with dripping fangs and a bloody knife which I called "It."

What was It doing? If It had gone about Its business, I was wasting time and if you had asked me where I wanted to waste time I certainly would have told you somewhere else. If It had not gone about Its business, then it was very certain that Its business was me and you can imagine what a comforting thought that was.

I almost wished a door would open and footsteps would come toward me because then I would know what to back away from and what to do. As it was, the silence was so terrific that I could have cut it into blocks and walled myself in with it.

I wondered what luck I would have trying to lock the doors and sit tight. One of these days dawn would happen but then maybe I would never live to see it. Dawn is sometimes pink and lovely and I am quite esthetic by nature and the thought of not seeing it one more time and indeed a whole lot of times after that was quite upsetting.

Well, you can't stand in one spot forever. Acorns do it and get to be oak trees and leaves grow all over them and by and by they can't move at all. I ran over the floor plan of the house mentally and thought about the windows, and I was sure they were all shut. Raising a window would make a noise so that was out. There were only two doors, one from the front porch into the living room and one from the kitchen into the back porch. If It was waiting for me, It would wait outside the back door in the first place but I had turned off the light and hadn't come out, so if It could put two and two together, It was probably waiting for me at the front door. I picked up my feet as carefully as I could and took them over to the front door and listened. After a while I was sure I could hear something breathing. I will bet you even money that I didn't breathe in or out for as long a time as you would spend taking the dog for a walk. Then I made up my mind. If It was at the front door, then the safest place for me was outside of the back door as fast as I could get there.

Having made that decision, I didn't wait. I ran across the room toward the kitchen door, tripped on something and fell heavily, scrambled to my feet, found the back door, took two steps and jumped off of the porch. I could hear light footsteps running down the walk by the side of the house and I struck out across the back yard. It was dark as pitch and after about four steps I tripped and fell again and almost at once something fell over me and nearly knocked my breath out. Before I could even roll over, something whistled past my ear and hit the ground and then a very hard object hit me on the head somewhere and I went out like a candle.

40

The world was revolving and voices came out of the whirlpool in little snatches that did not make sense. I was dizzy and sick at my stomach and pains shot all over me in every direction. I opened my eyes and when I could focus them I saw that I was in a neat bare room in a clean white bed with a nurse who had curves in the right places bending over me watchfully. I signaled for something to be sick in and she produced an object and I put in it whatever I had not put into the bathroom at Miss Katie's house. The effort made the room go round and round again and when I sat up and put my feet out I was as wobbly as a kid just learning to walk. The nurse said:

"Lie down. The doctor says you aren't to move."

"Tell the doctor I'll come back in a day or two and lie down all he wants."

I stood up holding to the end of the bed to keep from falling. I didn't have a thing on except one of these hospital nightshirt arrangements that hangs down to your knees. I said:

"Get my clothes."

"I won't do any such thing. You're lucky you aren't dead. Get back in that bed before I call an orderly. And don't wrestle with me. You shouldn't exert yourself." She took hold of my arm and wanted to help me get back in bed, but I shook loose.

"Later," I said firmly. "I wouldn't get back in that bed if you promised to get in with me. It'll take more than you and an orderly so you better bring two of them."

There was a closet in the corner of the room and I wobbled over and pulled it open and sure enough there were my clothes. I put my pants on first without bothering about underwear since a man without pants cannot make himself very useful in the world. The nurse ran out of the room. I shoved my feet into my shoes. I slipped on my shirt and the coat right on top of it and I don't suppose I was over ten steps behind her. I can't tell you yet what direction I took or how I missed the hospital authorities, but pretty soon I found myself in a furnace room tucking in my shirttails and feeling very woozy indeed. I didn't have to worry about my hair because there was a bandage around it.

A man in coveralls came in from the bright sunlight outside and stared at me and said:

"My great aunt Jezebel!"

I gathered that I was not such a beautiful sight. I said: "Nice day, isn't it," and walked past him and went through the door he had come in by. It was the brightest sunlight I had ever seen and it stabbed into my eyes like a pair of knitting needles. I was in a back yard with a pile of coal and there was a cinder drive. I didn't know where it led to but I walked on it and listened to the cinders crunching under my feet and it was like hearing a sound from another world. Pretty soon my feet didn't crunch any more and I saw I was in an alley with concrete underneath my feet and I kept walking and blinking my eyes and brushing up against objects of various kinds until I ran into a fire hydrant and found a curb and sat down on it. I could hear a car coming along the street. It stopped near me and I could hear as from a distance some questions and ejaculations which I didn't try to understand.

My tongue was big and dry and tied in a square or reef knot, like what you tie when you are a boy scout to get a merit badge. Someone raised my head and I was glad to have help because I could not have done it for myself. With a great effort I said: "Harper. Take me to the Harper home. Don't argue. It's important." A dark brown feeling started up from my heels and turned slightly purplish as it came up my body. There was a tingling feeling all over me. Two people had me under the armpits and were taking me toward the car and the last thing I saw was my feet dragging on the street like a dead man's feet. My neck was not holding my head up as a good neck should do and I gave up trying.

41

I guess I was not unconscious more than a couple of minutes because when I came to they were trying to get me out of the car and we were right back in front of the hospital again.

"Hell's fire," I said with considerable heat, "don't take me in there. That's where I just came from."

"You need a doctor and you are going to get one whether you like it or not."

"I don't need a doctor and I am not going to have one. I was so anxious to get out I even left my underwear. Look and see if you don't believe me. If you won't take me out to the Harper place, get out of my way and I'll walk."

My head was much clearer than it had been before and I got out of the car and started walking. The two men stood there looking after me and then got in and drove along beside me.

"OK, OK," said the driver wearily, "only instead of walking in the wrong direction, get in and we'll take you there."

I got into the back seat and said, "Thanks a lot. If I'm dead when I get there I absolve you of all responsibility and you can call a cheap undertaker."

The news about Miss Katie was, of course, all over town and I learned that she had been discovered and me along with her because someone had tripped over the telephone cord in the living room and what with all the excitement over the death of William Jasper Harper the telephone operator had told the chief of police and he had sent someone around to investigate. I thought it was better not to say that it was I who tripped over the telephone although I was glad that I had. It seems that both Tim and Ruth McClure had vanished.

It was then about seven o'clock in the morning. As we swung through town a train was just pulling in from the north and as we passed the station I saw a man get off almost before the train had come to a stop. I asked the driver to pull over to the curb and then I thanked him and got out and told him I had changed my mind about going to the Harper place and did I owe him anything.

He said I didn't and I doubled back to the station platform and followed Hillman Jolley to the taxi stand. When he got into a cab and said he wanted to go out to the residence of William Jasper Harper, I got in right behind him and said: "Just got in on the train I see."

From the look he gave me you could tell that if I had asked his permission to get in with him the answer would have been "No." I had never met Hillman Jolley and he had never met me and he didn't know who I was from a hole in the ground. I let him stare at me quite a while and then I said: "My name is Gilmore Henry. I stole some things from your office in Louisville but I sent them all back and I guess you got them. There is no use calling the police because they are all at the place we are going to."

When I mentioned my name and what I had done, he jumped and got red in the face but he didn't say anything. I didn't see any reason to be unpleasant so I borrowed one of his cigarettes and asked him for a match and took two or three drags that tasted good.

"Come all the way from Louisville?" I said.

"No. From Overton. I went down to Overton yesterday

morning and then last night I heard about the awful thing that happened down here and being a friend of the family and a business associate I jumped on the first train to see if I could help Janet."

"Janet?"

"Miss Harper."

"Old friends?"

At first he was annoyed as if what business was it of mine, but then he put on an expression of considerable dignity.

"That would be an understatement. Miss Harper and I have reached an understanding."

I was surprised and showed it. I didn't know that Hillman Jolley was in the field and from the amount of running back and forth that Mr. James Mead had been doing I had somewhere distinctly gotten the idea that he was having things his own way, although I must admit that my impression was gathered only from Mead himself and could have been prejudiced. I muttered something about congratulations and then shut my big mouth and began thinking about how, if at all, this new piece of information might affect things that were on my mind.

When we pulled up on the Harper drive, I let my companion pay the cab driver because it was cheaper that way. Right in front of us was a gleaming Buick roadster and I recognized the license plates and knew that Mr. James Mead was on the premises. I didn't pay any attention to Jolley but simply walked through the front door giving the guard a dirty look and getting one in return. I knocked on the dining-room door and stalked in without waiting for an answer. The sheriff, the chief and Mead were conferring over the table. They all looked at me in surprise and I gathered they thought and maybe even hoped that I had been buried by this time.

The sheriff said: "Well, I didn't expect to see you for a long time but if the doc let you out of the hospital, you can't be in such bad shape and we'll start in right now. What were you doing in Miss Byrnes's back yard and what do you know about Miss Byrnes anyway?"

"They tell me she's dead."

"As if you didn't know."

"Look," I said, "Did you find a busted basket full of busted eggs on the other side of the drive last night or this morning?"

The sheriff and the chief and James Mead exchanged puzzled glances and then all of them looked at me.

"Yes, we did," the chief told me. "What's that got to do with it?"

"I don't know much about this town and maybe I have a way of jumping to conclusions. Every time I've seen Miss Katie she has been lugging a basket of eggs around with her and she sells eggs to William Jasper Harper, among others. The basket might have meant Miss Katie was behind the bushes and saw something that happened here last night. Farfetched idea, but I thought it was worth a tumble. I went to see Miss Katie and I never got there. What was I hit with?"

"A monkey wrench wrapped in a dish towel belonging to the McClures. You never got into the house?"

"You didn't find me there, did you?"

"Wait a minute," the sheriff broke in. "One thing at a time. Where did you find out about the basket in the first place? We didn't find it until thirty minutes after Tim McClure—er—shot his way out. By that time we couldn't find you around. When we found you, you were in Katie Byrnes's back yard out cold. There was nothing in the newspaper about the basket. Give."

I drew in a deep breath. "That's easy. The place was alive with coppers and I didn't see what I could contribute. I got out on the road to town and Tim McClure came by in a car and picked me up."

The sheriff jumped up and made a strangling noise in his throat. "And you didn't tell us?" he shouted. "You knew he was a fugitive. Talk fast or I will have you under arrest."

"Don't get excited. He had a gun. Just how far do you think I would have gotten on my way to a telephone?"

"He didn't have a gun."

"My mistake. I thought he—er—shot his way out. Those were your very words."

The chief said: "Damn your impudence, Henry. We're not here to argue. Don't change the subject." Then an idea came to him and his eyes narrowed. "So Tim McClure was with you at Miss Katie's. That connects. The dish towel from his own kitchen. Now we *are* getting somewhere."

"No, you're wrong. Tim put me out in front of his place and told me to beat it and keep my mouth shut. He said he was going to find Ruth himself. He didn't think any of you were very smart. I didn't think it was the time to reason with him and I wanted to talk to Miss Katie anyway so I headed across the street and was going to use the phone over there."

They thought that over for awhile and then the sheriff said: "Could be. I won't say I believe it but the story is good enough to hold until we see if we can check it. Now about the basket. You keep changing the subject. Let's get back to the basket."

I was getting impatient but I was too close to being arrested myself to turn around and walk out. I said: "Tim said he landed in the basket when he jumped the second row of bushes. He had egg all over him. I touched his pants leg and thought it was blood. The significance of it didn't dawn on either of us for a while. Maybe it didn't dawn on him at all. Now let me ask a question. Two or three of them. First, where is Ruth McClure and why is she there? Second, where is William Jasper Harper's will? We ought to look at that right away and see who profits by his death. Third, will you give me five minutes alone with Mr. Mead?"

Mead broke in at that point. "The will idea naturally occurred to me, not only for its possible criminal implications but also in my capacity as attorney for the family and for the estate. I got

Harper's secretary out of bed in the middle of the night and she said she thought his will was with some other papers in the safe out at the plant office. We went out together and got it half an hour ago. I was just going to open it with you when Henry came in." He had a briefcase with him and he was unstrapping it as he talked. He brought out a long brown envelope sealed with wax and handed it to the sheriff.

"Just a minute," I said leaning over and taking the envelope out of the sheriff's hands. "Before we open it, let's satisfy ourselves that no one has been tampering with it."

The chief grabbed at the envelope and jumped up and bellowed, "Damn it, I've had about enough of your arrogance. You're getting in my hair and in a minute I'm going to comb you out and mash you between my thumbs. We'll do all the looking that needs to be done. Give it here."

I retreated to the window and had time to turn the thing over in the light while he was coming at me. The writing on the front of the envelope was in ink, badly faded, but you could see that it said "Last Will and Testament of William Jasper Harper—Not To Be Opened Until After My Death." The back of the envelope looked perfectly natural and as far as I could tell, the seal had not been disturbed. The chief was almost at me and he had mayhem in his eyes. I handed him the envelope meekly enough and said: "No offense, Chief, no offense. I was just trying to be helpful."

He was slightly mollified. "You do your helping by keeping your paws off of things," he growled. "I don't like your impudence and I don't think you're telling all you know. Let me catch you in a lie and I'll turn the heat on you. Think you're pretty slick, don't you?"

As a matter of fact I thought I was just a little slick but I couldn't see any reason for saying so. We went back to the table and everybody examined the envelope and it was agreed that there was no evidence of any tampering. Then the sheriff cleared his throat and put a finger under the flap of the envelope and broke it open. We crowded around and looked over his shoulder.

I think we all expected dynamite and we were all disappointed. The will was short and to the point and in one paragraph gave everything to his beloved wife, Alice Holt Harper, absolutely and in fee simple to do with as she might please. The following sentence said: "I am fully conscious of my obligations to our beloved daughter, Janet, but I am satisfied that her interest will be best served by leaving my entire estate to her mother without any legal restrictions whatsoever."

There was another sentence designating Alice Holt Harper as executrix and that was all. There were no witnesses and the thing at least purported to be all in his own handwriting. The paper was old and had turned slightly brown. The date was the 8th of May, 1915.

42

Nobody said anything. I read it two or three times but there was no possible way to get any other meaning out of it. After a while the chief said:

"Where does that get us? It don't give no motive to anybody but Mrs. Harper. What would she want to get in a hotbox for?"

"Not only that," Mead put in thoughtfully, "but why would she wait twenty-six years? This will was made in 1915. He could have written a new one anytime. How was she to know whether he had made a new one or not? It doesn't make sense."

I took the paper over to the light and looked at it closely and turned it over and looked at the back and then held it up and looked through it. I could see absolutely no evidence that there had been any erasures or changes. I studied the edges to see if anything could have been cut off but couldn't discover a thing. Unless there might be a later will, this looked like the business and it didn't fit in with the pattern that had been forming in my mind at all. I didn't like it. It didn't fit in. It wasn't right.

I went back and tossed the thing on the table and said:

"Well. Where does that leave us? Twenty-six years is a hell of a long time. Who would know if he made one later? Who was his lawyer?"

"Frank Gregory represented him for a while," said Mead. "How long I don't know. Old Gregory died two or three years ago and Harper didn't care for the other choices he had in this town and came to me. There wasn't much to do and he paid me a retainer for a lot of routine stuff and that was all. I didn't think it amounted to enough to even tell Henry here. He certainly never got me to make a will for him."

The sheriff said: "Old Frank Gregory was quite a lawyer. He represented everything and everybody around here. Died of old age at seventy-eight. I remember going to the funeral. The whole county was there and the Governor came down and we had everything except dinner on the grounds. There wasn't any other lawyer here worth mentioning and my guess is Frank Gregory represented Harper ever since the Spanish-American War. I wonder who would have his files."

"Looks like that's the next move," said Mead. "If this is his, we'll want to offer it for probate after a decent interval. But I think I ought to at least make a reasonable search before offering a will as old as this. Times change and people change their ideas. It seems almost certain he would have made another one."

"Holbert is a smart man," said the chief, turning to the sheriff for approval. "I'll get him in here and put him on the trail of Gregory's files and records. It may be a tough job but I think Mead is right. Could be a new will that would make the whole thing look different and might tell us a thing or two." He got up and went out and we could hear him on the phone.

When he came back I stood up and stretched and yawned and said: "Well, if you don't mind, I think I'll be running along. I feel like I'm starving and I could do with some sleep and the hospital won't like the way I walked out of the place."

None of them paid any attention to me. I started toward the door but before I could reach it someone was running in the hall and broke in breathlessly. It was a patrolman and he said:

"It's Ruth McClure. We found her. All trussed up like a

dressed chicken and where do you suppose? Right in the shed in back of her own house in the corner behind a pile of coal."

We were all standing. "Dead?" asked the sheriff.

"No, not even hurt much. Says she got a phone call and somebody said to make sure she wasn't being followed and come back to the shed and she could get some information that would clear her brother. Naturally she went and didn't even think about what might happen. Bingo. A blanket gets slapped over her head and she is tied up and nearly suffocates before she can think. Her feet get pulled up behind and tied with a rope that goes around her neck and if she moves an eyelash she's a dead duck. She hollers and nobody can hear her on account of the blanket and all she can do is squirm around a little and get her feet propped so they don't pull her head off and then everything goes black."

That reminded me of something. I put my hand into my coat pocket frantically, and was relieved to find that that was where the hospital people had put the junk they took out of my pants. I pulled it all out and when I didn't see what I was looking for I got down on my hands and knees and put it all on the floor and sorted it out carefully. The key wasn't there. I looked again but there was no doubt about it. The key was gone.

43

I looked through all the rest of my pockets and then went out and called the hospital and after the nurse at the desk got through being indignant at me, I finally had a chance to talk to the voluptuous little thing who wanted me to get back in bed. She wanted to give me a lot of back talk but I cut her short.

"Listen," I said, "and listen good and get it the first time. Go into that room I had and look everywhere. Look under the bed and in the bed and through my shirt and underwear and on the dresser. Look in the gobboon* and everywhere. It's a key I had and now I haven't got it. It's flat and looks like it's made of brass and I need it the worst way. Now run and don't argue and I'll hold the phone."

"I don't have to look. We put everything you had on you in one of the pockets of your coat and you have the coat. If it isn't there, you either didn't have it or you lost it since. We're not in the habit of stealing a patient's belongings. What are you trying to do? Put me on the spot?"

I said: "Woman, don't argue. I didn't say you stole anything. I only said it was gone. Now be a good girl and go and look and some day I'll come over and give you a great big kiss."

---

*A cuspidor or spittoon.

"You'll get a slap in the puss," she said shortly, but she didn't hang up the phone and I could hear her go away. She was gone a couple of minutes. "All right, I looked. It's just like I said. There is nothing there but your clothes and if you don't come and get them we'll put them in the incinerator."

She hung up with a bang and I doubted very much whether I would ever get any kisses.

I went back into the dining room and learned that they had taken Ruth to a doctor for a checkup and then she had raised so much stew they had given in and let her go home to get a bath. A man was waiting right outside of the bathroom door and she would be brought out for questioning in a few minutes. Mead and the sheriff and the chief were discussing this new development and getting reports on the search for Tim so I went out and across the hall and knocked on Mrs. Harper's door. It was opened quickly by a tall, prim woman of maybe sixty or sixty-five with white hair. She looked as pure and proper as the Chairman of the Women's Auxiliary of the ME Church but right now she was looking at me with the utmost severity and she had her finger on her lips and was "sh"-ing me. She stepped out and pulled the door shut behind her softly.

"Go away," she said in a heavy whisper. "Mrs. Harper is taking a nap. It was a great shock and everyone has been so noisy she hasn't had a wink of sleep until a few moments ago."

I wanted very much to have a talk with Mrs. Alice Holt Harper but I could see it was no use pressing the point. I nodded and said I would come back later. I assumed this was Miss Knight and I watched her go back in and close the door quietly.

I went over to the guard at the front door and asked where Mr. Jolley had gone. It seems that he had asked for Janet and had waited until the maid brought a message that he could come up to her room.

I went upstairs and looked around. A door was open and through it I could see Janet in a pretty snakey sort of negligee.

Hillman Jolley was sitting beside her on the chaise longue and he was holding one of her hands and they were talking together very low.

I could have been more diplomatic but I wanted to see what their reaction would be so I stalked into the room and said:

"Excuse it, please. Don't pay any attention to me at all. We found out something downstairs and I thought you'd be interested—both of you."

I turned to Janet but out of the corner of my eye I was watching Jolley as well.

"We opened your father's will. It leaves everything to your mother, lock, stock, and barrel."

I thought possibly I was dropping a bombshell but if so it didn't go off. Neither one of them batted an eye. Janet stood up but didn't seem to be either surprised or alarmed or annoyed or shocked. Jolley went over and put his arm around her and from the look she gave him I thought he was probably handing me the straight stuff when he told me that they had what he called an understanding. Jolley said brusquely: "Really, I don't think this is a very appropriate occasion to be discussing things. Janet was devoted to her father and she is naturally distraught. She has had a horrible night and what she really needs is a sedative."

I said: "Sorry, my mistake. I shouldn't have blundered in this way in the first place."

I turned on my heel and went out and down the stairs. I was nearly to the front door when the door of Mrs. Harper's room opened and a man in a chauffeur's uniform came out and looked around. The cook was dead right when she said he looked like Humphrey Bogart, only Humphrey Bogart never looked as tough. The guy looked around and saw me and I kept on going but he caught up with me on the front steps.

"Mr. Henry?"

"That's right."

"This way please. Mrs. Harper wants to talk to you."

"She probably wants to talk to Mr. Mead."

"No, she said you especially. This way, please."

I hung back. "There must be a mistake," I said. "I want to talk to Mrs. Harper but she couldn't have sent for me. She doesn't even know who I am. If it's because she thinks I'm still Mead's partner, tell her I'm not."

I wanted very, very much to talk to Mrs. Harper but I was sure she must be sending for Mead and I didn't want to talk to her while he was around. If he was the man she wanted then I might as well be spending this time trying to get in a word with Ruth McClure while I might have a chance.

Humphrey Bogart looked at me and his face got even tougher. He said: "Mrs. Harper knows you and Mead have busted up. She said you particular. Why is no skin off my nose but that's what she said and that's what we're going to do."

You couldn't look at him and doubt that I was going to have an interview with Mrs. Harper if he had to carry me in by the seat of my pants. We stared at each other and finally I shrugged my shoulders and said:

"OK, lead the way."

44

Mrs. Harper was sitting up in her wheel chair with a pillow behind her and Miss Knight was in a chair right by her side taking her pulse. There was a four-poster double bed which had been out of my line of vision when I looked in the night before, and rolled under the bed was a low pallet on wheels like they have in hospitals.

I was glad to have a good look at Mrs. Harper. She was either about eighty years old or she had been an invalid for a long time. Her face was almost like wax and was dead white and almost translucent so that her veins showed clearly and you could see the pulsations in the artery in her neck. However, her eyes were alert and bright, almost feverish. She looked tired and drawn.

She gave a little gesture of dismissal and said: "Thank you, Miles, that will do." The chauffeur looked as if he wanted to stay and see what was going on but after an instant of hesitation he went out and closed the door behind him.

I said: "I'm Gilmore Henry. He said you wanted to see me."

She fumbled for a pair of glasses, put them on and studied me closely. I half expected her to ask if she could look inside my mouth like you would inspect a horse. You could see every detail soak in, not excepting my missing tooth, the bandage, my funny proportions and everything. If I had been looking at myself, I would have gained a very poor impression but if she felt that way, there was no sign of it.

"You have dissolved your partnership with Mead and the others?"

"You know that?"

"So I was told."

"And you still want to see me?"

"I want to have something done. I want someone I can trust—not only trust in the usual sense but trust not to talk. Not to anyone. I haven't time to fool around. From what I've heard, I am inclined to take a flier on you, sight unseen and no questions asked. Yes or no?"

I didn't know what was coming. This was not at all what I had expected. I thought I would be asking questions and she would be answering them. Furthermore, as Mead represented the family and the estate, I had no desire to muscle in and I also had no idea of tying myself up in anything which would embarrass me in my representation of Tim. "I represent Tim McClure. He's under arrest and they think he did that," I said pointing in the direction of the study. "He's a fugitive. They would like to think he did the other thing too. You know about that?"

"I have been told about all of that. I still want to know. Yes or no."

"It would depend on the job. I'd have to know first. I can't give you an answer until I know."

"I don't want to tell you until I know your answer."

"Then get somebody else."

If that was the purpose of the interview, it was at an end. I stood up and said: "Sorry."

She fiddled with a handkerchief in her lap and looked out of the French windows and back at me for a long time. "I haven't very much choice. There is no one in Harpersville who will do and I don't know anyone in the city. Give me your word first. If you decline, this conversation will never go any farther."

I looked hard at Miss Knight and back to Mrs. Harper. She said: "Miss Knight is all right. She is more than a nurse. She is a friend and a companion and has been for years, ever since my first attack."

I put my hat on the bed, looked around and saw a chair with its back against a door that probably connected with the study. The knob had been taken out of the door and from the way the furniture was arranged it was apparent that the door was not in use. The chair was not too far from Mrs. Harper and was where she could see it so I went over and made myself comfortable. "All right, go ahead. Only remember that if it is something inconsistent with what I'm doing I can't accept. And if it is something that will help me clear Tim, I cannot receive it in confidence but will use it as I think best. You'll have to take that chance. If it doesn't suit you that way, don't start."

She bit her lips and looked me all over again and then made up her mind and drew in a deep breath. "I want to know if you can prepare a will that's no good."

Life is full of surprises but I had been getting them so fast and so continuously in the last couple of days that I was learning to roll with the punches. I said: "I can. Whether I will or not is something else. You don't ask a doctor to perform a bad operation. You shouldn't ask a lawyer either. If I start making bad wills, I've got to quit being a lawyer. What do you want with a will that's no good?"

"Why I want it is my business. All I'm asking is whether you will do it or you won't do it. I have ample means and I will pay well. Name your own price. I won't argue about it."

I got up and took a turn around the room and came back. I got out a pack of cigarettes and asked a question with my eyes and she nodded so I lit one and inhaled deeply. Miss Knight got up and found something I could use as an ash tray.

"Mrs. Harper," I said, "you are evidently troubled in a very serious way or you would not be talking to a lawyer you know nothing about. I am not as stupid as I look and I will take a guess that before we got through I would probably be in position to blackmail you out of your eyeballs. Do you realize that?"

"Young man, I wasn't born yesterday. I used to go to the races when I was younger and in better health. There are times when you want to put everything you've got on a horse—to win. When you do, you have to trust the jockey and pray."

"There are a lot of ways to make a will that won't stand up. I would have to know what's in your mind before I could pick the best one. For example, under Kentucky law, if the will isn't all in your own handwriting, you must have two witnesses and they must sign in your presence and in the presence of each other. We could have only one witness. Would that do?"

She shook her head. "The requirement of two witnesses is common knowledge, isn't it?"

"I would think so."

"Then it wouldn't do. The will must look good. I want to show it."

"It wants to be good enough to stand examination and not good enough to work?"

"That's the idea."

"If it is to be examined by someone who knows his business, I can't think offhand how it could be done. You could have someone forge your name but then if you are going to acknowledge that it is your will, it would be the equivalent of someone signing for you at your direction and it could be made to stand up. We can't get anywhere sparring in the dark. There may be a very easy solution if you would only trust me completely. It is silly to pay a lawyer and hold out on him."

She made a motion to Miss Knight who seemed to understand her perfectly and took the pillow out from behind her back. Mrs. Harper leaned back against the headrest and closed her eyes. Gradually her face relaxed and she lay there motionless except for her breathing which was scarcely perceptible. A corpse could not have looked more fit for burial. Finally she opened her eyes and sat up and drew another of the deep breaths which seemed to precede the making of all her decisions.

"Mr. Henry," she said slowly, "I want to make a will and I want everyone to know it is made and what's in it. But when I die, I don't want my estate to go the way the will says. I want it to go another way. That's what I want done and that will have to be enough information. You must not inquire as to my reasons."

I said: "If that's all, you should have put it that way in the first place. The solution is perfectly simple. There is nothing to it. We'll simply make two wills. The last will is the only one that's worth the paper it's written on except for the chance that it might be lost or destroyed or never discovered. The only chance you will have to take is that the second one shows up at the proper time."

"There are ways of arranging that, aren't there?"

"Precautions could be taken. You could make it reasonably certain."

"Then I will want you to draw both of them right away. Today. I'm an old woman and I want to get this off my mind. Could you go some place and fix them up and come back this afternoon?"

"I could but it isn't the best way. If they are both signed on the same day, there would be too much chance of doubt as to which was the first and which was the second. I think one should be executed today and the other should be executed tomorrow, with different witnesses or with witnesses whom you can trust enough to explain that there are two of them so that several years from now, a clever lawyer won't be able to confuse the witnesses as to the exact day. That will leave a gap from one day to the next, and during that period the first will be effective as your last will and testament. Is there anything wrong with that?"

She turned it over in her mind and her eyes narrowed in thought. "And if I died in that period?"

"Then the wrong will would stand up."

"I don't like it, but I'd rather do it that way than take any chances. Very well. The matter is in your hands."

I said: "Go on, you've just started."

"What do you mean?"

"It's in my hands, but what is it? You told me everything except what's supposed to be in the wills."

"But you will undertake to prepare them?"

"With the same reservation I made before. If what you tell me now is useful in representing Tim McClure, I'll use it as I think best. I'll promise not to broadcast it, if that's what you mean."

"You will understand that this whole situation is not of my choosing. Having gone this far, I have no choice but to rely upon your integrity. I think we understand each other perfectly. The wills are to be very simple. In the first one I want everything to go to Janet."

"And in the second?"

"In the second will the estate is to be divided equally between Janet and Tim McClure."

I did not know that it was going to be something I could remember without taking notes and I had out a pencil and an envelope on which I could write. At that moment I thought I heard a little sound on the other side of the door behind me. I wrote on the envelope. "Don't ask any questions. Go right on talking whatever happens. *Don't ask any questions.*"

I handed it to her with a finger on my lips and a warning frown. I said: "You will want to be thinking about whom you will have as witnesses. You shouldn't use Janet either time or you may jeopardize her chances to take under the terms of the will. I would like it a lot better if you would take me completely into your confidence and explain why. Perhaps it would have a bearing on how the instruments are worded."

Mrs. Harper read what was on the envelope and opened her mouth but then thought better of it although she was both puzzled and excited. She showed the envelope to Miss Knight who exchanged a glance with her and then looked at me. I made an impatient gesture and Mrs. Harper took the cue and said: "Miss Knight could be a witness to both of them. I think Miles would be all right for the other. Let me think the other thing over a minute. I do not want to say any more but neither do I want to make a mistake by saying too little."

She and Miss Knight were both watching me intently with bright eyes. While Mrs. Harper was talking I bent over, unlaced my shoes and slipped them off. The French windows were open and I walked across the room keeping to the rug and picked my feet up and put them down quickly but carefully. I said: "That sounds all right about the witnesses. You know them better than I do."

Miss Knight spoke up with a contribution of some sort and Mrs. Harper took up the conversation with her. Just before I got to the French windows a board in the floor gave a loud creak under me and I didn't waste any more time. I went out on the terrace at a run, dashed around to the windows of the study and looked in. The door from the study to the hall was just closing. The French windows were shut and when I tried them they were fastened on the inside. I ran back through Mrs. Harper's room and out into the hall. There was no one in sight. I could hear voices in the dining room and could tell that Ruth had appeared and was being questioned. I found a guard outside of the front door smoking a cigarette. "Anyone been in or out in the last few seconds?"

He dropped his cigarette surreptitiously behind him, turned his head in an effort to hide the smoke, and said: "Not a soul, Buddy, not a soul."

"I thought you were supposed to be inside."

"I was, only—well I thought I heard someone driving up

and if it was a reporter I got strict instructions to head him off, no pictures or nothing and no wandering around. We've been doing a good job keeping the newspapers out and I didn't want to make a bust."

I said: "You came out to smoke a cigarette. Hell, don't look at me that way. You can smoke a pipe as far as I'm concerned. How long have you been here? It's important."

He grinned sheepishly and pointed to the cigarette butt under his heel. It was about half gone. I went to the front door again and Hillman Jolley was coming down the steps from the floor above. I waited for him and said: "Did you see anybody come upstairs just now?"

He looked blank. "No, did someone go up?"

"I'm asking you."

"I didn't see anyone at all."

He was staring at my stocking feet but I didn't bother with any explanations. I ran back into the hall, opened the door that led to the basement steps and looked down. I couldn't see anything. I went back to the foot of the stairs and took a look at the situation. Anyone leaving the study could have gone to the basement or walked upstairs or into the dining room or into Mrs. Harper's room or out of the front door or through the big arch into the tremendous living room in front. The living room opened at the far end into a sun porch which in turn had a door leading into the yard on the other side of the house in front of the kitchen shrubbery. There was not a sign of anyone in sight. No one had gone into Mrs. Harper's room and even if the policeman at the front door were lying, there hadn't been time for anyone to get out of sight that way. Hillman Jolley reported that no one had gone upstairs. I was too late to do any good on the basement or the living room, so that left only the dining room.

I went over and walked in. Ruth McClure looked up and was relieved to see me. Mead was standing near the door. The sheriff and chief were across the table from Ruth and there were two patrolmen over by the window and a man taking shorthand.

"Pardon the interruption. Has anyone been in or out of here in the last couple of minutes?"

Mead spoke up quickly. "I've been standing here for quite a while."

The sheriff and chief looked at each other and shook their heads. I went back to Mrs. Harper's room and put on my shoes.

45

I promised Mrs. Harper I would be back sometime during the day and was about to leave when there was a knock on the door of her room. I looked at Mrs. Harper and raised my eyebrows and she nodded, so I opened the door. Janet was standing there with Hillman Jolley, and instead of going out I stepped back and held the door for them. I thought I could guess what was about to happen and I did not want to miss any of it.

When they came in, I closed the door behind them. Janet looked at me and was clearly of the opinion that it would have been much better if I had closed it from the outside and stayed there. Mrs. Harper looked at them expectantly, and I think she knew as well as I did. Janet went over and knelt in front of her mother. Mrs. Harper's hands were clasped in her lap and Janet took them in her own. She said:

"Mother, I know this is a curious time to talk about a matter of this sort, but I hope you will understand and give us your blessing. Hillman and I have been in love with each other for a long time, and we were planning to tell you and Father about it the next time Hillman came to Harpersville. Now that this horrible thing has happened Hillman thinks more than ever that his place ought to be made known so that he can be free to help us and stay with us without providing food for the gossips. Maybe we needn't make any public announcement for a while, and of course there won't be any celebration, but we're not going to try to hide it, and it had just as well become known. We want to be married as soon as it is decent under the circumstances."

Jolley went over and stood by her, and when she looked up at him there was a glow in her face, and it looked to me like the real thing. My mind was racing around like a squirrel in a cage, and I couldn't help thinking about someone who had been in the adjoining room a few minutes ago, and how that person could have been Mr. Hillman Jolley. If that is who it was, then it was certain that he knew Janet was in line for either half or all of the tremendous Harper fortune. He would have had time to slip out of the study and upstairs and then turn right around and walk down again as innocent as you please. There would also have been time since I left him for a trip upstairs and an impassioned plea to Janet, especially since she obviously did not need much persuasion anyway. I moved Jolley two or three places up in my list of suspects, although I had seen him come in on the train after the murders of both Harper and Miss Katie, and I couldn't quite see just how he could have done it. I was also stumped when I thought of the extremes he might have gone to without even taking the trouble to find out the contents of the will of William Jasper Harper. If he was counting on feathering his nest by marrying Janet, I found it hard to imagine that he would murder her father just on the theory that her mother would eventually die and probably leave Janet most of the property. More than ever I wanted to have some information on whether a later will existed, and I also made a mental note to check up and find out whether Jolley had actually been in Overton as he had told me. The whole thing did not fit together and make a great deal of sense, but neither did the rest of the business and I wasn't missing any bets.

All of this was tumbling around in my head, but I wasn't

missing any of what was going on. Mrs. Harper didn't seem to be surprised, and she was neither enthusiastic nor disappointed. She said:

"Well, Janet, since you put it that way I'll have to approve. Not that it makes a great deal of difference one way or the other. You have plenty of intelligence, and I am afraid I haven't been as close to you or contributed as much to your life in recent years as a mother should. You are perfectly capable of making your own plans and decisions, and I am sure I am not the one to interfere with them, even if I felt the inclination." She looked up at Jolley and managed a fairly warm sort of smile. "You must be good to her, Hillman," she said, patting his hand. "She's really a dear child and I am sure you will find her loyal and loving. Perhaps it is just as well for us to have a man to help us in the family. After all, I am not able to do much, you know, and I may not have long to live."

It was quite a domestic scene, and I didn't see much point in hanging around. I had heard the important piece of news and there were other fish to fry. I went out quietly and went across the hall into the dining room.

46

The questioning of Ruth McClure was about finished, and I was permitted, ungraciously, to interrupt long enough to find out that I could escort her home in five or ten minutes. I motioned to Mead and he followed me out. I led the way into the big living room and we sat in a couple of overstuffed chairs in sight of the arch leading into the front hall. I watched Mead closely and said, "Janet and Jolley have just announced they are going to be married."

Somewhat to my surprise he said, "Yes, I know. It has been coming for some time. Jolley is really a pretty decent sort, I suppose. He and Janet called me out of the dining room and asked me what I thought about making the announcement, and I couldn't see any harm as long as it was made known quietly and naturally without the fuss and feathers." He gave me a one-sided sort of smile which was decidedly forced and said ruefully, "I can't say it overjoys me. I've been pretty lonesome in that big house of mine since Edith died, and there's no use denying I have had some ideas about Janet myself. I have been down here a lot of times in the last three years, and I've entertained Janet and W. J. quite a lot. She's a great girl."

My mouth may have been hanging open. The fact that Jolley

was anxious to announce the engagement even before my conversation with Mrs. Harper was totally inconsistent with the theory I had been building up for the last five or ten minutes. Furthermore, the conversation Mead had just told me about must have been after I told Janet and Hillman Jolley about the contents of her father's will, since Jolley came in at the same time I did that morning, and I was with Mead in the dining room until the time when I went upstairs with the news. The chronology was all wrong. There was no escaping these facts: That Jolley found out Janet would get nothing under her father's will and yet he urged the announcement of his engagement to Janet even before my conference with Mrs. Harper. I was bound to be all wrong unless a more recent will of William Jasper Harper should turn up. I am a tenacious sort of cuss and I made a mental note not to forget my theory until this last point could be settled one way or the other. I decided again I would check on his presence in Overton. If a later will did not appear, and if Jolley actually was in Overton the day before, then it looked as if I would have to re-arrange the pieces of my picture puzzle, since I could not see that he would have any understandable motive for killing Harper and couldn't have been in Harpersville on top of that. And there was that disturbing Katie Byrnes business which was even more difficult to understand.

I was silent so long that Mead thought the conversation was at an end. He started to get up.

"Wait a minute," I said. "I never did get around to asking you for that list of the people who were at your house the night someone turned me over in the ditch. People don't hide in bushes and shoot at passing cars just for target practice. Someone wanted to get either you or me. The more I think of it the more it's obvious it was me. How could anyone know your car would be on the road to Harpersville that night unless it was someone at your house who heard your phone conversation with me? And if that is what happened, the same person would automatically know that the trip was my trip and not yours. I am not at all crazy about having people at large who try to bump me off."

He sat down and looked out of the window and I took an envelope and pencil out of my pocket again.

"Let's see," he said slowly, "that was only three nights ago, and the party wasn't a big one. There won't be any difficulty at all making out a complete list. I was there, of course. Smallwood and his wife. I asked Opdyke and Helen, but they had a previous engagement. Dr. Woodford Collins and his wife. William Jasper Harper and Janet. Hillman Jolley was in Harpersville and when I found it out I included him. How many does that make?" I counted up and said, "There were eight."

"Well, that's all of them, then. There were just eight. They were to come at six-thirty—rather earlier than would be customary, but Mr. Harper always showed up at the plant at a frightful hour in the morning, and he wouldn't accept an invitation unless he could get home early. We had some cocktails and as I remember the dinner was served about seven. After dinner we had a liqueur in the living room and sat around and chatted. You must have called around nine-thirty. The party was just getting ready to break up at the time. Harper had already said he wanted to get on back, and since Janet had come up with him she was upstairs powdering her nose."

"You say Janet come up with her father? Where was Jolley? How does he fit in? I would think Janet would have driven up with him."

"That's so," said Mead, with a thoughtful expression on his face. "How was that? I distinctly remember that Janet came with her father and was getting ready to leave when he said he was leaving. Wait a minute. Janet did come with her father. Jolley had borrowed one of their cars and driven to the city earlier in the day and he joined us from in town somewhere. He was a little later than the others. It seems to me there was something about a call he wanted to make in town before going back to Harpersville."

"Then if Harper came up with Janet it was probably in the big sedan. How about Miles? Did he drive them or did Janet drive?"

"You mean Miles, the chauffeur? Yes, I think he did drive them up. After I had talked to you I hung up and the crowd was all filtering out into the hall to get their wraps. You asked me that night when you called me from Harpersville, and I told you then that I hadn't seen any reason to keep any secrets so I told them that it was my junior partner and you were borrowing the car to go to Harpersville."

There was nothing more to learn. I had hoped for something helpful, but if I had it I certainly didn't recognize it. There had been a time the night before when I had felt convinced I was about to see the whole pattern of the thing, but every time I found a piece it seemed to be a different color and the wrong shape, and I was worse off now than ever before.

Ruth came out of the dining room looking rather worn out. I excused myself to Mr. James Mead and joined her in the hall. She gave me an odd smile, but her lower lip was trembling and I could see she wasn't far from tears.

"Take me home, Gil," she said, squeezing my hand. "I have had about all I can stand right now. They say there is no news of Tim, and I am practically frantic. I am sick of violence and all things I can't understand."

The telephone pealed through the house like a fire siren. The sheriff snatched open the dining-room door, found the telephone on the stand in the front hall, and scooped it up. We all listened as if transfixed. My heart sank as I saw an expression of satisfaction on his face. Presently he put down the receiver and almost beamed at us. "They've got Tim McClure again," he said. "And not only that, they've found a gun hidden in the McClure house, and I'll bet ten to one it will prove to be the one that did for Harper." We stood stock still. You could tell that he was holding out something and that it was the biggest news of all. He let us gape at him and after a long while he said, "It's Tim's gun. I think this case is about closed."

47

My first thought was of Ruth. She had been shaky enough before this last telephone call came in and if ever she needed someone to help her hold up her head it was now. If she had burst into tears or fainted I would not have been at all surprised, but when they chose the material out of which Ruth McClure was cut they evidently picked the finest grade of Scotch wool unmixed with any cheap substitutes. Instead of weakening, her head came up and there was a flash in her eyes that was magnificent.

"You're a bunch of stupid idiots," she said furiously, "all of you." She turned to me. "They're all against Tim. I'm for him. I'm going straight down to the jail and see him now. If you think the ship is sinking, you can leave it like any other rat."

"Don't be silly," I said as mildly as I could; "I'm a rat all right but the ship isn't sinking and I'll at least stay aboard until it does."

I took her arm and maneuvered her out and down the front steps to the drive, and then it dawned on me that I had come in a taxi and the police had brought Ruth so we were without transportation. I was not in any mood to take sheep-dip off of anyone so I stalked back in and peremptorily demanded the keys to one of the police cars. Believe it or not, I got them.

We were halfway back to town before either of us said

anything. I looked at Ruth out of the corner of my eye and the reaction had set in. Her lower lip was trembling again and a great big gob of tears was in the eye nearest me, about ready to run all over her make-up. I handed her my handkerchief and she blew loud and long. When she handed it back she said with a catch in her voice: "I didn't m-m-mean it about the rat. I don't know what got hold of me. If I didn't have you I'd be lost."

"Never mind," I said cheerfully. "I've another rat in mind and I think it is me. I'm thinking about the nursery rhyme where the rat began to gnaw the rope, the rope began to hang the butcher, the butcher began to kill the ox, and so on down until the pig got himself over the stile and the poor old woman at last got home."*

---

*The traditional version of the tale is: An old woman was sweeping her house, and she found a little crooked sixpence. What, said she, shall I do with this little sixpence? I will go to market, and buy a little pig. As she was coming home, she came to a stile: but the piggy would not go over the stile.

She went a little further, and she met a dog. So she said to the dog, Dog! bite pig; piggy won't go over the stile; and I shan't get home to night. But the dog would not.

She went a little further, and she met a stick. So she said, Stick! stick! beat dog! dog won't bite pig; piggy won't get over the stile; and I shan't get home to night.' But the stick would not.

She went a little further, and she met a fire. So she said, Fire! fire! burn stick; stick won't beat dog; dog won't bite pig (*and so forth, always repeating the foregoing words*). But the fire would not.

She went a little further, and she met some water. So she said, Water! water! quench fire; fire won't burn stick. But the water would not.

She went a little further, and she met an ox. So she said, Ox! ox! drink water; water won't quench fire, &c. But the ox would not.

She went a little further and she met a butcher. So she said, Butcher! butcher! kill ox; ox won't drink water, &c. But the butcher would not.

She went a little further, and she met a rope. So she said, Rope! rope! hang butcher; butcher won't kill ox, &c. But the rope would not.

She went a little further, and she met a rat. So she said, Rat! rat! gnaw rope; rope won't hang butcher, &c. But the rat would not.

She went a little further, and she met a cat. So she said, Cat! cat! kill rat; rat won' t gnaw rope, &c. But the cat said to her, If you will go to yonder cow, and fetch me a saucer of milk; I will kill the rat. So away went the old woman to the cow.

But the cow said to her, If you will go to yonder haystack, and fetch me a handful of hay; I'll give you the milk. So away went the old woman to the haystack; and she brought the hay to the cow.

As soon as the cow had eaten the hay, she gave the old woman the milk; and away she went with it in a saucer to the cat.

As soon as the cat had lapped up the milk, the cat began to kill the rat; the rat began to gnaw the rope; the rope began to hang the butcher; the butcher began to kill the ox; the ox began to drink the water; the water began to quench the fire; the fire began to burn the stick; the stick began to beat the dog; the dog began to bite the pig; the little pig in a fright jumped over the stile; and so the old woman got home that night.

James Orchard Halliwell, ed., *The Nursery Rhymes of England, Collected Principally from Oral Tradition* (London: Printed for the Percy Society, 1842), 159–60.

You could tell that she was taking her mind off of something else and pointing it in the direction of what I had said and you could see the knobs turning as she brought the lenses to a focus. I let her soak for a while. Finally she said: "You mean there's a chain of events all hooked together and you're ready to identify the links?"

"I don't know whether I'm ready but I think I have most of them on the table in front of me. I don't know what follows what exactly and I've got an awful feeling that one or two of the most important links are somewhere at the bottom of the sea, but we'll find them if I have to put on a diving helmet and go down myself. First of all, you'll have to humor me and put off your visit to Tim long enough to get me something I need."

"Can't it wait?"

"No, but don't worry, it won't take over a minute. OK?"

"If you say so."

I turned at the next corner and we drove around and pulled up in front of Ruth's house. I didn't even turn off the motor. I said: "I think I saw a picture of your father in the living room. Be a good girl and hop out and get it and I'll take you straight down to Tim."

She hadn't the faintest idea why I wanted it but she got out and ran in. Inside of a minute she was back and we were off.

"The suspense is what gets me, Gil. I don't understand any part of anything. All I know is that Tim couldn't and didn't kill Mr. Harper. He's not the sort who would shoot a man in the back of the head. He probably wouldn't shoot at all. He's as strong as a steam shovel and if he wanted to do anything like that he would just take your neck in his hands and break it all in little pieces without half trying. Can't you tell me just enough so I can manage not to go crazy?"

"I would, Ruth, but I'm not sure I know that much. I know that there are two sets of circumstances that are at work. Whether they're working separately or together or whether only one of them is responsible I can't tell any more than you. Furthermore neither one of them is complete in my own mind and the one that I think is the most important is terribly jumbled up and there are some things evidently of the greatest importance that I don't know and can't understand or figure out."

"Maybe if you'd think out loud I could help."

"Think you can take it?"

"After what I've already taken, can you doubt it?"

"No, I guess not. All right, but don't say I didn't warn you. Ready?"

"And waiting."

"I think you must have figured part of it out for yourself already. I don't think there is any doubt that Tim is the son of William Jasper Harper and I've a pretty good idea that his mother was Miss Katie. Some deal was made and your father and mother adopted Tim. Or maybe there wasn't a deal. At any rate it seems certain that both your father and Miss Katie have been living off of William Jasper Harper for a long number of years, probably ever since Tim was adopted in May, 1915."

I do not know how much of it was new to Ruth McClure but at least some part of it was a terrific shock. When I looked at her I was sorry I had dished it out so fast. The color was completely gone from her face and her fists were so tight that the knuckles were white. I pulled over to the curb and shut off the motor.

"I'm sorry," I said penitently, "I ought to have known better than to put it so bluntly. You look ill. Are you going to be all right?"

With a visible effort Ruth pulled herself together and looked at me unflinchingly. "I'll be all right," she said in a small strained voice. "The ugly implications were too much for me all at once, that's all. I won't get anywhere closing my eyes and ears. I want all of it. Go right ahead."

"I don't think it's wise. Let's wait until another time. I think a drink of whiskey would do you good. You've been through a lot and it's a wonder you're operating under your own power as it is."

"No, give it to me straight. I'll be all right. Don't be afraid for me."

"Very well, if you say so. But remember that I'm on your team and remember that when I say what I think is a fact, it doesn't mean I believe all the distorted implications that may suggest themselves. This thing has to be worked out and the answer has to be found and as you say, we won't get there by closing our eyes and ears and kidding ourselves. Obviously, Miss Katie has not been making a living either from her garden or from her chickens. She probably hasn't gotten enough eggs for her own breakfast. She bought them at the grocery store and what she didn't give to you and Tim she ostensibly sold to Harper, but that won't work because she called them country eggs which they weren't and sold them at less than they cost her. You don't have to be a cash register to know that you can't make money that way. Even Harper didn't expect me to believe she was living on profits and he told me himself he gave her something every few days or weeks for sweet charity, and I don't believe that either. You and Tim know you didn't go to flossy schools and dress nicely and have a car of your own on thirty-five dollars a week. Your father's bank account is a thirty-five-dollar-a-week bank account but every item that would be of any real interest isn't reflected there. Harper offers to buy your stock at an absurd price, which is one thing, but he adds a condition that smells to high heaven. Why would he want to be in charge of your father's estate and take over all the records he could find if the records didn't connect with him somewhere? We can be as loyal as we want but we mustn't be fools."

"Then you think my father stumbled into the picture and found a way to make a good thing out of it? To be brutal about it, you're thinking about blackmail." Her voice was dead and matter of fact like a voice that comes up out of a big cold lump in the middle of your body.

"That would be one explanation. There may be others. I'm not saying I think that's the right answer."

"But you're afraid it is."

"I don't know. That's the trouble with talking when you're only halfway through a room full of confusion."

"And it also means that Tim is—well—a bastard."

"That's something I'm sure of. But remember that Tim is Tim no matter who his father and mother may have been and no matter what the circumstances. It's a cockeyed world that visits the children with the sins of their parents. Personally I don't give a tinker's dam who Tim is or where he came from, and neither do you. He's here and he's one hundred per cent in my book and he'll stay that way. What we call society, which includes all of us, is a bunch of dopes. Whatever else you may think about William Jasper Harper, don't you ever forget that whatever the reason might have been, he went for better than thirty years and took care of his own after his own fashion and did something from what must have been a distorted sense of shame or justice or fair play or something to shield the human product of his wild oats."

"But there is a fatal weakness in the story."

"Yes, I know. You know your father didn't play ball that way. I never knew him but I know you better than you think and you're right. There is something wrong and we've got to find out what it is. At least we've got to proceed on the conviction that something's wrong. Somehow I feel that the whole thing's too easy figured out this way. Either too easy or totally cock-eyed. It doesn't explain anything. It doesn't explain why William Jasper Harper got bumped off. He was the goose and the supply of golden eggs was probably inexhaustible."

"Yes, that's true. But the sheriff and the chief won't figure that way. They'll figure Tim finally found the pieces and put the puzzle together for himself. They'll figure he lost his head and killed Harper on some wild idea he could thereby cover up his own history. They'll figure he escaped and went after Miss Katie as soon as he had had time to brood about things in jail and come to the same conclusion you have come to. It'll all be cut and dried. There'll be nothing to it. I wouldn't bet an old hat they won't prove Tim's gun did it. The whole thing will look simple and beautiful."

"I'm way ahead of you. That's why we have to hurry. If it isn't Tim, then someone's loose and for all we know there may be other chapters to come. We don't even know the plot and characters. We've got to hurry."

"What next?"

"It's twenty minutes to ten. County court opens at ten o'clock. You go in and tell Tim to keep his chin up. Then meet me in front of the Court House and we're going to get you qualified as executrix of your father's estate right now. We've got something definite to learn and we'll never get to first base unless we are clothed with evidence of authority."

She did not say a word but she reached over and turned the ignition switch. I drove her to the jail, let her out and then went and parked in front of the Court House.

48

The office of the telephone company was right across the street. I swapped a five dollar bill for a handful of small change, went into the booth and placed a station-to-station call to the office of Yoland & Jolley in Louisville. After a minute I recognized Miss Judson's voice. I said: "This is the chief of police in Harpersville."

"What?"

"Harpersville, Harpersville, do you get it?"

"Yes, I get it, Harpersville. Who did you say you were?"

"I said I'm the chief of police."

"Oh, I see. To whom did you wish to speak?"

"You'll do. It's important that I reach Mr. Jolley at once. I understand he's out of town. Where can I reach him?"

"Could you give me an idea what you want to talk to him about? Perhaps someone else in the office can give you the information."

"Lady, if I wanted to talk to somebody else I'd say so. I want to get in touch with Mr. Hillman Jolley. Where is he? Is it a secret?"

"Of course not," hastily, "I was only trying to be helpful. Just a minute."

I knew that "Just a minute" stuff was a gag but there was nothing I could do about it so I hung on and waited. I could hear heels clicking and a door opening and shutting. Pretty soon a door opened and shut again and then Miss Judson said: "Mr. Jolley was in Overton yesterday. One of the junior accountants was talking to Mr. Yoland today and reported that Mr. Jolley heard about—that thing in Harpersville and left a message at the hotel that he was going down on the night train. Isn't Mr. Jolley in Harpersville?"

"If he was would I be calling you? What business did he have in Overton? I'll call down there myself and see what I can find out."

"Well, I guess it's all right. He went down to start the annual audit for Overton Christian College."

"Why didn't you say so in the first place?" I said and hung up.

I waited maybe thirty seconds and then put through a call to the business manager of Overton Christian College. Yes, Mr. Hillman Jolley had been there. No, he didn't come with the junior accountants. They had come several days before to start the dirty work. Mr. Jolley came in the morning, pretty close to noon. He was there for lunch and as a matter of fact had lunch with the business manager. Yes, he stayed after lunch for a while and then said he was going to discuss another account and told the junior men that he could be reached at the Palace Hotel. No, he didn't know the name of the other account.

I hung up and called the railway station. Overton was on the main line from Louisville through the city and on down through Harpersville. It was about 100 miles from Louisville. There was one train that left Louisville about 10:00 in the morning and it would get you into Overton about 12:30. There was a train in the evening leaving Louisville at 10:10 and getting into Overton at 12:42. Yes, that was the train that arrived in Harpersville at 7:38 in the morning.[*]

---

[*]The geography is this: Louisville to Overton to "the city" to Harpersville. Neither Harpersville nor Overton can be found on a map. Harpersville seems to be quite a distance from Louisville, a seven-hour train ride. Louisville is right on the northern edge of Kentucky, and a look at a map of Kentucky, searching for a "city" that is still central to the state (leaving enough distance for the more remote Harpersville to still be in Kentucky on a "line," close to the eastern border of Kentucky) suggests either Lexington or Frankfort as "the city." Frankfort, the state capital, would have the most lawyers, but Lexington is a little farther east and so most likely to be the closest "city" to Harpersville (where Ruth McClure would go to find a lawyer). Furthermore, if "the city" were Frankfort, one might expect some reference to government buildings.

I don't know whether it was what I expected or not. Taken at its face value, it looked as if Hillman Jolley might be on the square.

49

I crossed the street and found Ruth waiting for me by the police car. It was ten o'clock. There was nothing much doing in County Court. Ruth produced her father's will and it not only appointed her as executrix but waived bond and surety so we were through inside of fifteen minutes. I asked the clerk for a couple of extra attested copies of the letters of administration and we had these in another ten minutes. It was 10:25 when we crossed the street to the Farmers & Traders Bank. I said: "We're doing this just because it's easy. There won't be any results. I think your father had a lockbox somewhere but I don't think it was in his name and he couldn't have gotten by with an assumed name in Harpersville. Just the same, it's stupid to start beating the bushes until you have explored your own back yard."

I was right. The Farmers & Traders Bank had no safety deposit box in the name of John McClure. Everyone in the bank knew him like they knew everyone else in town and there could be no mistake about it. From there we went to the Citizens Bank & Trust Company and from there to the First National Bank of Harpersville, all with the same results.

"Well, that's that," said Ruth. "It's a big world, where do we go now?"

"First we take the police car down to headquarters and turn in the keys. The chief would like nothing better than to haul me in for attempting to steal public property. Before we go there, we can stop by your house and pick up your car. Mine's still parked on the Harper drive and I forgot all about it this morning. You pick me up at the police station and we're heading for the city."

"Why there?"

"Why not? Put yourself in your father's place. He wouldn't be going to some little town because there would be too much chance of him being recognized after awhile. Here's a city only twenty-five miles away and big enough not to care about who comes in from the country. If he went any farther he wouldn't be able to get to the box conveniently when he had to."

At 11:15 we parked the car in a downtown garage in the city. On the way up I had remembered that neither of us had eaten any breakfast so we found a restaurant and I insisted that we have a cocktail before eating even at that odd hour of the day. The meal was a long time coming and the cocktail felt fine. While we were sitting there, I called for the telephone directory and copied down the names and addresses of all of the banks. I knew the town like a book but I wasn't taking any chances of overlooking something.

"We'll probably have to call on every one of them," I said. "I'm damned if I know whether I would go to one of the biggest on the theory that its size and bustle would offer obscurity or whether I'd go to a smaller one on the theory that I'd be less likely to run into somebody from Harpersville and it might be embarrassing."

Ruth looked at the list and it was fairly long. She said: "We'd better hurry. Remember that the banks close at two o'clock and if the answer is here I don't want to wait until tomorrow to find it."

We ate in a hurry and started the rounds. With the letters of administration to back us up we had no difficulty accounting for ourselves and at each place the procedure was the same. First was there a safety box in the name of John H. McClure? If not, did the vault employees recognize his picture under any other name. It was a maddening process because we were at the hours when some one or more of the vault staff were at lunch. We couldn't wait them all out so I made a careful memorandum of the names of the people we didn't see and we went on.

It was eight minutes to two before we had any encouragement at all. The cashier of the Haymarket State Bank & Trust Company thought he could recognize the picture. In considerable excitement, we trailed him down to the vault where an old fellow with a droopy mustache who had been there for forty years adjusted his spectacles, studied the picture and said: "Yes, that's John McCall. Comes in once every week or ten days. Been doing it for years."

I said: "His real name was McClure. Don't ask me why. He died about two weeks ago and this is his daughter who is the executrix of his estate. I'm her attorney. Call Mead, Opdyke, Smallwood, Garrison & Henry and verify it if you want. The number is Main 8247."

They took the letters of administration and studied them and went off together and muttered. When they came back the cashier said: "Understand, Mr. Henry, we don't doubt you or anything like that, but after all we need more than this. We're satisfied Miss McClure is executrix of the estate of John H. McClure like it says here but we have to establish definitely that John H. McClure was John McCall before we could let you into the box. If we made a mistake, we would be wide open."

I drummed on the desk with my fingers. I couldn't stand it to be so near and yet so far away.

"Look," I said to Ruth, "I hate to bring this up but it is the best way I can think of. Your father's picture was in the *Harpersville Gazette* the day after his accident; I wonder if we could possibly locate a copy here in the City."

"Newspapers have exchange departments," she suggested.

I picked up the telephone and called the office of the *Inquirer* and asked if their exchange department would have back numbers of the *Harpersville Gazette*. A grumpy woman said they kept back numbers of the country weeklies for a while and then threw them away. She might have the *Harpersville Gazette* of two weeks ago and she might not. If we wanted to come and look for it, we were welcome but she had other things to do and couldn't be bothered. I told Ruth where the *Inquirer's* office was located and she said she would drive over and see what she could find. In the meantime I learned that the box was number 1087 and I could look through the bars and see it. Then I remembered that I didn't have the key and that brought up a new problem.

"Of course you have to have the key," said the cashier with considerable condescension. "It takes two of them. We have a master key that fits the top key hole and the box-holder has the other. Unless they are both put in and turned at once, the box won't open."

"Don't people ever lose keys? I do. I lose about one a day. Other people are human. What do you do then?"

"Naturally, Mr. Henry, we haven't any duplicate box-holders' keys. They are made one at a time. If we had a duplicate, we'd have a thousand law suits a year from people who would scream that we had browsed around in their boxes and filched all their valuables. If the key is lost, we have to bring in the locksmith and drill the box. There is a standard charge of three dollars which includes a new key." I said: "Then call the locksmith. You'll be satisfied with our story as soon as Miss McClure comes back with the newspaper article so you can see we're telling the truth."

The cashier and the vault custodian withdrew and had another conference and looked at the clock. "I'm afraid you'll have to come back tomorrow, Mr. Henry. Rules of the bank, you know. We don't mind accommodating a box-holder after hours but it would be some time before we could get the locksmith and even then, of course, assuming your story is proven to be correct, as I am sure it will be, still you can't open the box of a deceased person without a representative of the State Tax Department being present. That's something we can't help."

He was perfectly right and I mentally kicked myself. At the same time there was nothing I could have done about it since I had had no way to tell whether we would have any luck or not and I couldn't have carried a locksmith and a State revenue man around in the car with me all day. I went to the telephone and called the office of the local representative of the State Tax Department but the man was out and probably would not be in the office again until tomorrow morning. They didn't know where he could be reached.

It was maddening. Even if I could reach him, there was that business of satisfying the bank and calling the man to drill the box and it was already 2:30, and if I got into the box there was no assurance I would find anything helpful. After all, suppose it did have a lot of stuff about money received from William Jasper Harper? I knew that already. I fumed around cursing my luck and at quarter to three a call came through from Ruth and she said the Inquirer did not have the right copy of the *Harpersville Gazette*. She'd have to get one in Harpersville. I hung up the receiver in despair, found my hat and was just starting out when the cashier asked if he could make arrangements for some time in the morning. I said he could. If he would have the locksmith and the tax man there at nine o'clock, Ruth and I would be back and we would have all the ammunition we needed. In the meantime, old droopy mustache had been talking with the uniformed guard and he was getting pretty excited. He came up and said: "The guard just reminded me. There was someone else here today asking about that box. Had the key and everything. Said John McCall was sick and it was urgent. I was out at the time. The guard referred him to Miss Crenshaw and Miss Crenshaw said he would have to have a power of attorney before we could let him get in. He was quite impatient and upset but finally he said all right he would get a power of attorney if he had to but Mr. McCall wouldn't like it."

"Did you say he?" I asked. "It was a man?"

"I didn't see him myself but that's what the guard said."

I talked to the guard and it was a man all right but the guard could no more describe him than I could describe the governor of Maine. He couldn't remember whether he was tall or short or fat or thin or blond or brunet. I gave them my name and the number of my ex-office and the McClure number in Harpersville and told them if the man showed up again they were to call the police and get me on the phone as quickly as possible. I promised I would swear to a warrant and guaranteed to keep them out of trouble. I referred them again to the firm of Mead, Opdyke, Smallwood, Garrison & Henry because we were one of the best known offices in town. I didn't see any reason to tell them I was no longer connected there.

I went out and waited for Ruth and then I remembered that I had to find a typewriter somewhere and prepare a couple of simple wills and get the hell back to Harpersville.

50

Ruth was as upset as I was over our failure to get into the lockbox. Both of us had a growing conviction that somewhere in that box we would find a paper or a record of some sort that would at least take us a long way through the maze that surrounded us. We were both so disappointed that we hardly said a word while I drove around to the parking lot nearest my office building.

As we walked down the hall I must confess that I felt pretty bad when I looked at the firm name on the door as I had done a thousand times before. I cannot say that I regretted my decision to leave the place or that I even thought of backing up, but I had had a lot of good times there and the prospect of moving out gave me a feeling of the deepest depression. Ruth sat in the outer office while I went in and riffled through the mail that had come in. Myrtle brought her book and in fifteen minutes I disposed of everything as briefly as possible, mostly with short memorandums asking some other member of the firm to take over. When I was through I sat back and Myrtle looked at me with such a long face that I knew she had heard of the breakup. I couldn't trust myself to talk about it so I grinned with the muscles of my face and she managed to grin back with the sort of thing you might put on for the benefit of the surgeon just before he starts to cut your arm off.

I told her that I had to do a couple of wills and they were so confidential I couldn't even dictate them to myself so we went out in the main room and she got me out some legal size paper and maybe put in a surreptitious sniffle or two. Of course, she was beginning to have a cold or something and I made allowances.

I am not much of a hand at the typewriter and I picked out two wills slowly and carefully, so as to avoid the typographical errors that habitually spot my work. Since this was my first job working strictly for myself, and since I was going to charge all the traffic would bear, I was careful to start with my best or "In-The-Name-Of-God-Amen" form. When I got through it was nearly four o'clock and my two wills were as alike as two peas in a pod, done in single space so that the signatures and everything would be on one sheet of paper in each case, and without a typographical error or even a smudgy fingerprint. I washed my hands and then folded each one carefully and put it in a separate envelope and stuck them in my pocket.

As we went out I gave Myrtle a big wink so we didn't talk about the situation any more and then out in the hall I said to Ruth: "I know it's late but I think Mrs. Harper can wait a few more minutes. While you were at the *Inquirer's* office, I thought of something. It's a wild shot but as long as we're here, I'm going to follow the hunch and see where it gets me."

"Anything I can help you do?"

"I can probably do it myself in fifteen minutes but maybe with you along we can cut it down to ten. We're going by the newspaper office and haul out some back numbers in August, 1909, and look for a fire. I figure there must have been a fire about that time either here or somewhere else and we might as well look here because we don't know where else to look."

"Fire? What kind of a fire?"

"Probably a residence. Maybe a boardinghouse or a hotel but I don't think so. A fire in which a woman was badly burned. By the way, I've been meaning to ask you, do you know a Miss Phoebe Murdoch or a Mrs. somebody who used to be a Miss Phoebe Murdoch?"

"You mean in Harpersville?"

I nodded.

"I never heard the name in Harpersville at all. I don't even know how you would spell it. That doesn't mean there isn't someone there by that name—maybe working in the factory or something but I certainly never heard of it. What's the connection?"

"When we look for this fire, we're going to look for the name of Murdoch. Could be the name Phoebe will appear in the story but she isn't the one who was burned. If we're on the right track and my hunch is any good, I think we'll find that a Catherine Murdoch was burned practically to a cinder, either on August 7, 1909, or pretty close to that time and unless I miss my guess, it was Catherine Murdoch who was murdered in Harpersville last night."

I know Ruth wanted to ask three hundred and twenty-one questions but we were parking in front of the newspaper office by that time and she didn't ask them.

My hunch was right. It was quite a prominent story in the *Inquirer* on August 6, 1909. A gas heater had exploded in a residence on Murray Street, then evidently a nice enough residential section. The fire was reported by Phoebe Murdoch when she returned from a shopping trip. Her sister, Catherine Murdoch, school teacher, age twenty-eight, had been knocked unconscious by the explosion and was rescued with severe burns by the daring action of the fire department. At the city hospital she was placed on the danger list. There were pictures and details running over to page seven but that was the substance of it.

In the issue of August 7, 1909, there was a short item obscurely placed near the bottom of page two. Despite the gravity of Catherine Murdoch's condition, upon the insistence of her sister Phoebe, she had been rushed on the night train to Louisville with a doctor and nurse in attendance, for special treatment.

Just to be sure we did not miss anything, we pored over every issue of the *Inquirer* for the ensuing two weeks but there was nothing more about the case.

51

When we left the building I thought of something else and instead of taking the route to Harpersville I pulled around the block and stopped in front of the office of Killion, Wintersmith & Black. Brokers are not usually in their offices at that time of day because they go home as soon as possible after the market closes in New York but my friend, George Black, was in his cubbyhole and that was quite a break. He said: "Hi, Gil. What's the good word?"

"I wouldn't want to be quoted on it."

"Take your weight off your feet. What's on your mind?"

"Information."

"What sort of information?"

"Harper Products Company."

George took his feet off the desk and went for a file. Before he opened it he said: "Down to eighteen today. The news of the old man's death doesn't set so well with the market."

"The price was twenty-three the first of the week. Five points is a lot of drop overnight isn't it?"

"Not so much considering. Old William Jasper Harper was supposed to be quite a whiz and he never delegated anything he could do himself. The rest of the management isn't too highly regarded. And besides that, the stock has been a puzzle for a couple of years. Dividend cut in half, earnings not so good. Then, of course, the news from the last directors' meeting put the skids under her for six or eight points inside of a week."

"What news was that?"

"Harper himself. Said he had received a lot of inquiries from stockholders about how things were going. He said the stock-holders were loyal and had held on through a tough period and the market quotations did not reflect the true value. He said the stock was really worth as much today as it had ever been worth and the future looked bright. He announced that before he would let the price go down much farther, he would peg the price himself by buying in the open market. Damnedest popping off I ever heard of. He may have meant well but what would you do if you heard an announcement like that?"

I studied the proposition a minute. "I don't know that I'd like it so much. I didn't care for that reference to the stock going down some more. I think I would quietly unload and take my loss before it got worse."

"You and a lot of others. Sounds like whistling into the wind. Then in a couple of weeks Harper gets snuffed out and since he's the one who was going to put the floor under the thing, a kind of panic sets in. I wouldn't be surprised if it doesn't go down another five points tomorrow."

I said: "Everybody knows that you were his brokers. Did he ever place a general buying order?"

"I'm not supposed to discuss a client's affairs."

"I know, but this is important. Believe it or not, I'm working on the great Harper murder case and I'm not doing so good. I won't breathe a word of it to a soul."

"Well, on that basis, it's still not all right but I'll trust you. He placed a general order to buy at twenty if it got down that far. No limit on the amount. It didn't go to twenty until after his death and naturally we aren't filling any orders for dead people."

There were some other things that I wanted to know and I thought George Black could find a way to get the answers for me but I wanted to be sure I didn't approach him in the wrong way so I sat still for a while and thought about it. Finally I said: "George, there's a big good-looking fellow in the hoosegow in Harpersville who's going to be indicted for the murder of William Jasper Harper in the next twenty-four hours unless I turn up something before they get around to it. They'll convene a special session of the Circuit Court and they'll rush him to trial and crucify him in less time than it takes you to eat your breakfast. I don't think he did it. I know he didn't do it. But the police and the sheriff think he did and the facts look pretty bad. That's the situation. You've already told me one thing you didn't want to tell and I appreciate it. I wouldn't ask you to go any farther if things were less serious. But the chips are all down and the bets are all in, and it's up to me to call or turn my hand over. The time is short and I don't know anyone else to turn to. I want you to peep at a couple of hole cards and tip me off."

He didn't like it. He didn't like any part of it. He got up and walked to the window and stuck his hands in his hip pockets and stood there looking out. I went over and stood beside him. I said: "That's my car out there. That girl's his sister."

He didn't move for a long time. "How do you know I can get the information for you?"

"Maybe you can't. It's possible you have some of the answers right here. Maybe not. Maybe there won't be any way you can get the answers. You can't help that. All I want you to do is to try."

"What do you want to know?"

"I want to know who's been placing orders for big blocks of Harper stock. Not everybody, of course. I'll give you the names."

"How would I find out something like that?"

"That's your problem. You'll have to trade on some friendships. You've been in deals with most of the brokerage firms in town. Probably all of them. You may cut each other's throats but you know who you can trust and who you can't. Tell 'em I'll use the information if I have to but I won't reveal the source and I'll cover up so that nobody will know."

"It's a great deal to ask. What if I have to refuse?"

"We'll deal with that when we come to it. If we do."

There was another long silence. Time was not standing still but I knew I couldn't rush things. He turned around slowly and gave me a big wink and said: "When do you want to know?"

"Right now. It would have been better if I had known yesterday."

"Give me the names. I can't find out right away because most of the offices are closed but I know who does the trading in each outfit and I'll get on the phone and see what I can do. It may be tomorrow noon for all I know. By golly, I hope you appreciate this because every time you do a favor, you've got to look for one right back at you and it's no telling what this will cost me in the long run."

"Swell. Feed it to me as fast as you get it. Don't bother too much about details. Just give me the yes or no in each case. I'll remember it and I've got a memory like an elephant." I went over to the desk, found a scratch pad and wrote down the names of Janet, Mrs. Harper, Mead, Jolley, Miss Knight and Miles. Then I thought a minute and added the names of Tim and Ruth McClure just to make certain. I told him to try me at the Harpers' and the McClures' and if he didn't reach me at either of those places, then to try the sheriff and the chief of police on the theory that I might be tagging along with them wherever they went.

52

I did a lot of thinking on the way back to Harpersville and the more I think the slower I drive. It was 5:45 when we got there. I called the Harper house and got hold of Miss Knight. Mrs. Harper had been in a state all afternoon because I had failed to show up but her own impatience had finally worn her out and she was then asleep. I couldn't see any reason to wake her up to sign a will that could be signed any time so I said I would get something to eat and maybe see Tim and be out there around seven o'clock. The late afternoon paper from the city was being hawked around on the streets and we bought one. Sure enough a special grand jury was being convened Monday and the coroner's inquest on Harper's death was set for ten o'clock the next morning. The Circuit Judge was reported as saying that if an indictment was returned by the grand jury, he would convene a special session of Circuit Court so that a speedy trial could be had. The commonwealth's attorney had spent the day going over the evidence and interviewing some of the witnesses and he was pretty smug about his predictions. It was clear enough that they were getting ready to put the bee on Tim McClure and that they would waste no time doing it.

There was a separate item about the gun. Ballistics experts

from the city had taken their pictures of test bullets and it was definitely established that Tim's gun had done the job. The sheriff and chief of police had done a fair job muzzling the newspapers as far as concrete facts were concerned but someone had dug up an old picture of the Harper house and the paper had gone to town with what it had on the case. Ruth set her jaw and read everything there was and she seemed to shrivel up right in front of my eyes.

"Look," I said, "they put a fellow named Holbert on the job of running down the possibility of a later will. Do you know him?"

"Yes, like I know nearly everyone else in town. He's young and pretty decent. I had a couple of dates with him in summers between years at college."

"Think he would talk to you?"

"Probably as much as he could."

I drove down to the police station and we found Holbert without any trouble. The reporters had just been there and gone and the chief had given them a statement on the subject so there was no reason why we should not be told. Holbert had gotten in touch with a young lawyer in the city who had started out as a cub in Frank Gregory's office and with his help, it had been a simple job to trace his files and records. All the files relating to Harper and Harper Products Company had been delivered to Harper himself and they had been found in the basement of the company office building. There was no trace of any will at all and no correspondence about a will. The young lawyer had been with Gregory from 1933 until the time of Gregory's death and he was positive no will had been drawn during that time. As a matter of fact, he thought he recalled a conversation in 1937 in which Gregory had asked Harper about his will and Harper had said it had been taken care of long ago and wouldn't talk about it.

I was conscious of a let-down feeling. For no reason at all, I had been sure that the 1915 will was not the last will and testament of William Jasper Harper and I had been speculating about what would be in the later will when we found it. This new information seemed definite enough and instead of helping, it left me more confused than ever.

Frankly, I was discouraged. I had been running around for two or three days sticking my nose into other people's business and chasing every shadow I could find and if there was a pattern, I was apparently no nearer to it than I had been when I started. As a matter of fact, I was farther away than ever. If it was blackmail, why would anyone kill the source of the whole thing? If it was not blackmail, what was it?

Twenty-six years ago a kid had been adopted and within twenty-four hours a will had been made but the will didn't provide for the child nor did it provide for anyone else except Mrs. Harper and why would she want a lot of dough? She was only one jump out of the grave herself and she had everything she wanted and could scarcely move a muscle. Obviously William Jasper Harper had something to do with the adoption of Tim by the McClures but if he was covering up the fact that Tim was his own son, what kind of deal could have been made that didn't ultimately involve a handsome provision for Tim out of the estate? And where was Phoebe Murdoch? What did Miss Katie see that got her throat cut for her? Why did Jolley want to marry Janet after he found out she would get nothing of her father's estate for the time being, and before he or anyone else could have known of Mrs. Harper's intentions? And how could Jolley figure in it anyway? He was in Overton the day it happened and the train he came in on didn't even leave Overton until after midnight. Who put a slug in the tire of the car I was driving and why?

I don't know how long I had been standing there but I realized that Holbert and Ruth were staring at me and I also realized that I had a heavy frown on my face and my eyes had been focused on nothing in particular.

Suddenly a thought occurred to me and it scared me right down to my shoetops and made my mouth dry. The whole Harper estate, generally estimated at between ten and fifteen million dollars now belonged to Mrs. Harper. It was generally said that she had a couple of hundred thousand of her own and certainly she must already have a will. I had been thinking so hard about the two wills I was preparing for her that I had altogether forgotten this perfectly obvious fact. If someone was in position to gain under Mrs. Harper's existing will, then it would not be a bad scheme at all to kill Harper first, providing the contents of his will was known. That would mean that Mrs. Harper had been in danger since nine o'clock the night before and she would be the next on the list. I cursed myself for a doddering fool. I could hardly make my mouth ask the next question but I managed to do it and with a certain degree of unconcern at that. "What about Mrs. Harper? Find any sign of her will while you were scratching around?"

"Sure," said Holbert. "Found that the first thing, right where his will had been. We had quite a confab as to whether we had any right to open it but we asked Mrs. Harper and she told us to go ahead."

I said: "Well?" and held my breath.

"Nothing to it," said Holbert. "Exactly like his. The works to her beloved husband, William Jasper Harper. Even the wording was the same."

"And the date?"

"Exactly the same. Some day in 1915. Put up in the same kind of envelope and sealed with the same kind of wax."

I said: "This is the damnedest case in the world. Come on. I need about a pint of whiskey and the biggest steak that ever walked on four legs."

53

Ruth would not think about eating until she had seen Tim, so I told her to go on in and see him, and I would get some whiskey and come back for her. I found a liquor store, bought a pint of Bourbon, and took two big pulls out of the bottle.

Before going back after Ruth I thought of something so obvious that I couldn't imagine why I hadn't thought of it before. I drove around to the office of the telephone company, went in, laid a couple of bills on the counter, and asked the cashier to give me some change. I had done the same thing that morning, and the old battle-ax remembered it. She stopped chewing gum, looked at me sourly, and said, "Is it for a phone call?"

"No," I said, giving her a cold stare. "I'm doing my homework. The teacher wants to know how much change I can get for two one-dollar bills and I want to make a hundred so my daddy will take me to the circus. If you don't like that, you can say I came in to grow a beard."

The look she gave me would have operated a blast furnace. She snatched open the change drawer, slapped a collection of small coins on the counter, and muttered something under her breath that sounded a good deal like a reference to "dirty little snips." I looked at the change on the counter and said: "I'll never get to the circus that way." Without even looking she practically threw another quarter at me which made up the two dollars, and I went on in and placed a call for the head man at the airport at Louisville. I don't know why I wanted to give the needle to the cashier, but I was worn out and exasperated, and if there is anything I hate it is people who want to make wisecracks because they are asked to do what they are paid to do.

I could hear two or three operators feeling their way over the State of Kentucky. They finally got things straightened out to their mutual satisfaction, and after awhile I could hear a phone ringing and a voice came on the other end of the wire.

"Hello," I said. "This is the chief of police at Harpersville, Kentucky. Do you get it?"

"You said it in English, didn't you?"

"I thought so."

"OK, you can argue about it if you want to. You're paying for this call, not me."

"All right, skip it," I said, in my best conciliatory manner. "No offense, this is business and it is important. You keep a record on all planes that leave the field, don't you?"

"Yes."

"Well, I am working on the Harper murder case down here—you know—William Jasper Harper. I need some information. Look at your records, if you will, and see if any planes were chartered out of Louisville yesterday."

"That's easy. Chartered planes all you want?"

"Yes, just the chartered planes. Never mind the commercial flights."

"Hold the line. I don't even have to look to tell you there was one, but I guess you want the details."

I hung on all right, and I was practically trembling with excitement. Jolley had been in Overton, and he had come in on the train that morning, but there was nothing about the story that would be inconsistent with a trip by plane. He could have chartered a ship, stopped at Overton long enough to put in his appearance at the college, check in at the hotel, and gone out on something that was supposed to be business. A plane could have taken him to the city or even Harpersville, and he would have had plenty of time to get in his dirty work, fly back to Overton, and get on the train. Or he could have driven up to the city and gotten on the train there. My hand was sweating so I could hardly hold the receiver. Pretty soon I could hear the man in the airport humming "The Music Goes Round and Round," and then he said, "Hello."

"OK, shoot."

"Plane chartered out of here yesterday afternoon down your way. Fella by the name of Henry. Can't read the scrawl, but looks like it might be Wilbur or Gilbert or something. The porter says he was a funny little mutt who looked like he had been fighting Two-Ton Tony Galento.* Took off here about—."

"That's swell," I answered hastily. "You've been a big help." I hung up abruptly and stood there feeling like an old man. My spirits reached a new low. When I went out the cashier gave me a mean look. There was a mirror on the wall and when my back was turned, I could see her going through the motions of giving me a Bronx cheer. I felt so bad I didn't even care. I took another drink out of the bottle and hoped that I wouldn't pass out. In the last three days I had swallowed more whiskey than in the preceding three months, and it occurred to me that if I went on investigating murder cases I would probably turn out like these private dicks in detective stories who inhale the stuff oftener than they breathe. The liquor did not have much effect, but it did relax me a little, and I remembered what a small meal I had had that morning and how long ago that had been. I also felt drowsy, and I believe I could have sat right behind the wheel and slept for three solid days in front of police headquarters if Ruth had not come out and jumped in the car at that time.

---

*Domenico Antonio "Two-Ton" Galento (1910–1979) was an American heavyweight boxer. Known as a brawler and famous for gorging on six chickens, spaghetti, and beer or wine before his fights, he lost spectacularly to then-champion Joe Louis in 1939.

She had taken longer than I thought she would, and it was a quarter to seven already. I had promised Miss Knight I would be out with Mrs. Harper's will at seven, and since this was my first employment on my own I reluctantly came to the conclusion that there would be no time to eat until later. Ruth did not seem to care one way or another, and she was about as communicative as a deaf-mute who has not learned sign language. All the way out to the Harper place she stared straight ahead and I did not bother her with conversation because among other things my eyelids were so heavy that I could hardly keep from running off the road.

When we went up the front steps and into the hall the telephone was ringing. Mead came out of the dining room and answered it. I stood and watched him because I was conscious of the fact that the call might be for me.

It was. Mead listened with a funny look on his face and then glanced up and saw me. He held out the instrument. "For you. It's George Black. How did he know you were here?"

"I was expecting the call. Told him to try the McClure house and then here."

I wasn't sure I liked the way things were turning out. James Mead knew George Black as well as I did, and I could tell he was wondering just what was going on. George Black's voice was coming over the wire. "Gil?"

"All right."

"Ready?"

"Shoot."

"I have some dope for you. You don't want to know where it came from, do you?"

"Yes, give me the whole thing. I won't use names unless I have to."

"Well, I tried Joe Fulton of Carpenter & Shearer. I had a devil of a time getting him out at the Country Club. No soap there at all. Never heard of any of your names except the Harpers, and never had any dealings with them. Tried Bill Anderson over at Dobson & Company and did a little better. One of your people put in an order the first of the week. Said to buy at the market whatever it might be and keep buying until further notice. Who do you reckon it was?"

"Haven't time to guess. Give it to me for pete's sake."

"Jim Mead."

I looked up and Mead was still standing there not over five feet away and his ears were doing everything but shimmying. I couldn't tell whether he could hear anything or not. When I caught his eye he looked away and then back again, and then he turned abruptly and went into the dining room. I said: "Thanks, George. Don't stop. Keep at it and call me every time you have anything. If I am out of reach for a long time, I will call you myself."

"OK. I hope you remember this. Next time ask me something easy."

54

I knocked on the door of Mrs. Harper's room and Miss Knight opened it, looking as prim and virginal as ever. As soon as Mrs. Harper saw me she squirmed around in her chair, and I could see she was trying to work up a good mad at me.

I held up my hand and said: "Skip it. It's no good for the blood pressure and too much of it will give you gallstones."

I smiled and after a moment of uncertainty she smiled back at me in a reluctant sort of way. "There's something about you I like, but I don't know what it is. You look funny and you do things in a queer way and when you're gone I wonder why I trust you."

"But you do trust me. The rest is immaterial."

"Yes, I do, and for all I know, you may skin me out of my eye teeth."

I said: "Maybe I will, at that."

I sat down in the same chair over by the door to the study and then I got up and walked out through the French windows and took a long look to be sure that someone wasn't eavesdropping again. When I returned Mrs. Harper was watching me. She said: "You look like you're dog-tired."

"I think I've been bit by tsetse flies. I'm the original sleepy man."

"I'm ready to attend to the will thing. Then you can get a room at the hotel and charge it to me and sleep until next March if you want to."

Miss Knight was sitting by her side looking very inoffensive and uninterested and I didn't think her mind was wandering. I pulled out the two envelopes, looked in one of them, put it back and handed her the other. "I believe Miles is to be the other witness. While you are reading it, Miss Knight can go after him and we'll be ready to sign as soon as they come back."

Mrs. Harper made a gesture and Miss Knight went out and closed the door behind her. Mrs. Harper got out her glasses and read the will slowly while I held my breath. The skin around her eyes crinkled with concentration. When she was through she looked at me intently for a long time. I looked right back at her.

"You don't think I'm going to live very long, do you?" she asked calmly.

"I hope you do. I want you to be careful."

"Now let me see the other will."

I took it out and handed it to her and she read it with her finger marking each line as she went through. Then she looked at me again and I thought I saw a little twinkle. She folded the second one, put it back in its envelope and handed it to me.

"Do you think it's as bad as that?"

"I don't know. I think it's important, don't you?"

"Do you know or are you guessing?"

"Guessing, now. But I'm going to know."

She gave me another of her long quivering sighs and looked down at the hands clasped in her lap. "If I'm wrong in trusting you, I'll come back and haunt your gizzards out of you."

At that point Miss Knight came in with no expression on her face and Miles followed her and closed the door. I took out my fountain pen and handed it to Mrs. Harper. Miss Knight handed her a stiff magazine and she put it across her knees. I held my hand over the will to keep it flat and she signed "Alice Holt Harper" in a beautiful spencerian hand.*

I said: "Now go up there and put in the date. There's also a space for you to put the day of the week. It's Thursday and seven-thirty P.M. Maybe a minute one way or the other."

When she was through I beckoned to Miss Knight and Miles and said: "Mrs. Harper, do you acknowledge this to be your last will and testament in the present of these witnesses?"

"Yes, I do."

I turned the will without picking it up and handed the pen to Miss Knight. She hesitated so long that I looked up at her and there was some strange conflict that she resolved just as I caught her eye. She hadn't intended for me to see it and she bit her lip in annoyance. She took the pen away from me a bit ungraciously and wrote "Genevieve Knight" and walked away.

"I'm sorry, Miss Knight," I said at her back, "you'll have to come and watch while the other witness signs. Requirement of law. Witnesses sign their names in the presence of the testator and in the presence of each other. That means you're looking when it happens."

She came back and watched impassively while Miles signed his name in a bold angular scrawl.

When the ink was dry Mrs. Harper folded the will herself, put it in the envelope and sealed it. I suggested that she write her name across the sealed flap and she did so. I put it in my pocket.

Miles was standing very stiff and straight, and I wondered who he was trying to make an impression on. He bore a faint resemblance to the Petrified Forest.† He said: "Is that all, Madam?"

Mrs. Harper looked at me and I said: "That's all there is to it.

---

*"Spencerian script" was a cursive style of writing prevalent in the U.S. from about 1850 to the mid-1920s, based on the system of Platt Roger Spencer in the 1840s. The advent of the typewriter largely displaced its teaching.

†Gil is referring to the 1936 film starring Humphrey Bogart, in which Bogart plays the desperate gangster Duke Mantee.

Janet is all taken care of. Since she's named executrix, it might be a good idea to send for her and tell her all about it now."

Miles went out in a rather precise sort of way. Mrs. Harper looked at Miss Knight and nodded her head toward the door and Miss Knight went on out to find Janet.

I looked at Mrs. Harper and she said: "You wanted them out of the room. What now?"

"This thing ought to be put in a safe somewhere. I don't feel much like carrying it around with me. Where is the safe?"

"In the study."

"Know the combination?"

"I used to. I think so."

"Well, let's go. You can put it in with your own hand and lock the thing. I don't want to even know how it works."

"You'll have to do it. I haven't walked that far in years."

"Don't kid me. It's your heart that's weak, not your legs. It'll do you good."

She tried to stare me down but I outlasted her. I remembered that the French windows of the study were fastened from the inside so I went out into the hall and around to the study door. The case was so completely solved as far as the law was concerned that there was not even a guard in the hall although I could hear voices in the dining room and someone was shuffling his feet outside the front door.

The study had the flat dank smell of a room that has been shut up tight for awhile. I closed the door behind me, crossed over and opened the French windows and went around into Mrs. Harper's room by way of the terrace.

There was nothing wrong at all with the way she walked. I gave her my arm, escorted her back to the study and watched from a distance while she slid back a panel in the wall, fiddled with a dial, opened the safe and put the will inside. When she had locked the safe and restored the panel, we went back into her room again. Miss Knight was still gone.

The telephone rang out in the hall and I started to go out and take care of it when Mrs. Harper said: "You can take it in here." There was an extension phone on a stand by the big four-poster bed. It was George Black again.

"More news?" I asked.

"Sure. How'm I doing?"

"Fine. Let's have it."

"I couldn't get hold of the man in Farjean, Tully & Andrews. He's on his vacation and won't be back for two weeks. I don't know the man who takes his place. That just leaves Holcraft, Munday & Company. Baker Trask is the man over there. He got a toothache and had hauled his dentist away from his dinner and down to his office to get it worked on. It was a devil of a job but I got him to the phone and I don't think I had better see him again for about ten days."

"Very interesting. You lead a tough life, but where's this getting me?"

"I'm getting to that. Don't be impatient. Let's see, I've got your list here. He never heard of your McClure people. Has a client named Miles but he's Vice-President of the Transit Corporation and I don't think he's the man you're talking about. No orders for Harper stock anyway. Doesn't remember any Miss Knight but then he says he could have a customer by any name and he wouldn't necessarily remember it. Says he's sure she isn't a big trader, whoever she is. Nothing on Mead, but of course I gave you the dope on him. Doesn't know Mrs. Harper. Got all that?"

I said: "What the hell. You haven't said anything yet."

"Just getting the routine out of the way. That leaves Janet Harper and your Mr. Jolley. Jolley has been buying Harper stock off and on for several months but nothing doing lately. I squeezed it out of Trask that he's in fairly heavy on margin and with the stock going down fast, they may have to sell him out. Janet Harper placed a standing order last Saturday. Anything else you want to know?"

"No, that'll do. Thanks a lot. We'll skip the fellow who's on his vacation. I'll do you a favor sometime."

"OK, Bub. Keep your nose clean."

He hung up. Before I broke the connection I heard something that sounded like a faint click. I put the receiver down in the cradle.

"Nice little gadget you've got here." I said to Mrs. Harper. "Got 'em scattered all over the house?"

"Four or five extensions. You can plug them in almost anywhere but we don't move them around much. There is this one, and one in the study and one in the hall where most of the calls are taken. Then there is one upstairs and one in the butler's pantry and one out in the servants' quarters that you can switch on or off."

"Do you take your own calls or does a flunky take them and see who it's for?"

"Ordinarily we take the calls ourselves. Whoever is closest. If it rings more than two or three times, one of the servants will answer it in the butler's pantry. If we are all going to be out of the house, we throw the switch and the servants can take it out at their place."

I would have given a lot to know who had been listening in on my conversation with George Black but there didn't seem to be much possibility of running it down. I wanted very badly to have a chance to sit down and add these last nuggets of information to the store of apparently unrelated material I had scraped together but at that moment there was a knock on the door and Miss Knight came sailing in with Janet Harper behind her. Janet's face was flushed and there were sparks in her eyes. Despite the slightly horsey cast of her face, she was almost beautiful but she was furiously angry and I hoped the anger was not directed at me.

She said to Mrs. Harper: "You sent for me." She was controlling herself with an effort.

"Nothing particularly important," said Mrs. Harper taking it all in. "I just wanted to tell you that I have signed a new will and you're provided for. The will's in the safe in the study."

"Thanks. Is that all?" There was a touch of impatience in Janet's voice and manner.

Her mother said rather shortly: "Sorry. I must have interrupted something. You look as if you would burst a blood vessel. Come back when the storm is over and we can talk about it then."

I couldn't tell whether Janet was going to say anything or not and I don't think she could tell either for a minute. She turned as if she would leave the room and then thought better of it and blurted out: "The storm's already over. Maybe I've been mistaken about Hillman. Don't give out any more about our plans. I doubt very much if they will come off."

She had cooled off a little but not enough. She looked as if she could not trust herself to say any more and ran out of the room, slamming the door behind her.

Everything was silent for maybe a full minute and then Mrs. Harper said: "Nice day, isn't it."

"Very nice," I agreed. "There are a few clouds but I doubt very much if it will rain before morning."

"Are we all through?"

"All but a little incidental matter that I'd rather we didn't overlook."

"Oh, yes, the fee."

"That's right."

"Well, I said I wouldn't argue about it. Tell me how much and that's the end of it."

"All right. A thousand dollars."

She didn't change expression as I would have done if someone had asked me for a thousand dollars but she was nobody's fool and she gave me one of those hard steady stares that I was beginning to expect.

"Nothing cheap about you, is there?"

"Not particularly. You can make it two thousand if you want."

"Never mind. I heard you the first time. How long did it take you?"

"Maybe an hour. Maybe more. Maybe less. What do you want me to charge you? Fifty cents and a beer check?"

Her eyes got the twinkle back in them. "You'll do," she said. "I think maybe I will want to use you again sometime. But for heaven's sake, put a tooth in that hole in your face. Give me my checkbook, Knight."

"Look," I said, "about this check business. I'll settle for fifty dollars cash."

"Is that all you think my checks are worth?"

"No, but I'll settle for fifty dollars cash just the same."

"No dice. You'll take a check. I know what you've got on your mind and I think I'll just keep you on my side."

When I had the check in my pocket, I went across to the dining room and got hold of the sheriff.

"Listen," I said, "Mrs. Harper is worth a lot of dough. I want you to put a man on the terrace and a man by her door and keep them there all night. Tell 'em to sleep there."

"I'm running this thing," said the sheriff frigidly. "I'll think up the orders and I'll give 'em. You go away and peddle your papers. I still think you ought to be in the jailhouse and I'm liable to slap you in there any minute."

I shrugged my shoulders. "OK, don't say I didn't warn you. Mrs. Harper's in danger. This thing isn't over yet. You think up the orders and you give 'em but if anything happens to her, it's going to look awful funny when I tell the newspapers I tipped you off and you were too damn smart for your own britches."

"What do you know that you haven't told?" he fairly roared at me. "You haven't warned me of nothing."

"All right, I warn you now. The killing isn't done. Somebody is going to be next and I'll take a guess it's supposed to be Mrs. Harper. I don't know any more than you know but I'm telling you, if anything happens to her, I'll pop off plenty to the newspapers and you'll be on the hottest spot you ever saw in your life."

Somehow I got it over. He grumbled around and scratched his head and finally said grudgingly: "I don't know why I pay any attention to little dumb squirts but there can't nobody say I ain't willing to take precautions. OK. I'll put Duncan and Parker on for the night and if nothing happens I'll let them take you apart tomorrow."

I found Ruth in the big living room curled up in one of the big chairs sound asleep. Her face was peaceful and relaxed for the first time in two or three days. I hated to wake her up but I thought she belonged in her own bed so I shook her gently by the shoulder. Her eyes popped wide open in a second and the look of terror and anxiety came back into them.

"Look, girlie," I said, "take yourself home and put it in a hot tub of water and then take it to bed."

"And you?"

"I've got some things to do. Do you want me to drive you home or will you take the keys and run along by yourself? Too sleepy?"

"No, I'm all right."

On the way out to the car I said: "By the way, there's something I've been wondering about. How did you happen to pick me?"

"You really want to know?"

"That's why I asked."

"You won't feel bad?"

"Should I?"

"Well, you might. To be frank I thought Mr. Mead might have something to do with the proposition Mr. Harper made me about the stock and I thought the best way to find out would be to try to hire someone in his own firm. Then probably you'd know Mr. Mead represented Harper and his company and you'd ask him and then if you turned me down, I'd know. You were the last name on the door, and I thought I could pump you easier than anybody else. Mr. Jolley told me where your office was."

I stopped in my tracks and took her by the arm, maybe a little more roughly than I should have. "Who told you?"

"Mr. Jolley. Mr. Hillman Jolley. You know—Janet."

"What did he have to do with it?"

"Didn't I tell you? I rode to the city with him that morning. He was very much interested."

I remembered what the man had said in the basement of the hospital and it was the only thing that occurred to me at the moment. I said: "Oh, my great-aunt Jezebel!"

55

After Ruth had driven off I went back into the house. Janet was just coming down the stairs still looking pretty mad about something. I went over to the bottom of the steps, leaned against the newel post and said: "Hi, Toots."

She said: "What makes you say things like that? I don't know whether I like it or not."

"I'm lonesome and hungry and sleepy. I won't ask you to sleep with me but you would probably enjoy eating with me and maybe drinking with me and getting a load off your mind."

"I'm not hungry and I'm not thirsty and I'm not lonesome. Go away."

"You might," I said, "be interested in talking to me. I'm a very clever fellow and you would like me if you only knew me. We can drive one of your cars if you like and if it would make you feel any better, I'll let you pay the bill."

"You make it sound very attractive but if you don't mind I'll refuse."

"Oh, but I do mind. I particularly want to talk to you but then it makes very little difference whether I raise my voice and talk here or whether we go someplace where we could maybe neck a little on the side."

She began to get the idea and there was indecision in every line of her body. After a while she said abruptly: "I'll get my hat," and went back up stairs.

She didn't want to get her hat any more than I wanted to get mine which was not at all. She was going upstairs to marshal her forces. When she came down, she had evidently made up her mind to be agreeable because she managed to give me quite a nice smile and hooked her arm in mine rather more chummily than I had expected. She pressed a button somewhere and when the butler appeared she gave directions that Miles should trot out the Packard roadster.

While we were waiting on the front steps, she handed me a ten and two fives. If she thought I was going to feel badly, she was mistaken. I put them in my pocket without saying a word. Janet watched me with a queer look and then laughed. It was the first time she had ever laughed in my presence and it was quite an attractive laugh with genuine amusement in it. She said: "I never met anyone like you in my life. Are you this way all the time or only on Thursday?"

The laugh was contagious and almost made me forget how hungry and tired I was. About that time the big black roadster came swishing around the house and Miles got out and held the door open. Janet said: "That will do. Mr. Henry will drive. Where are we going anyway?"

"I don't know. Preferably some place where we can get curb service, at least for the drinks. I doubt if there is any place in the world where they would bring out to a car the kind of meal I'm going to eat but if you think there is, we'll try it."

She studied a moment. "Mind drinking straight?"

"Not at all."

"Fine. It'll save time. I'll get some in the house and we won't have to go through town. We can take this road on out to Sheely's Tavern. Unless you want something fancy."

I said I didn't. I was thinking about steak, French fries and coffee that I had left untouched in my room at the YMCA. While she was gone, Miles stood as still as a bottle of beer, his face expressionless and his eyes on nothing. He wasn't stiff or formal, just inconspicuous. I would bet that if his ears had been on feelers, they would have been hanging right over my shoulder while Janet and I were talking. And wiggling.

Miles put Janet in one side of the car and then came around and put me in the driver's seat as if he were packing a suitcase. His eyebrows asked if that would be all, and mine said it would. We whirled out of the drive and turned left, away from town, the headlights cutting a slice of night out of the road. We drove maybe five miles, and Janet didn't say a word. She was as tense as a watch spring wound up tight.

When I saw a level piece of ground beside the road, shadowed by half a dozen immense trees, I turned the ignition switch and coasted to a stop under the branches. I turned off the lights, without even looking at her. Then I crossed my arms over the steering wheel and put my chin on them and waited.

Pretty soon she said: "Well?"

I said: "You're strung as tight as a bowstring. Come off it. You won't enjoy eating."

She gave a long sigh. "Is it any wonder?"

"No, but it isn't good for you. Get out the whiskey."

She took a drink, but it wasn't big enough and I made her take another. She got the second one down, shuddered and said, "Whew!" So did I. It was good whiskey, but we didn't have anything to chase it with. My hair stood up a little straighter.

Janet slid down in the seat and leaned her head back. I moved over and kissed her. It was a fairly long one, and she took it without giving any part of it back to me. I moved back over behind the wheel.

Janet said: "Do you like me?"

I said: "Yes."

"What do you like about me? Fifteen million dollars?"

"If I did, it would be imagination. You haven't got fifteen million dollars."

"I know, but it's in the family. I have a little of my own on top of that. There is no use being technical about it. Whoever marries me won't have to eat cheese on rye."

I said: "You'll have to lower your sights a little. Your father had maybe that much money. He left it all to your mother. By the time the state and federal governments take their slice she may have half of it left, but I doubt it. Then let's say at her death she leaves it to you. The taxes take another big hunk—probably half of what's left. You may have to hobble around on a mere four million."*

She didn't say anything.

I waited awhile and then said: "Which brings up a thought. Your father wasn't any wooden Indian. He understood all about these things. Why do you suppose he detoured the property through your mother so the tax men can take two bites out of it instead of shortcutting it to you with a life estate or something else to take care of your mother? After all, at her age and in her condition it doesn't stand to reason she will have it long enough or get enough good out of it to be worth the difference in taxes."

She still didn't say anything.

I waited a little while longer. "And another thing. I wonder why Miss Janet Harper suddenly places an order to buy a lot of stock of Harper Products Company after all these years."

That one got her between the ribs. I couldn't see her expression but she gave a little squirm in the seat beside me. "Full of questions, aren't you?"

"Might as well be. I don't get any answers."

"What do you know?"

"Not quite enough."

"Is that what you got me out here for?"

---

*It was not until 1948 that a "marital deduction" (the exemption from tax of property passing from a decedent to a spouse) was introduced into the federal estate tax rules, but the deduction was limited until 1981, when the current unlimited marital deduction rule was introduced.

"Partly. I also thought it would be nice to kiss you and find out what kind of a girl you are."

"Well, you've done that and you've asked the questions. Shall we go on out to Sheely's or shall we go home?"

She leaned over and turned on the ignition switch.

I said: "Sore?"

"Some."

"Hungry?"

"Some."

"Well, let's make it Sheely's then. I haven't had a square meal since I can remember. Besides I'd rather have you cool off before I leave you. I rather like you even if it turns out you haven't more than four or five million dollars. We may want to get married one of these days and if we separate in a huff, we'll have to go after it the hard way."

She surprised me with that laugh again. It was not a sarcastic laugh. She put her hand on my coat sleeve in an impulsive gesture. "Really, Mr. Gilmore Henry," she said, with a chuckle in her voice, "you're the biggest fool I ever met, but you're so damnably foolish that I can't stay mad at you. I was all set to smack you down and now if you don't mind, I'll join you in another drink and if you care to kiss me again, we can make up and eat in peace. I am honestly beginning to doubt whether you have a grain of sense in your head and for once in my life, I'm wondering if there is a man in the world who isn't thinking about my money." She was turned sideways in the seat facing me. I took her face in both my hands and said: "Honeybunch, don't you ever doubt for a minute that I'm thinking about your money. I've been thinking about it ever since I knew there was that much in the world. If all you had was a nickel and a car check, I wouldn't waste my time with you. When we're married, I think I would like to have a small checking account of my very own. Nothing big. Maybe fifty or sixty G's for weekends and such."

I kissed her again. This time it wasn't as one-sided as before. It wasn't bad at all. Then we each took another pull out of the bottle and I drove on out to Sheely's.

56

The tavern was a half mile off of the State Highway down a country lane. It had once been a farmhouse. Two or three partitions had been knocked out on the ground floor so that there was one big room with a lot of tables and a few small private dining rooms. There were booths all around the wall of the big room and not a great deal of light, and a small dance floor. There was no orchestra but there was a tremendous, ornate juke box. The crowd wasn't at all bad for a place ten miles out of a small town. We found a booth and ordered the two biggest steaks in the house and all of the side dishes that I had been thinking about for three days. I felt the whiskey and it felt good. Janet put her elbows on the table and put her chin in her hands and looked pretty satisfied with the world.

I took a dog-eared envelope and a pencil out of my pocket. "Now, Miss Moneybags," I said, adjusting the point of the pencil, "I think I would like to take a short inventory of some of the tangible property that I'll share with you after the wedding. We can start with the Packard roadster. You can keep that in your own name. The LaSalle coupe would, I think, do nicely for my personal use and we might transfer that to me so that I will not be embarrassed. The other cars are a trifle big and heavy and I shan't bother with them often. I'll let you keep the house, but if you have a couple of trifling camps or summer homes or lodges scattered about, I might find one of them useful on occasions. I'm afraid I can't supply any more of the picture. I do hope that too much of your fortune isn't tied up in real estate. Not liquid enough."

"Well," she said, thoughtfully, "let's see. I have a flock of dresses but you wouldn't want them. The jewelry is entirely feminine but could be hocked. Until we get down to our last million I'll keep it if you don't mind. Nothing personal, you understand. Just sentiment. But, of course, there's the red monoplane. You might want to fly that sometimes."

Something in my chest froze up tight. I said: "Monoplane?" I was excited and hoped that the excitement didn't show. I'm afraid it did because I noticed that Janet changed expression in some indefinable way. I thought maybe I had better get off the subject for awhile. I put the bottle on the table and grinned and said: "Want another one? I don't think it would hurt you."

I guess it was too obvious. Janet was looking at me. "What about the monoplane?" she asked.

"Nothing. Flying's no good for me. I'm afraid of high places. The mere mention of airplanes upsets me."

"Like hell it does."

"Well, then it doesn't. I'm a bull. Red monoplanes make me mad."

"Stop talking in circles."

I played with a fork on the table without looking at her. I also took another drink of whiskey. As it went down, I realized that I was getting tight but it was too late to stop.

Janet said: "When you're through stalling anytime will do."

"Very well," I said slowly, wishing my mind were a little clearer, and being careful not to muff any of the words, "you want to know, so I'll tell you. I have an awful feeling that a red monoplane may be the answer to all of my questions. Do you fly it yourself?"

"Sometimes."

"And who else?"

"Years ago my father used to fly it sometimes."

"Go on."

"Miles can fly it."

"Jolley?"

"Yes. He has a private license."

A whole lot of things that had seemed impossible before didn't seem so impossible now. The waiter came with shrimp cocktails and I asked for a bottle of horse-radish. I counted the shrimp very slowly without knowing how many I had counted and didn't look at Janet. I said:

"We can quit the kidding now. There was something about you and Jolley being engaged, and then there was a fight. How does it stand?"

"Do you mind if I keep my business to myself?"

"No, keep it to yourself if you like. It'll have to be the same either way."

"What do you mean by that?"

"Where was the plane the day your father was killed?"

"It was in Louisville for repairs."

"It's not there any more?"

"No, it's at the landing field in the city. I run up and use it from there when I feel like it, which isn't very often. There's a field between here and town that we could use if we wanted to but it's not so good and there's no hangar."

"Know who flew it down from Louisville?"

"No. Someone from the flying service I suppose. I told them I would pay to have it flown down if I didn't send for it."

I felt sure that this was the end of the road. It fitted perfectly. I was so excited that my insides were shivering but instead of feeling elated or triumphant, I felt depressed, liquor and all. I looked up and found that Janet was studying me with an intensity that was almost fierce. I wondered whether she had taken the drinks that I thought she had taken or whether she had fooled me. When I caught her eye she looked away. Then she said: "Excuse me," slid out of the booth, and walked out of the room.

I called the waiter and pointed to the door she had gone out by. "Is that the way to the ladies' rest room?"

"Why else would she go there?"

That was a stumper. I sent him after the horse-radish again. I wondered where the telephone might be but I didn't want to go looking for it just at that moment because first of all I wanted to have a long interview with that steak to keep from falling flat on my face one of these days and in the next place I didn't want Janet to come back and not find me.

Janet was gone a good deal longer than I expected. The steak came and it looked so good I could hardly keep my hands off of it. I watched the thing getting cold and it made me feel positively ill. Janet came back and the minute she was seated I said:

"Judas! There's nothing wrong with me but malnutrition. I feel like a famine in China."

Janet's mood had completely changed. There was no sign of laughter any more. The atmosphere was cold and almost hostile. She was not inclined to open a conversation, which was entirely satisfactory to me since the steak and I were on the same wave length and tuned down to a fine point. I finished before she did. I said:

"It's my turn to be excused. Do you mind?"

She shook her head. I went out through the same door she used and looked around me. The first thing I saw was a telephone booth and behind that the ladies' rest room and then the men's rest room. I suddenly thought about how long Janet had been away from the table and I looked at the telephone booth pretty hard and then I didn't want to use the telephone as I had intended. I wanted to get out of that place and I wanted to get fast.

I went into the men's washroom and put cold water on my face and then went back to the booth. Janet was smoking a cigarette, I picked up the check and said, "Ready?" She nodded, slid out of the booth and waited while I got hold of the waiter and paid off.

We went out to the car and I helped her in and closed the door. I walked around to the other door and when I had my hand on the handle I heard a sound and turned around. I was not quick enough. The last thing I remember is that I went down on my knees and the lights from the tavern were spinning around in a most confusing way.

57

The first thing I was conscious of was my head and I would have been willing to trade it in for two little heads with cash to boot. It felt about as big as a ripe watermelon. I kept my eyes closed in the hope that pretty soon I would just go to sleep again and forget the whole thing, but every time my heart beat the pulsations went through my skull like hammer blows.

I was lying on something very hard and I must have been in the same position for a long time because my hips were aching and every muscle was practically in cramps. I was lying on my right side and my right arm might just as well have been amputated at the shoulder since I didn't know where it was. I tried to move my left arm and found that it was behind me and the hand was tied to something. It took me quite a while to figure out that it was tied to the other hand. I would never have known whose hand it was tied to except that when I pulled gently I could feel something move under me and there wasn't anything under me except my right arm.

I could hear breathing—not even, peaceful breathing like when people are sleeping, but something irregular and almost explosive.

The next thing my troubled mind got around to focusing on

was my mouth. It was full of a big dry tongue about the size of a cow's tongue and I couldn't open it because there was tape all over my face. I wondered if I could open my eyes but didn't much care whether I could or not.

There wasn't any use rolling over on my back because I would be lying on my own hands and that wouldn't be any fun at all. I just lay there and hoped that I was dead and didn't know it.

I must have moved or maybe the tempo of my breathing had changed because someone walked heavily across a wooden floor and kicked me in the pit of my stomach. It was enough. I went out again.

The next thing I knew I was soaking wet and gasping and with an effort I did not know I was capable of, I wrenched myself up to a sitting position and put my head down on my knees. I experimented with my eyes and they came open, somewhat to my surprise, and I was looking down at rough boards with cracks in between them. Someone cuffed me hard on the side of my head and I nearly fell over again. I didn't feel the sting but what it did to my head was a special kind of torture that should be reserved only for the Japs.* An anger that took me as close to insanity as I ever want to be boiled up from somewhere and if my mouth hadn't been taped up I think I would have taken a blind bite in the hope of getting a shinbone in my teeth. If that had been possible, what I would have done with it would have made a Doberman pinscher go home and take lessons.

I raised my head and turned and looked up at Miles. He was grimmer and tougher than ever. If they have bouncers in hell, the head man of them all must wear a chauffeur's uniform. He didn't even need horns and a tail to complete the illusion.

"Well!" he said, "we have company again."

He reached down and tore the adhesive tape off of my face with one gesture and if he didn't take half my skin with it, it's because he took the whole face. The stuff had stuck to my lips

---

*The book was published at the height of the war with Imperial Japan.

somewhere and he took off a strip that burned like fire and I could feel the blood running down my chin. If he had been a little closer, I would have bitten his foot off like a shark. The circulation was beginning to operate in my right arm again and the pain made me close my jaws tight until they ached.

Miles said: "You and I are going to have a nice little talk."

I said: "Go ahead."

He made a motion with his hand and I thought he was going to hit me again and I cringed like a dog. He laughed.

"Yellow, aren't you?"

"I guess so."

"You ain't seen nothing yet. Start singing and I mean start right now."

"What do you want to know?"

"Don't give me that stuff. Start talking."

I looked around for the first time to see where I was. Janet was in a chair with her hands tied together behind the back of it, and tape over her mouth. Her eyes were open and she was watching with a sort of horrified fascination. I went on from there and found we were in a one-room cabin with no ceiling, so that the rafters showed. There were two windows and two doors and it was still night outside. Over by the second door was something I had to look at twice before I believed it. Hillman Jolley was lying on the floor pretty much as I had been except that I couldn't see any goose egg on his head. His feet were tied together and his hands were out of sight behind him. His eyes were open, too, and they were bright and watchful.

I stared at Jolley and he stared back at me. I was so surprised that I almost forgot where I was. I looked up at Miles and he evidently had no trouble reading my expression.

"Fooled you, didn't I?" he said with a chuckle. "Old Perry Mason himself. Runs around all over everywhere finding out all kinds of bright things and making all kinds of smart cracks and all the time he's fooled like a third grader. I'll bet you still believe in Santa Claus."

I said: "No, not any more. I'll talk. What do you want to know?"

"What was in that safety deposit box?"

"I don't know. We never got in."

"You're lying. Tell it or I'll kick your ribs in."

"That's all. They wouldn't let us get into the box. Said they couldn't be sure John McClure was John McCall and anyway you can't get into a dead man's box without the tax people being there. We had to make a date for this morning. If it still is this morning."

That stumped him. I evidently sounded like I was telling the truth because instead of kicking me as he had promised, he went over and sat down in a cane-bottom chair by the table under the window and drummed on the table top with his fingers.

Presently he said: "If you're kidding me, you're going to be sorry."

The blood was drying on my chin and it itched. The circulation had got down to my right hand and it was throbbing. I said:

"I wouldn't kid you."

"Well, what did you expect to find?"

"I don't know. I haven't the faintest idea. It would never have occurred to me to try and get a look except somebody wanted that key awfully bad."

"You wanted to stick your nose into the books of Harper Products Company. What's the big idea?"

"How did you know that?"

"I'm asking the questions. Keep talking or I'll smack you down."

"Is there something in the books I shouldn't see?"

He crossed the room swiftly, put his foot on the side of my head and shoved me over hard.

"That'll give you an idea, Mr. Wisenheimer. Maybe you think you're playing mumbly-peg in the backyard."

He grabbed me by the collar and jerked me up to a sitting position and hit me in the mouth so that my lips started bleeding again. I said:

"You don't have to do that. Give me time. I don't even know what you're getting at."

He went over and sat down again.

"You were plenty curious about something. I want to know what."

"Somebody paid me to look and I was looking. I didn't know what I was looking for. I walked out of Jolley's office with some financial statements and after I got them they were just a jumble of figures. If I saw anything, I don't know what it was."

"You lying little bastard."

"Why would I lie to you? I didn't understand the figures. That's nothing new. If anything was there, the bankers and brokers didn't seem to understand it either. I'm no accountant. What makes you think I could find something even the directors don't seem to know, assuming anything's there?"

He was tough but he wasn't too bright and when his mind turned over it was like a cold motor. If he wanted to count up to ten, I'll bet he did it on his fingers.

"Well, maybe so and maybe not. It said in the papers you were traced in Louisville after you swiped that stuff and you were asking a lot of questions about somebody named Murdoch. What was that all about?"

"I don't know that either. I don't know who she was or who she is or where she is. That's what I wanted to find out. I thought you would know. I don't know where you get the idea I know all these things. If I knew as much as you think I know, I wouldn't be here and you would be on your way to the electric chair."

I shouldn't have said that. This time he took a gun out of a holster under his arm and held it by the barrel and walked over and hit me with it. I didn't go out completely but I made out like I did. Everything seemed red and hazy and there was a roaring sound in my ears. There was a gurgling from Janet and the chair creaked a little. From the exclamation that came out of Miles, I gathered that she had fainted.

Miles came and stood over me and then there was a sound of some sort outside because even without looking I could tell that he had stiffened to attention. For a long moment the room was very still and then he tiptoed over, turned the oil lamp down low, and went out quietly, closing the door behind him.

I squirmed around so that I had my back to the wall and could see whatever might happen. Janet was slumped over in her chair with her head hanging down. Jolley was as bright-eyed as ever and his face was red with effort. The sweat was standing out on his forehead and I could see that he was working with his hands. Pretty soon he gave a grunt and one hand came out from behind him and then the other. He pushed himself up and leaned his back against the wall and rubbed his hands together, flexing the fingers to get life back into them. Then he bent and untied his feet and wiggled his ankles a little. He looked over at me, caught my eye and made a movement indicating silence. He didn't bother right away with the tape over his mouth but tiptoed over to the table, keeping out of line with the windows. There was a gun on the table. He broke it open, twirled the cylinder with his thumb and clicked it together again. He started over to Janet and then brought up short in the middle of the floor, listened a second, gave me that same gesture of silence again and slipped out of the door across the room from the one Miles had used. I heard his first step or two and then the place was still again and under the floor a cricket started its senseless chirping.

There was not a sound for a minute or two and then I heard what could have been a couple of footsteps on gravel, quite a distance from the cabin. Then there was an exclamation and three shots followed by what could have been someone crashing around in the underbrush. Then a car started with a roar and there was a scraping of tires as it went into gear with a jerk and then it was gone.

58

I supposed Mr. Hillman Jolley was dead. Probably Miles had shot him in the dark without knowing who it was, and then had taken flight on the assumption that someone had followed him and was beginning to close in. If so, it was the rankest kind of assumption, since there I lay and there Janet sat without anything happening at all. After about ten minutes it seemed plain enough that help was not on the way, so I started experimenting around with the ropes. Miles was no amateur, and when he tied me up it was for keeps. I worked with my wrists until I had rubbed all the skin off. The knot didn't feel like it was slipping, but the rope was fairly old and it stretched just enough to give me a little hope.

Janet stirred and raised her head. She was the color of one of these "white papers" that the State Department is always talking about. She opened her eyes and looked straight at me, but there was a fuzzy look in them and I knew she was looking through a fog.

I said: "Hey!"

Her eyelids fluttered and then popped wide open.

I said: "Hi, Sport. It isn't as bad as all that." She brought her eyes around to bear on me like the main turret of a battleship. The sky was clearing fast. When she took me in, the horror came back and she made a convulsive move to get up, but the chair teetered around dangerously and she was lucky that it didn't fall over. She was wide awake, but with all that stuff over her mouth all she could do was look like a haunted house. She said, "Mmm-mmm-mmm-mmmm-m-m-m." I said: "That's a hell of a thing to say to your prospective husband. Save language like that for the revenooers.* I'm the fair-haired boy, remember?"

A spot of color appeared on her cheekbones, and she began to look better. I wriggled around in the rope some more, but my wrists were so sore that I stopped to think it over. You can't lie around tied up like a Christmas package forever. Even Christmas packages don't have any fun until December 25. I don't like rats, but I could have made a nice deal with even that kind of loathsome creature if I thought it would gnaw through the rope like in the nursery rhyme I had quoted to Ruth when I was a comparatively young man.

There didn't seem to be but one thing to do. My hands were pudgy like the rest of me, and flesh will give even if a rope won't. I was hurting in so many places already that I didn't think it would make much difference if I opened up a new front. With a great effort I rolled over and by getting in the corner of the room and doing a lot of hunching against the wall, I finally managed to stand up. By acting like an animated pogo stick I somehow got across the room and fell against the table while I caught my breath. Janet was watching me with a mixture of encouragement and perplexity. I squirmed around with my back to the table, bent my knees a little and got the rope hooked under the corner. Then I turned a little sideways and rested my weight on the table to keep it from coming off the floor. The stage was all set, but I rested there a minute to get my courage up.

When someone else hurts you there is nothing you can do about it, but when you hurt yourself you have got to have your

---

*That is to say, the IRS (then known as the Bureau of Internal Revenue)—hence, the "revenu-ers." The "revenooers" enforced stamp taxes on liquor manufacture and so were unpopular with "moonshiners" operating outside the law.

mind made up or your muscles rebel when the going gets tough. After a while I drew in all the air I could hold, set my teeth hard, and gave it everything I had. I gave it plenty with my left arm, leaving the right arm as limp as I could to make it easier. It came out, but the way it felt I half expected to hear my right hand come off and fall on the floor. I hadn't expected it to be that easy, and I lost my balance and fell off before I could catch myself.

The pain was pretty bad, and I just lay there for a minute and damn near bit a piece out of my tongue. I'll never know whether I whimpered or not, but tears came out of my eyes and stung me sharply where Miles had ripped the sticking plaster off. My right hand was raw and swelling a little, but I was able to worry the knot at my feet with the other hand and it finally came off. One foot was sound asleep. When I put my weight on it, it turned under me and I finally had to go over to Janet on my hands and knees. With my one good hand I got her loose with an effort, and then I lay back on the floor while she untied her feet. She pulled gently on the tape over her mouth, and when a corner of it came loose she went down on her hands and knees beside me and said: "We'd better get out of here. Can you make it?"

I said: "Can you?"

"Oh, I'm all right. All they did was tie me up. It will be a while before I feel like riding a horse, but I'm a long way from being non compos mentis, or whatever you call it." Then she touched my face gently and said: "Poor Humpty Dumpty. I'm afraid all the King's horses and all the King's men will never put you together again. Is it too bad?"

"The first time he hit me it was too bad," I answered wearily. "After that it didn't matter much one way or the other. The next time I meet that son of a bitch I hope I have a 37mm. gun and I don't mean with blank ammunition either. If you will rub my ankles a minute, I think I can recognize my feet again. I know what they mean when they talk about having one foot in the grave."

59

It was beginning to rain when we got out of the cabin, and if it is darkest just before the dawn, that's what time it was. I couldn't tell whether we were on Brooklyn Bridge or in the middle of a broccoli patch. Janet held my best hand and we stood there waiting for the darkness to get thinner, but all we got was wet. I said: "Well, it's lots of fun holding your hand, sweetie, but I can think of things I would rather do just at the moment. Which direction would you say is up?"

"Don't you hear something?" she asked.

"Sorry, but I don't. Do you mind?"

"No I mean seriously. Sounds like running water."

The revolver butt had clipped me on one ear, and it was about like a disconnected telephone. I don't know whether you can strain an ear or not, but plenty of good writers say you can, and I strained the other one to the best of my ability. All I could hear was my hand swelling and it sounded like the *Lost Chord*.* Janet must have been doing a better job, because she started walking, pulling me after her.

The ground fell away rather sharply and under foot there were rocks and gravel. I stumbled along after her and we ran

---

*A powerful, dynamic tune by Sir Arthur Sullivan, written in 1877 and still performed in the twenty-first century.

into a few trees and miscellaneous things. There was a path, but we did not have much luck staying on it and every now and then one of us would have to get down on the ground and feel for it. Presently I heard the sound she had been talking about. It was the burbling of a mountain stream and it wasn't far away. We got there eventually and the water was pretty cool even at that time of year. I found a pool, knelt down on a rock beside it, and stuck my whole head under water. It felt swell. When I got up my foot kicked against something metallic, and when I found it I had a revolver in my hand. Janet was splashing water on her face, and I didn't tell her. I broke the thing open and felt the cylinders. They were full. Evidently this was the one that Jolley had taken with him. If that were so, then his body was probably close by, but it might have been in any direction and I did not see any use looking for it. We hadn't heard a sound except for the running water and we didn't hear any now.

"Let's go," said Janet. "I feel better. I also have a rough idea of where we are. Foothill country is east of Harpersville, and that is the only place we have a stream like this. There is usually a trail of some sort down the bottom of these valleys. Let's look."

To call it "looking" was just a figure of speech. It was strictly feeling, and after this I would rather do my feeling in the inside of a concrete mixer in full operation. Between the boulders, the trees, the vines and the briars, it was no fun at all. When I finally stumbled into the rutted mountain road I felt like singing. Janet was fifty feet away in another direction, and we called back and forth while she blundered over to me. I didn't dare move for fear I would lose the road and never find it again.

When she reached me she said: "I couldn't tell where you were, and I got to thinking about snakes and I was scared and lonesome." Then she found my shoulder and put her head on it and cried, and I had a little feeling of my own that it was not being afraid so much as being lonesome that had done it. I got out my handkerchief for her and she blew her nose and then we stumbled our way down the road together maybe three-fourths of a mile. When we found the State Highway, dawn had still not yet begun to break.

60

We had about as much chance to catch a ride as a pair of mangy Pomeranians with worms. Claudette Colbert could have pulled up her dress and exhibited her legs like in *It Happened One Night*[*] but for the first twenty minutes she wouldn't have stopped any cars because there weren't any. Then a car with a Michigan license came along and the driver started to slow down, but when he got a good look at me in the headlights, he put his foot on the floor and shot past like a rocket. An old lady with white hair took a look at me out of the back window and screamed. I must have looked like something out of the zoo but I was too mad to worry about it.

It had been raining continuously and the water didn't even bother to slow down when it hit my clothes. It was running over my skin and down into my shoes. In about five minutes a Model T touring car with curtains, vintage probably 1922, came along and stopped. The back seat was full of a lot of baskets of vegetables but I will guarantee that I could have found a place to sit if I had been given the chance. The driver was a farmer in

---

[*]The 1934 "Best Picture" Oscar®-winning film starring Clark Gable and Claudette Colbert. In the film, Gable attempts to demonstrate his prowess at hitchhiking by waving his thumb in a flashy manner. After he fails to get a car to stop, Colbert hikes up her skirt and achieves immediate success in attracting the attention of a passing car.

overalls and he seemed willing enough, but his wife was a sharp-nosed old bitch and between the vegetables and her new seat covers she had just made with her own hands, there wasn't a chance. The driver looked apologetic and opened his mouth as if to remonstrate but she gave him the kind of look that kind of woman can give and he closed his mouth so fast it almost made a popping sound.

We had better luck the next time, or worse luck, depending on your point of view. An old truck came wheezing along and squealed to a stop twenty yards down the road. Two men were in the cab. The body was one of these things something like a bathtub and had been used for hauling tar ever since Hoover defeated Al Smith. We were in no position to look down our noses, so Janet got in the cab and thoroughly wet one of the men before he could get out of the way. I suppose you could say the tar container was empty, but even when a tar container is empty it has got more tar in it than you would want your children to play with. I stood up just back of the cab and didn't touch anything I could avoid, but the first time I tried to move, I knew that my shoes were there to stay. I called down to Janet and she mooched a cigarette off of one of the men, lit it and handed it out to me. By making a tent out of my hands, I was able to get a few drags before it got wet and fizzled out on me.

Harpersville was about twelve miles but it took us thirty minutes. Janet got them to put us out in front of her place. I had to unlace my shoes and leave them and when I started to crawl out, I thought for a minute I would have to leave my pants too. I had visions of double lobar pneumonia with the most insidious complications. Janet thanked them without a great deal of enthusiasm.

The house had lights everywhere and there were plenty of official-looking cars crowded on the drive. I took off my socks and walked in the grass since it was more comfortable that way. The house was two stories and above that the roof went this way and that way in the best country type of years ago, with two or three dormer windows in various places. There was a light in one of them and someone was moving back and forth. I pointed and said:

"Who would be up there?"

Janet glanced up and said:

"That's Miss Knight's room. She spends most of her time with Mother but technically that's her place and she is at liberty to hang out up there when she isn't needed."

"That's fine. She seems to be there now and a conference between the two of us is long overdue." Then I added without looking at Janet: "I assume you have noticed that something is up."

She said: "Yes, and I'm scared to death. It must be Mother." She broke into a run and I trotted along behind her, stepping on sharp objects at almost every stride. There was a guard at the door wearing a big black raincoat. He looked slightly miserable. Janet ran up the steps, made a motion toward the parked cars and said anxiously: "What's all this? What's happened? Is it Mother?"

The guard was excited when he saw her. He threw open the front door, stuck his head inside and yelled:

"Joe! Joe! Tell the chief Miss Harper and the little fat guy have showed up. Step on it!" Then he turned around. "What's happened started out being you. In comes a call from out at Sheely's about some kind of ruckus going on outside and there's your car with some blood on the running board on the driver's side and where are you? The chief gets out of bed in his night-shirt and everybody in God's world goes charging around the county and the city trying to find you. Then on top of that Mrs. Harper has herself an attack maybe an hour ago. Mr. Jolley has come in before that with his arm in a sling and the motor boiling over and he don't know nothing about this part of the country and don't know where he came from so off goes a bunch of squad cars—"

A door came open with a bang and the chief of police ran down the hall and grabbed Janet as if he were afraid she would fly away.

"Miss Janet!" he said, with considerable relief, "thank heaven! Are you all right?"

"I'm all right, but what about my Mother? Mr. Dudley says she had an attack. I see the doctor's car. What does he say?"

"He says it's pretty bad. We had an awful time getting him and he's been working on her ever since he got here. Won't let me in but sent out a message it was plenty tough."

"I'm going in," Janet said abruptly, pulling away from him. She went over and walked into Mrs. Harper's room without knocking.

The chief looked at me and whistled shrilly through his teeth. "Damn!" he said, "what happened to you?"

"I haven't taken inventory. Where's Jolley?"

The chief jerked his thumb toward the dining room. "In there, answering questions. Says somebody clapped a blanket over his head, like they done to Ruth McClure, and dragged him out in the country somewhere and then there's some scuffling around and another drive up into some hilly country and it turns out it was Miles and here he is with you and Miss Janet. Says he got loose and shot it out in the dark with Miles but probably missed him and thought he had better come for help when he ran into a car parked on the road. Seems to have fallen and hit his arm on a rock somewhere because he got it in a sling and says it hurts like hell. We'll be through with him in a few minutes. Stick around. You're next."

I sat down on a fancy chair in the living room and ruined it. As soon as the chief closed the dining-room door behind him I walked up to the third floor and knocked on Miss Knight's door. Before I knocked I could hear her moving around but afterwards the room got perfectly still and nobody told me to come in. I tried the knob and the door wasn't locked so I threw it open and stepped in. Miss Knight was flattened against the wall by the door and she had a pewter candlestick in her hand and she recognized me just in time to keep from fracturing my skull.

"Oh, it's you," she said. She looked scared to death.

I said: "Yes, it's me. Who were you expecting?"

"I don't know. That's the trouble."

I looked around the room. There were a couple of suitcases on the bed and clothing was lying around in neat piles, part of it already packed. I nodded in that direction and said: "Taking a little vacation?"

"Permanent. There's too much going on in this house. I'm frightened."

"Too much such as what?"

"Too much murder. First Mr. Harper and now Mrs...." She clapped the back of her hand against her mouth and didn't finish.

"What do you mean? They said it was a heart attack."

"That's what they say."

"What do you say?"

"I don't say anything. I don't know anything."

"Were you there?"

"Yes. It was just a heart attack, like they say. If you don't mind, I think I'll go on with my packing. I want to catch the first train out of this town in any direction."

"What made you say it was murder?"

"I didn't say it. How could it be murder? She isn't even dead, is she? You can't have murder until somebody is dead."

She went over to the bed and took some of the things out of the suitcase and put some other things in and then took those things out again and put the others back. Her fingers were trembling and she didn't have the faintest idea what she was doing.

I said: "Who else was there when it happened?"

"Nobody. Nobody but me. She just took this medicine and pretty soon she had a heart attack. It could happen like that any time. You don't have any warning and they can come whether its morning, noon or night or even in your sleep."

"What kind of medicine?"

"Just regular medicine. She gets it when she has a bad night and doesn't sleep so well."

"Pills out of a box?"

"No, it's a liquid. She gets it in warm milk."

"And where does the milk come from? She doesn't have it there in the room with her, does she?"

"What difference does it make? What's milk got to do with it? She had a heart attack just like I said."

"I know. Where did you say the milk came from?"

She didn't answer me for a long time and then she suddenly said: "Who are you?"

"I might ask you the same thing."

"What do you mean by that?"

"Just what it sounds like, Miss Phoebe Murdoch."

The color drained out of her face like water running out of a bathtub. She took on a kind of mottled look and gave a funny gasp and felt out with her hand blindly until it hit the foot of the bed. She stood unsteadily for a moment and then sat down by the suitcase and said in a very small distant voice: "What did you say?"

"Shall I repeat it?"

She shook her head dumbly, pulled herself up with an effort, walked over, closed the door, turned the key in the lock and leaned back against it as if she were exhausted. She looked at me with something like desperation in her eyes and then she went over to the dresser, pulled open a little drawer and faced me with a .22 automatic that she held in both hands. She said:

"I think I'm going to kill you."

I didn't like the way she said it. I didn't like what she said either. Compared to me, the Sphinx and the pyramids are moving objects. I said:

"You don't want to kill me. I'm the only one around here who's even halfway smart and I'm so stupid I ought to be disbarred. If you kill me, what'll it get you?"

"Who else knows about me?"

"Just you and me. If you kill me everybody will know. I think you owe your life to the fact that one person or maybe two people don't know it. Stop and think."

I knew then that she wasn't going to shoot me. The only time she could have done it was when she was scared and the idea was fresh. Now she was perilously close to folding up into a little puddle on the floor but the effort to concentrate on what I was saying was holding her up.

"What should I think about?"

"Let's think about the eighth day of May, 1915. Probably in Louisville. You were there and your sister Catherine was there and William Jasper Harper and Alice Harper and John McClure. Maybe John's wife was there too. Any more?"

"No, that was all."

"Think some more. Let's check them off. Ruth McClure died some years ago. It was probably a perfectly natural death. John McClure went out two or three weeks ago. It wasn't natural at all. Then comes William Jasper Harper and the same night Miss Katie. Now something has happened to Mrs. Harper. Who does that leave?"

"I know. Me."

I could hardly hear her. The last word was whispered. I knew why she had waited for me with a pewter candlestick raised over her head.

I said: "Was it in writing?"

She nodded.

"Then that's the trouble. It's an outsider who's been guessing. He couldn't tell whether it was written or not and he didn't know how to find out. He searched the McClure home twice and then he tried to get into a lockbox up in the city but he didn't have any luck. I guess he thought he had a good plan to begin with but when it didn't work so smoothly he got panicky and thought he could kill everybody in the world. He did some pretty good guessing at that. Who had the written instrument?"

"John McClure."

"Then it's probably in the lockbox after all. That's what comes of going off halfcocked when you don't know what you're doing. Murderers aren't so smart. I'll bet this one never even heard of Phoebe Murdoch and didn't know that Catherine was Miss Katie. I'll bet he doesn't know it yet. I'll bet he never thought of doing anything to Miss Katie but had to because he got caught."

"You seem to know a lot. Who is it?"

"I think I know but it took me too long to find out even when I had the pieces in my mind. No use worrying now. It's too late. You stay up here and keep your door locked and don't go out even to the bathroom. Don't go out for anybody. Understand?"

The revolver I had picked up out in the hills was stuck in the waistband of my trousers. I thought about swapping it for the little .22 automatic but I didn't do it. It occurred to me that anytime I got in such shape that I would need a gun, I wouldn't want any toy pistol. Phoebe Murdoch let me out of her room and locked the door behind her.

61

I went about halfway down the stairs to the second floor and sat down on the steps to think things over. Now that I had all the strings in my hands and was ready to tie a knot in them I suddenly felt weary and exhausted almost to the point of collapse. I had spent several days stumbling around to the best of my ability but instead of being proud or elated over impending success, I was disgusted at the length of time it had taken me and especially over the fact that I had not learned the truth in time to prevent the perfection of the murderer's plan. All I could do was to deprive the guilty person of the fruits of the carnage. Despite the fact that the murderer had more than earned anything that might be coming, I could not look forward with any degree of pleasure or satisfaction to the immediate future. The whole thing was so distasteful to me that I actually toyed for a moment with the thought of walking out on the whole thing. The days when I lived a life like other people, worked at sane peaceful pursuits within reasonably certain hours, ate, drank and slept in a more or less normal way, were remembered more as dreams of early childhood than as actualities of a week ago. If I had rested my head against the wall beside me, I think I could have slept until Labor Day.

I sat there only long enough to make sure the story seemed logical and connected and that the chapter I was reading was the last chapter in the book. Then I got up, stretched my aching body and walked on down to the first floor. I didn't exactly know what was coming but the palms of my hand were perspiring freely and my stomach was drawn up in a nervous knot.

I went into the dining room without knocking. The sheriff and the chief were both there. Jim Mead had appeared from somewhere and was looking smooth and urbane and neat even at that hour of the morning. Hillman Jolley had apparently been questioned sufficiently and was sitting in a chair by the door with his right arm in a sling. Janet Harper was sitting by the window looking all in with her wet hair straggling around her face and tearstains on her dirty cheeks.

I went over and sat down across the table from the law in what had been used as the witness chair during the last few days. I said: "You said you wanted to question me."

The chief cleared his throat and looked at some notes he had taken in a little black book. "Miss Harper says you were getting into the car out at Sheely's Tavern and somebody gave it to you in the back of the head."

"That's right."

"Who?"

"I didn't see. I think it was Miles. Has he showed up?"

"No. He apparently exchanged some shots with Jolley and then got scared. Jolley took the car and came for help and Miss Harper says Miles didn't come back to the cabin so he must be loose on foot up in the hills somewhere. Does that check?"

"I guess so."

"Miss Harper didn't see the man either. She says it was dark and she heard a thud and thought you must have tripped and fallen. She slid across under the wheel to see what had happened and someone opened the door on the other side of the car, grabbed her and put a hand over her mouth before she could even scream. Then she was gagged and tied up and put on the back seat and something—probably you—was put on the floor next to her and this bird drove up to the cabin. I believe you know the rest. If it was Miles, how did he know you were at Sheely's?"

I said: "He was standing right by me when Janet and I discussed where we were going." I was also thinking about the length of time Janet had been away from the table and I was thinking about the fact that the telephone was near the ladies' rest room, but I didn't look at Janet.

The chief was looking at me with a calculating look and he was a bit more grim and hostile than I could see any excuse for being. When he spoke, I understood his expression. He said: "Let's suppose it was Miles. He could have been working with someone else."

"That's so," I admitted. "Who for example?"

"You might think about that."

"I am thinking. Who are you driving at?"

"You."

I said: "Well, it's all right to think about me. It shows you have an open mind. I suppose you have it all figured out why I was working with Miles and particularly why I had hired a rough number like that to slug the stuffing out of me. Ask Miss Harper."

"She told us about it. Very smart. Could have been a blind to throw us off."

"And did I lie down in Miss Katie's back yard and slap myself silly with a monkey wrench, or did I hire Miles to do that too?"

"Take your choice. It's the same difference. We know you went to Miss Katie's house about the time somebody sliced her and we know you were in the back yard and we don't know anybody else that was there. We checked up on your trip down from Louisville in the chartered plane and we find you got to the city in time to have got down here for the Harper job too."

"You seem to be doing all right by yourself. What about John McClure? I believe that was a couple of weeks before I came to Harpersville the first time."

"That's what you say. And that ain't all. You say somebody shot out a tire on your car. I got to thinking just now. That's what you say. Same for Mr. John McClure—a lot of talk. No evidence. You have a wreck and you got slugged a couple of times but always who says so? You. Nice cuts and bruises and lumps on you but I don't notice you ever got hurt anything serious."

I said: "Whose idea is all this? Don't tell me you thought it up by yourself. I don't think the sheriff thought it up either."

The sheriff broke in and said: "Don't change the subject. It don't make any difference who thought about it. Let's have some answers."

A door opened and closed and there were footsteps in the hall. Then the dining-room door opened and a man with gray hair said in a low voice: "Miss Harper."

Janet jerked her head up and looked at him. He said: "I'm sorry. Mrs. Harper just passed away. There was nothing I could do."

Janet had evidently been expecting it. She stood up and looked around rather blankly and then nodded and sat down again and looked out of the window. Then she put her arm on the window sill and put her head down on her arm. There was no sound in the room except long shuddering sobs that were almost inaudible.

62

The doctor went over and patted her clumsily. I wanted to do something of the sort myself but it would have to wait. I had other things on my mind. I turned to James Mead and said:

"The way you're dressed, you didn't jump out of bed and run out here on any hurry call."

He flicked a bit of tobacco ash from his trousers and said blandly: "No, I didn't for a fact. I spent practically all night going over and discussing the evidence with the Commonwealth Attorney in preparation for the Coroner's inquest and the grand jury. Then there was all this fuss about you and Janet disappearing so naturally I came out to see if I could be of any assistance."

"Then you were here before the heart attack."

"Oh, yes, I had been here an hour and a half or two hours. There wasn't much I could do but I conferred with the sheriff and the chief from time to time as news came in and advised with them as to the steps which should be taken."

"You say from time to time. Then you weren't with them continuously."

"No, I was restless. I wandered around the house a time or two."

"Did Mrs. Harper spend a quiet night?"

"I would say not. The nurse came out several times to insist on quiet so she could get some sleep."

"You've been in this home quite a lot recently, haven't you?"

"I should say so. Yes."

"What happens when Mrs. Harper has a rough night?"

"I don't understand you."

"She's had bad nights when you were here, hasn't she?"

"Oh, yes. She has been having them quite frequently."

"Well, what do they do for her?"

"I couldn't answer that in any technical sort of way. They seem to have medicines that they give her, but I wouldn't know what they are."

"Something that she drinks in milk, for example?"

"Really, I wouldn't know. Possibly so."

"Recall anything like that?"

"Well, I would say yes. I think Janet and I were together one evening and Mrs. Harper wasn't doing so well and the nurse got Janet to warm up some milk, presumably for some such purpose."

I wondered why the law had let me ask so many questions without interrupting, but when I looked around I understood. They were obviously listening with considerable attention. Even the doctor was studying me with a little frown on his face and Janet had recovered enough to be looking a little astonished.

I turned back to Mead again and said:

"I believe you were in Harpersville the evening William Jasper Harper was shot."

He stiffened perceptibly. There was less urbanity and his eyes opened a little wider. "Yes, it happens I was. Just why do you ask?"

I said: "The night somebody shot a tire off of my car, you knew I was coming."

He stood up and glared at me and turned toward the others. "If you're trying to infer that I was in position to do the ghastly things that have been done in the last few days, perhaps I was and perhaps I wasn't. I can tell you most emphatically that I had nothing to do with them whether I was here, there or elsewhere and furthermore I have not held back any information from the authorities and it is fairly obvious that you have done exactly that. I think it's fair to inquire by what authority you are entitled to divert attention from yourself by attempting to embarrass me?"

I looked at the chief and said: "Hell, I don't care who asks the questions. Take over and ask them yourself."

"You're doing all right. It's your party. Keep right on going."

"Thanks. I believe I will. I believe I will ask Mr. Mead if he was not instructed to take certain action on an income tax matter for Harper Products Company and if he did not strongly advise a decision to the contrary. I would like to know if Mr. Harper did not overrule him in the matter and if he did not within a very short time place an order for the purchase of a good deal of the stock of the company. Instead of putting it that way, let's just make the statement that these things happened and ask Mr. Mead just why they happened."

Mead took an expensive cigar out of his pocket, turned it over impassively in his fingers, got out a penknife, cut the end off of the cigar, found a match, lit it and took a long draw. Then he looked up and said:

"Professional matters between myself and my clients are privileged as a matter of law. I don't think it is proper for me to discuss or disclose confidential communications. I'm surprised that you have seen fit to do so, especially with regard to information which you have obtained in an unauthorized manner."

There was a bristling silence.

"Mr. Harper was murdered. Katie Burns was murdered. I think John McClure was murdered. I think Mrs. Harper was murdered. Somebody tried to give me the old ashes to ashes and dust to dust at least once and possibly two or three times. I would rather be professionally improper than dead and I don't propose to split hairs about it."

"That's your position. You've heard mine. Is there anything else?"

"Wait a minute," said the sheriff, breaking in. "You said Mrs. Harper was murdered. What do you know that you aren't telling?"

"Ask the doctor."

Every head turned. The doctor's frown was a very big and dark one. He said:

"I'm afraid I fail to follow these conversations in any respect. I have just been with Mrs. Harper continuously since I came to this house. She—ah—I dislike repeating it in the presence of Miss Harper—but, well she is dead. No one entered the room while I was there and there was no evidence of any violence. She had a chronic heart ailment and this occasion was substantially the same as others when I have been summoned. I would say that she died of natural causes of long standing. The day and hour were not of course to be anticipated or predicted but I must say that it was no surprise to me. Of course it is a great shock in any event but I believe the family understood the situation and cannot be unduly surprised."

I said: "In her condition, Doctor, it wouldn't have taken a great deal to kill her, would it?"

"Less than in the case of a normal and vigorous person certainly."

"Would you say she was not poisoned, or would you be able to say at all?"

He considered that for a moment. "Well, it would take a post-mortem examination to make a definite determination."

"You knew she had heart trouble. She had had several spells before. When you were called you found a condition comparable to what you expected. You did everything you could in her extremity and no one is reflecting on your judgment. All I'm asking is this: Were the symptoms which you found in any way inconsistent with conditions that might be caused by some of the common poisons?"

"The idea is new. I didn't consider it. Have you any reason to believe that such a thing happened or are you merely trying to demonstrate the possibility?"

"I'm not asking questions purely for the malicious purpose of trying to confuse things. Mrs. Harper was having a restless night. The nurse brought her some medicine in warm milk as I believe had been done on prior occasions. Shortly afterwards she became fatally ill. I believe the milk supply is kept in the refrigerator in the kitchen. To anyone who was familiar with the situation, it would have been simple to visit the kitchen and put something in the milk. Someone was seen to enter the kitchen not long before the nurse went there for the milk that she gave Mrs. Harper. It is entirely possible that this sequence of events has no sinister meaning, but in view of the high fatality list, I think it should be investigated."

The chief of police was on his feet. "Who saw who going into the kitchen? This is another example of obstructing justice. I've had enough of it. You're under arrest. How much more are you holding out on us?"

I jumped up and faced him. I was pretty mad and I didn't much care what I said or how I said it. "You'll play hell putting me under arrest, you half-witted baboon. I found out just before I came in here. Instead of giving me a chance to tell you anything, you start in on me to show what smart things you can think up. You can always put me under arrest if you haven't anything better to do. Right now I think it would be a whole lot smarter to take into custody all the milk bottles in this house on the off-chance that my guesses are right and that whoever did it hasn't had a chance to pour out the evidence."

"Don't you tell me what to do," he roared hoarsely.

The sheriff said in a rather mild way, "Might not be a bad idea just in case."

I said: "Fine, we'll do it right now."

Jolley said hastily: "He's under suspicion himself and he's pretty clever. Better not let him get out of your sight."

"That's OK," said the sheriff, drawing his gun, "I'll tag along and see that he doesn't misbehave."

I went out through the swinging door into the butler's pantry and from there into the kitchen. There was only one bottle of milk in the refrigerator and it was unopened. I looked at the sheriff and he looked back at me. I think I had talked him into my theory pretty well and he was as surprised as I was. Apparently if any milk had been poisoned, it was another bottle that had already been removed and possibly washed and put out for the milk truck as innocent as any other bottle.

I took the risk of giving the sheriff a wink, not knowing just how he would take it. He didn't understand, but he took it all right. I went over to the sink with the full bottle of milk, took out the cap, poured about half of it into the sink and then looked at him again. He was pretty dumb but he had sense enough to get the idea. I took out a handkerchief, held the bottle clumsily as if I was being careful not to smudge any fingerprints and preceded him back into the dining room. Then I went in with the bottle held conspicuously in front of me. I might have been a snake charmer and the assembled group would in that case have been some well-charmed snakes.

"Well," I said, with as much evidence of satisfaction as I could muster, "at this point I won't say I'm right, but at least we can say that we haven't run into an inconsistency or a blind alley. I wonder if there is not someone who would very much like not to have this bottle examined for fingerprints."

There was a sudden movement. Someone shouted: "Look out, Chief, he's got a gun." A shot rang out and in that enclosed space it sounded like a two thousand pound bomb. The milk bottle jumped in my hand and wasn't there. There was another deafening roar and something caught me in the side with an impact like a kick from a very young and vigorous mule and I spun around and fell heavily on the floor.

I tried to get the revolver out of my belt with my right hand but it was so swollen and lacerated that there wasn't any grip in it. I rolled under the table, got it out with my left hand, steadied my wrist for an instant against the table leg and aimed for the broadest spot I could see. I wasn't taking any chances. This was for keeps.

There was another shot and a bullet tore through the table over my head. It takes a long time to tell it but the whole thing happened before either the sheriff or the chief could get his artillery into action. My two shots hit Hillman Jolley in the solar plexus and he was all through for the night. He clasped his hands together over his chest. The revolver that he had concealed in the sling slipped out of his hand and fell to the floor. He sagged at the knees. His head fell forward on his chest and he went down like a sick bull.

Janet was screaming. There was a great running around and chairs were overturned and somebody kicked my wrist and sent my gun spinning half way across the room. The chief jumped on my back, got his knee on me and twisted my hands around behind me. Mead had got out of the room so fast I didn't know how he ever got the door open. Only the sheriff seemed to be halfway coherent.

63

The chief of police was a good deal heavier from underneath than he was on an eye-to-eye basis, and his knee had certain bony qualities which would recommend him to a button factory, if buttons are made out of bones. Since I was half under the table, he was not even squashing me in a good honest top-to-bottom way, but was operating from an angle that hinted at a diabolical turn of mind heretofore unsuspected. My right hand was either sprained or had a bone broken in it because when he twisted it he gave me one of the most excruciating sensations I ever hope to experience.

The sheriff picked up my gun and Jolley's and said rather mildly: "OK, I think you can afford to let him up. My guess is the meal is over and it's time to gather up the dishes." The doctor got his bearings rather quickly and bent over Jolley who had a fixed stare in his eyes and was obviously in one hell of a shape. The doctor looked up after a moment and shook his head.

The sheriff said: "Any use trying to move him?"

"None at all. We can make him comfortable and I can try to stop the bleeding, but I don't think he'll last very long."

He straightened Jolley on the floor, took off his coat, folded it and put it under his head. Then the doctor rolled up his sleeves, got the shirt unbuttoned and ripped the undershirt with a deft motion. He looked up at Janet and said: "A lot of clean cloth. Napkins will do if you haven't anything else. Hurry."

Having something to do was probably the best thing that could happen to Janet. She looked like an obituary notice but she got up and went into the butler's pantry in a purposeful way and I knew she would come through for the moment at least.

Jolley was conscious and in a vague way he was getting the drift of things. When he spoke, it was through his teeth and with a great effort. "Am I all washed up?" There was a bubbling in his chest and blood came to his lips.

"You keep still," the doctor said rather sternly. "I'll do what I can."

The chief got off me and I drew enough air to fill a blimp. I could feel my face losing its purple, strangled appearance and coming back to within a few shades of normal. I felt my right hand gingerly and found that the fingers would still work, although not enough so that I would want to try to pick my teeth with them.

Anybody could tell by just looking at Jolley that in a few minutes he would not care what the chips were selling at or whether he would have any luck drawing three cards to a pair. I went over and knelt beside him. He recognized me but there was no hostility or bitterness in his eyes—only anguish and agony and a funny look as if maybe he was seeing something in another world and wondering how he would like it.

"You might just as well let us get the story," I said, with a gentleness which rather surprised me. "The decks are awash and it is about time to abandon ship. There is one good thing you can do in this world and you have got to hang on until you have done it. Tim McClure's in a jam and you're the guy who can get him out of it. I'll do the talking and all you do is nod if I'm right."

Even the worst of us can find the last spark of decency when we are about to walk through the pearly—or otherwise—gates. There was no fight left in Hillman Jolley. His teeth were set tight and he was squeezing the blood out of his lips, but he heard me and gave a nod of assent.

I said: "The juggling of the inventory and cost accounts was your idea, wasn't it?"

He nodded.

"When the stock went down you were going to get aboard and when it went up, you were going to get well in a big way. Right?"

He nodded again.

I looked up at the sheriff who was right beside me. "There's no time for a stenographer. Are you getting this?"

"Every word of it. Hurry."

I turned back to Jolley again. "You thought the stock was down as far as it would go and you climbed in up to the ears. You thought it was time to reverse the picture but in the meantime Harper was working at his mental adding machine and two and two was beginning to be four. He wanted to drive the stock down a few more points and your money was gone and you were going to be sold out of your gold mine. You thought getting Harper out of the way would simplify things for you and you put a slug in him and it only made things worse. Then in desperation you tried to do a salvage job by playing your hand with Janet a little too fast. How about it?"

He gave me another nod. He wasn't doing so good. The sheriff said, "Hurry," into my ear and I went on.

"You thought we were snapping at your heels and you didn't know how long it would take us to figure out the airplane. To throw us off you had Miles tie you up while he was getting Janet and me out of the way for tonight's operations. Then you knew Miles was too far into the thing for his own good so you gave him the old doublecross. He's dead somewhere up in the hills, isn't he?"

He gave another nod but it was apparent I wouldn't get many more of them.

"You were going to come in by the French windows without anyone knowing and have one last go at reasoning with Harper. Then you overheard his scrap with Tim and the chance was just too good to lose so you let him have it right there. The only trouble was that Miss Katie was watching from behind the bushes and you caught a glimpse of her before she got away. You followed her and got her cornered before she could get to the telephone. One more thing. I was right about the poisoning, wasn't I?"

The nod came but it was awfully slow.

"John McClure was your work too. I was supposed to be but I got a break. Right?"

Jolley stared up at us and there was something desperate about him. He waited a long terrible moment and then with his last effort said, "Right," almost inaudibly and that was all for Hillman Jolley.

64

In the excitement no one had noticed the wound in my side. The bullet had hit me when my coat was open and the bleeding had not been very visible while I was kneeling by Hillman Jolley. When I got up there was a pool of it on the floor, and the right leg of my trousers was soaked. It ran down to my shoe and when I took a step I felt like I was standing in a bucket of mush. The pain was pretty bad, and I leaned against the table. The doctor stared at the floor where I had been, and then looked at me and said: "Good God Almighty! Let's have a look. Why didn't you say something?"

I didn't feel any too good at all. I started going down like a slow-motion picture, but I hung on to the table for dear life and got down on the floor without a bump. I felt like the Thirteenth Chapter of First Corinthians where it talks about seeing things through a glass darkly instead of face to face. Janet said, "Oh, my dear," in a small voice and sat down on the floor and took my head in her lap. If the doctor enjoyed tearing people's clothes, he was certainly having a field day.

My eyelids were very very heavy, but I got them open and looked at nobody in particular and said: "Look out or I'll bleed on you."

"Go right ahead," said the doctor. He seemed more cheerful about it than I would have been.

Things did not hurt nearly so badly now. I heard the doctor say: "Pretty deep, but just flesh as far as I can tell. Loss of blood is about all. Probably could use a transfusion." He took me by the face somewhere and gave me a pinch and said: "Hey, wake up! You don't by any chance know what kind of blood you have, do you?"

"Red," I answered.

The doctor chuckled: "Sassy little mutt, isn't he? All right, we'll find out as soon as we get to the hospital."

I wanted to go to sleep more than anything, but I had a thought and grabbed hold of it and pulled myself back out of the darkness long enough to say: "Let Tim out of jail. Tell Ruth to go to the bank and bring everything she finds in the box straight to me."

Then I went sliding down on a long slick inclined plane and down into a dark hole that had no bottom. I felt as if my pants were coming off, and even in my dreams the embarrassment made me pop out in a cold sweat. The hole was black and chilly. That's all I remember.

65

"...partly unconscious but mostly asleep, if you ask me. Take away the hole in his side and a double handful of bruises, contusions and lacerations and he's sound as a nut. He'll wake up when he gets hungry enough." I kept my eyes closed. The smell was definitely a hospital smell. Except for a very sore place in my right side and a hollow feeling where steak and potatoes ought to be, I felt all right. The thought of steak and potatoes made me a little giddy. I heard a door close and took a little peep to see what was going on.

The room was full of flowers. Great big ones and little bitty ones with clouds of fern leaves or whatever you call them. Janet was in a rocking chair by the window smoking a cigarette. Ruth was in a straight chair with a book open on her knees but the book was upside down so I didn't think she was bothering it much. The same curvy little nurse was pulling flowers out of vases and snipping off the bottom of the stems and putting them back in again. None of them were looking at me and I enjoyed watching them. My back was tired like you get when you've been in bed too long, but I didn't know whether I ought to move without help or not. I wanted a steak the worst kind of way—very big and very thick, with mushrooms and gravy and probably hot rolls and shoestring potatoes and head lettuce with Roquefort cheese. After a while I said: "It's either heaven or a harem, I don't care which. Could I have a cigarette?"

There was a great flurry and bustle but I don't remember all of the things that were said. Janet tried to get me a cigarette, but she shook all over and the package fell on the floor. I finally got one and Ruth lit it and the nurse blew out the match to keep it from burning off two or three fingers. Then the nurse's stiff uniform swished and her rubber-soled shoes padded out into the hall and pretty soon the doctor came in like the first breath of spring.

"Well," he said heartily, "you *have* been living the life of Riley.[*] How goes it?"

"If you get these women out of here and help me get my pants on, I'll feel a lot better. Then get a pencil and a piece of paper and start writing down about half of the things I want to eat and call a restaurant and let them in on the secret. Don't tell me I can't eat or I'll have a relapse."

"Anything you want. You ran a little fever for a while but you've got a constitution with twenty-two amendments and when your side has had a little more time to heal, we'll let you out of here. Forget about the pants. You'll be with us a little while longer and I don't trust you."

Janet was holding one of my hands in both of hers and she was as starry-eyed as a girl on her first date. "How do you feel?" she asked.

"Hungry."

"Love me?"

"Right in front of all of these people?"

"I love you."

I looked around the room and the rest of them were still there and I said: "When your fever goes down, you'll get over it. What day of the week is it?"

---

[*]The source of the phrase—meaning "living in luxury"—is unknown, though it became popular during World War I. "Riley" was a proverbial figure in Irish ballads of the nineteenth century, but luxury was not associated with the figure.

"Don't change the subject," she said.

"Hell, woman, this is so sudden. Don't rush me. I've got a girlish modesty about these things and besides they shouldn't be discussed on an empty stomach."

"You can have a bank account of your own with fifty or a hundred thousand dollars in it for weekends and trifles, just like you said."

I looked at her and said: "You have a very musical voice when you talk like that. You are also strangely attractive. You don't look like you've slept for two or three days and after all, I count on living quite a while yet. Give me a kiss and then run along and get some rest."

She patted my hand and said: "Swell. I'll attend to the food myself."

I think she was glad she had something to do. She got her pocketbook, found a pencil and piece of paper, wrote down all the things I said I wanted and probably added some ideas of her own. When she was gone I looked at Ruth. "Tim out of jail?"

"Yes, they let him out right away. The sheriff and the chief of police have been calling every few hours. They don't quite understand it all even yet and the newspapers are after them and they don't know what to say. They're outside now."

"OK, bring them in."

The chief was a little embarrassed but his attitude had changed completely. He pulled up a chair and said, "Hi, Sport. How's every little thing?"

The sheriff stood behind him and studied me carefully.

"There ain't anything wrong with him. Let's get down to business. The reporters are beginning to think we don't know anything about this case and I don't want them to find out how right they are."

"You got most of the story from Jolley," I said. "There isn't much to tell. He got himself hired as the accountant for Harper Products Company in '38. He was ambitious and greedy and he couldn't keep his shirt on. He wanted to get rich quick. The company had staggered through the depression but had been a little slow on the pickup and the stock was still selling at a pretty low figure. Business was good and the earnings for '38 were going to bring the price up sure. He was a smooth-talking buzzard and smart as a whip and he was able to convince old Harper that the accounting system was all wrong and by the time he got through, a good year looked pretty bad. That was fine. The stock dropped a few notches. Jolley saw to it that the right sort of talk got around where it would do the most good and the stock fell a little more. He persuaded Harper that the thing to do was to take the cash on hand and pay off as much of the indebtedness as possible so that the cash position was always weak and it looked as if the banks were cracking down. He stepped up the depreciation rate and that cut the profits even more."

"How was he going to make money that way?" asked the sheriff.

"He wasn't. He was going to use his scheme to get the price down and buy up all the stock he could get. He knew the government wouldn't swallow his cost and depreciation figures so when the income tax people got around to bearing down on the tax returns, he was going to back up and let them figure the profits their own way. As soon as the news got out everybody would know the corporation was something of a gold mine, whereupon the stock would go up to what it ought to be and he would be wading in four leaf clovers. By that time he wouldn't care whether he was an accountant or not and the whole thing had been handled so adroitly that he didn't think they could pin anything on him except ignorance and maybe not even that."

"But something went wrong?"

"Everything went wrong at the wrong time. The stock was down as far as he thought it would go so he took every nickel he had and bought on margin. The income tax people performed on schedule but instead of giving up, old Harper set his teeth and wanted to scrap about it. Scrapping with the government takes time and the first part of it isn't public, so there was Jolley with his tongue hanging out and the brokers getting nervous and no more credit. Every time the stock went off a point he nearly had a hemorrhage. He got desperate and thought with Harper out of the way he could persuade the Board of Directors to give up, pay off and open the doors to fairyland. He was so desperate he lost all his shrewdness and couldn't see that Harper's death would knock the bottom out of the stock and bring his house of cards about his ears. When the stock went down five points the day after Harper's death, he was fit to be tied. He had built up a pretty good case with Janet and he probably could have done all right if he had taken his time, but the brokers were breathing down his neck and he took a chance and proposed that they get married immediately. Everything looked fine and he thought he had gotten away with it, but she wouldn't marry him right away. My guess is he thought he had Janet eating out of his hand and he tried to get her to sign a note with him. That would have taken the pressure off for a while. Maybe he even asked for a big chunk of cash. Anyway she blew up and he backed off as fast as he could, still with the idea that she would get over it and marry him. Am I boring you?"

"Hell, no," said the chief. "My tongue's hanging out. I have been fighting reporters for two days telling them there were some angles and details we were cleaning up. They're waiting out there now."

"Well," I said, "there isn't much more to tell. He sneaked off and took a trip to the city and tried to get by with his creditors on the story that he was going to marry a skirt full of green-backs but after all, the money wasn't hers yet and it looked as if Mrs. Harper might go right on living. My guess is the prospects were a little too remote for the moneylending fraternity. Of course, Janet had some money of her own, but she had evidently heard her father or Jolley placing orders for the stock and she had climbed out on the limb herself so she was pretty well committed as far as her cash would go. Having gone as far as he had, Jolley couldn't stop. He hired Miles to get me and Janet out of the way and had himself tied up for good measure, thinking everybody would be fooled by a move like that. Miles wasn't supposed to tie him very tight and didn't. Miles is no Einstein and all he could think about was that he had climbed aboard the gravy train. He couldn't even see that he had stuck his head in a noose. After he had served his purpose he was far too dangerous to bother with, so Jolley let him have it and dashed home to take care of the poisoning job, although ostensibly to get help. That was the weakest part of his whole plan and maybe it wouldn't have been so weak if he hadn't been obliged to think it up on such short notice. He was pretty clever at that. He came in with his arm in a sling and we were supposed to accept his story that he exchanged some shots with Miles but lost him in the dark and thought the best thing to do was to grab the car and come after the law. I don't think it would have worked at best, but he didn't have a chance when I happened to stumble over Miles's gun and there wasn't a shot fired out of it. I'll take a guess that you found Miles with three neat holes in him from such close range that there were powder burns. Miles knew that Jolley was supposed to get loose and he met him down by the car as innocent as a little lamb."

"That's right," said the sheriff, "couldn't have been shot from over eighteen inches or two feet away. It had us wondering. Looked awfully funny."

The chief broke in. "Who was it saw him fiddling with the milk?"

"Nobody. I made that up. I suppose the sheriff has also told you I made up the milk bottle. Probably Miss Knight went out and got the milk, used it all up fixing Mrs. Harper's medicine, emptied the bottle, washed it and put it out, as a good nurse would do. Jolley thought he was backed into the corner and lost his head. I'm glad his aim wasn't any better. He saw a gun sticking in my belt and thought he would have a better chance to talk himself out of shooting me since the chief was inclined to think I was the boy in the woodpile* anyway. But he was afraid of the milk bottle more than anything and wasted a shot on it. That gave me just enough time to move and throw him off. I hated to shoot the guy but I wanted to live."

"Never mind about that. We already had the Coroner's inquest and the jury cleared you without leaving their seats."

I said: "That's all there is to it. Any more questions?"

"No, that'll cover it for now. We'll get you to write us out a statement for the file when you get out of the hospital."

When they were gone Ruth went to the dresser, took out a package and brought it to me.

"I had a little trouble but I finally convinced them my father and John McCall were one and the same. The sheriff was awfully nosey, but I told him that it was a private affair. I looked at all the stuff myself and couldn't find a thing out of the ordinary so I finally let the sheriff look just to keep him satisfied. I don't know what you and Mr. Jolley were looking for but whatever it was, you were wrong."

I put my hand on the package but made no move to open it. I just looked at Ruth. Pretty soon tears came into her eyes and she said: "Yes, I know. I don't know how to thank you. Somehow you've got it all explained and I have a feeling you deliberately left out the real story. I would like to think you did it for me and Tim. Anyway we appreciate it. Tim and I are going to be married, you know. This certainly makes it a lot easier and after all, we'll be sort of kin to you. You may not know it but about half the blood in your veins used to be in Tim. When he found out his blood classification was the same as yours, he told them to take all they needed even if it was all he had."

"Don't thank me. Thank yourself. You're a swell kid and it

---

*Proverbially, a concealed fact or motive. The original phrase used a racist term in place of "boy."

was obvious from the first that you were head over heels in love with Tim. He's not a bad guy himself. And then there was Janet too. After all, it's something none of you are responsible for. Old man Harper knew it was going to cost several million dollars in extra inheritance taxes to handle it the way he did, but he went through it without a squawk and kept the thing covered up for half a lifetime. I couldn't see anything to be gained by dragging it all out into the open now when justice could be done another way. I guess they've opened Mrs. Harper's will, haven't they?"

"Yes, they opened that almost immediately to see if it would have any bearing on the case. I won't pretend I understand but there it was, dividing the estate between Janet and Tim and doing it so beautifully with a lot of talk about love, affection and gratitude for John McClure as the oldest and most trusted employee and all that sort of thing that it seems to have gotten by. Mr. Harper always was fond of Father and Tim and showed it and no one in town seems inclined to look for a seamy side. I guess the story has been covered up so long that most people have even forgotten Tim was adopted. I definitely don't understand about the wills. I remember you prepared two of them but Miss Knight says only one was executed."

"That's right. I knew if my thinking was straight Mrs. Harper was in considerable danger. I had guards posted at the door in an effort to ensure her safety until I could figure the thing out. Jolley seemed the most likely, but I was stupid and I couldn't get around the fact he was in Overton the day before and came in on the train that didn't leave Overton until after both Harper and Miss Katie were murdered. By the time I heard about Janet's airplane, it was too late. Miles took care of both of us while I was just starting back to town and by the time we got out of that damn cabin the work was done. It's funny how you can figure out the tough parts and trip on some little silly thing like that. I even came down from Louisville in a plane myself and should have been able to figure, but I checked with the airport and all chartered planes were accounted for and the private plane just never occurred to me. When I drew up the wills I was afraid something might happen to Mrs. Harper. Someone had listened in on my conference with her and knew there were sup-posed to be two of them. I drew them both just alike so that if anything happened, twenty-five years and a couple of million dollars would not be wasted. Mrs. Harper was smart. She read both wills and knew exactly what was on my mind and went right through with it. Jolley knew the first will was supposed to give everything to Janet and since he still had an idea she would eventually marry him, he saw a neat way to keep the whole thing in the family while he was getting himself out of his financial jam at the same time."

"Aren't you even going to look at these papers?"

"Yes, I guess so. You say there's nothing here?"

"Not as far as I can see. What was it supposed to be? I never have understood that either."

I squirmed around in the bed and my side didn't come apart as far as I could tell so I said: "Do you suppose there's anything wrong with putting a couple of pillows behind my back and let-ting me sit up for a while? Get me another cigarette while you're at it." It felt much better sitting up. The package was tied up in brown paper and when I opened it there was nothing but a gray ledger such as the drugstore down on the corner might use. The thing was full of neat meticulous entries in regular amounts cov-ering deposits and withdrawals beginning in May 1915. There wasn't a thing to identify where the money came from or where it went to. There were no loose papers. I examined the backs of the ledger carefully but couldn't find any evidence that they had been tampered with. I sat and stared at the thing.

"Your father was a careful man," I said. "He kept a strict account of every penny he got from Harper and he was careful to make the entries so that in the event of his death, this book wouldn't mean a thing to anyone who didn't know the facts.

Harper didn't know whether your father had been careful or not. He wanted to make sure that his secret didn't get out. His one big mistake was in offering you much too high a price for your stock. If he had offered to take it off your hands at the market or maybe a little better, the chances are you would have accepted his help and thought nothing of it, but he was so afraid the one scandal in his life would come out while he had to face it that he overplayed the thing and not only offered you something too good to be true, but made such a point of wanting to get all the records that naturally you got suspicious. Yet somehow I can't believe that this book was all he wanted to get his hands on. It doesn't quite ring true."

"You've had an idea all this time and you've been looking for something," said Ruth. "Jolley was looking for something too. He searched our house twice and it must have been just as hard for him to locate the lockbox at the bank as it was for us. William Jasper Harper also had something in his mind. What have you been looking for?"

"Maybe I'm wrong, but this is the way I have it figured out. Before he was married, William Jasper Harper had an affair with Catherine Murdoch. He was probably in love with her—a little school teacher up in the city whom he probably went off and spent weekends with. He was a big shot from a family that practically owned this town and controlled half of this end of the State. For generations the family had been presidents of this and that and directors of everything else and trustees of churches and colleges and patrons of the Red Cross and the children's hospital. Whether he ever intended to marry her, no one will ever know, but I guess he was young and hotheaded and thought he could postpone his problems. He wasn't going to be able to postpone them very long because little Catherine Murdoch got pregnant and he must have been worried to death. Then there's an explosion in the house one day and a fire, probably accidental. Katie is horribly burned and her sister, Phoebe, gets her to the hospital and then rushes her off by train to Louisville with a doctor in attendance. Maybe they were rushing to a specialist. Maybe not. I haven't had a chance to go over this part of it with Phoebe, but the adoption papers didn't say anything about a birth certificate and it sounds to me as if she was rushed out of town because they were afraid the baby was going to be born prematurely and if it was born in the hospital, there would have to be a birth certificate and people would find out about it and Katie Murdoch would never live it down. The baby was either born on the train or in a private residence in Louisville and the doctor probably listened to reason in the form of a sizable chunk of William Jasper Harper's bank account. Once he took the money and conveniently forgot what had happened, he couldn't bring up the subject later without confessing to his own professional misdoing."

"Well, where does that get us?" Ruth asked. "I'm a long way from following you."

"Well, Catherine Murdoch didn't die. She and Tim lived in Louisville. Probably not with Phoebe or I would have run across their trail when I was looking for her. Catherine was horribly disfigured and couldn't make a living any more and I guess they lived off Harper and were satisfied with the arrangement for a while until it must have occurred to them that as every year went by they would have a weaker and weaker case to present if Harper ever got the idea he wanted to get out from under. Furthermore if Harper died, they didn't know whether they could ever get anything from the estate to take care of Katie and Tim. So there must have been something put in writing. John McClure might have been satisfied to adopt Tim without any written guaranties but I can't figure Miss Katie giving him up unless she were absolutely sure that he would be provided for permanently.

"In the meantime, William Jasper Harper has got himself married to a blue blood. Before he did that he could have married Catherine Murdoch, burns and all, and things would have been bad enough, but once he was married and had a little girl of his own, he was in a worse predicament than ever. I don't suppose we'll ever know the truth about it but there are cases in the law books where a contract is made to prevent the institution of bastardy proceedings. That is a court proceeding for the purpose of proving the paternity of a child and forcing the father to support it. Such a contract is perfectly valid and can be enforced against the man's estate so long as it doesn't try to give everything to the illegitimate child to the exclusion of any natural children.

"Now look at it this way. William Jasper Harper makes a will at the same time the adoption is perfected. But it isn't the kind of will that Catherine Murdoch would have been satisfied with because it makes no provision at all for Tim but leaves everything to Mrs. Harper. We find that Mrs. Harper made a will at the same time leaving everything to her husband. It can't mean but one thing. Harper wanted to keep scandal away from his family as long as he could, even in the event of his own death. So he makes a clean breast of it to his wife and she gets in on the agreement. They each make wills leaving everything to each other and when one of them dies the other is to make a will providing for Tim and Janet on an equal basis. This postpones the evil day until both of them are dead which is all they can hope for. If the survivor fails to make the kind of will provided for in the agreement, the agreement itself can be produced and enforced so that the same object is achieved. This means that Tim is going to be taken care of as long as that contract is in writing and nobody loses it. Now do you begin to get the idea?"

"I think I do. But does a contract like that have to be in writing? Couldn't the people who were there prove it by their testimony?"

"Yes, they could," I told her, "but in order to testify, my little chickabiddy, you have to be alive. Hillman Jolley didn't know whether there was an agreement in writing or not, but either way he had to close the mouths of all the witnesses—at least all of whom he knew about. You see, as accountant for Harper Products Company, he probably advised with William Jasper Harper about personal income tax matters and returns as well as those of the company. He stumbled on to some of the essential facts and drew some pretty intelligent conclusions and inferences but whether he picked up his information from Harper's personal records or whether he figured them out from observing the way John McClure and his family lived, probably we'll never know. At any rate, he was feeling around in the dark. When I was questioning him just before his death, I gathered that he didn't know about the Murdoch girls and had never identified Miss Katie as being Tim's mother. From the facts before him, he must have figured that Harper himself and probably his wife were parties to the agreement. Of course, John McClure had to be a party since he was going to assume the burden of caring for Tim. It seems almost certain that your mother knew about it too, because you can hardly adopt someone without your wife knowing a good deal about it. If there were any other parties or witnesses, Jolley could only hope that they had disappeared completely or were dead. He didn't know who the mother was and he didn't know where to start looking for her. Old Harper must have been pretty careful not to have any such information lying around, since he proceeded with extraordinary care in every other respect.

"Now we can go on from there. Your mother has been dead for a number of years, which eliminates one of his problems. He accounts for your father and no one would ever have suspected if he hadn't tried the same thing on me and failed. He would probably have figured out some very inconspicuous way of removing Mr. and Mrs. Harper from the picture, except that his financial difficulties on the stock transaction forced his hand and he had to act on the spur of the moment or lose everything he had spent three years working for. Miss Katie would, I think, still be living but she showed up at the wrong place at the most unfortunate time. She kept a sharp watch on you and Tim and it looks like somehow she found out that Tim was going out to have a showdown with Harper so she tagged along to make sure he wasn't mistreated."

Ruth interrupted and said: "She didn't find out somehow. She knew for a certainty. She was at our house when Tim got to discussing the thing and she did her best to sidetrack him. But Tim's got quite a temper and naturally he was curious about his own past. He flung out of the house determined to raise hell until he found out everything Harper knew. Miss Katie was frightfully upset and left the house immediately. I guess she followed Tim out there."

"That fits," I observed. "Tim came out through the French windows and walked down the drive to where his car was parked on the street. He must have passed right by Miss Katie and probably she didn't speak up because she was afraid he would either resent her meddling or jump to the conclusion which suggested itself to me within twenty-four hours after I got to Harpersville. While she was waiting for Tim to get clear away from there, she notices Jolley and stays to see what is going on. The rest you know from what Jolley said himself, if you heard the story. He killed Harper, saw Miss Katie leave, followed her and murdered her before she could notify the police."

"You mentioned Phoebe Murdoch," said Ruth, "who's she?"

"Never mind. The story's over and the book's closed. You'll never have any trouble from her and the less you know about it the better."

Ruth went over to the window and stood and looked out for several minutes. Then she came back and stood by my bed again and looked down at me. "You know, Gil, it all seems like a nightmare. I guess Mr. Harper thought he was doing the right thing, or the easy thing, at the time, but when you stand in the way of the truth and try to keep secrets about people's lives, all you do is take a little trickle of trouble that would run off down the hill and be forgotten, and build it up behind a dam until the pressure gets too great and the dam breaks and everybody in the path of it is obliterated. Until a couple of weeks ago, life went on so quietly and happily and now we've all been caught in the maelstrom and those of us who have survived are tossed up on the banks to treat our wounds and get over them the best we can. It's been a terrible thing, but all we can do is put it behind us and try to start living again. I'm making my start right now and I'm going to look forward and not back and try to cover up the horror that we've all been through. I would like to think that Tim's secret is safe forever but your reasoning has been perfect and it looks as if there's bound to be a written contract somewhere that will bob up to haunt us tomorrow or next week or next month or maybe our children after us."

I took her hand and said: "No, I doubt it. Jolley couldn't find it. Harper didn't know where it was and we haven't been able to find it. Your father knew its importance and wouldn't have tucked it away any old place where it couldn't be found for Tim's protection. Of course, it's possible that with the passage of all these years the thing began to lose its significance to him. Tim has grown up and he's a big fellow with a bright mind, able to take care of himself and make his own way in the world. I wouldn't be surprised if your father didn't simply destroy the instrument, preferring to let Tim stand on his own feet rather than take the chance of having somebody discover the one thing which might hurt him in the eyes of his friends. I think we can assume that the written agreement is no longer in existence. Take my word for it and don't worry your pretty head."

She lit a cigarette for me and I took two or three drags in silence. At length she sighed and smiled at me and said: "Well, Janet will be coming back in a minute with something to eat and I expect you'll want to be alone with her. I don't know what to say to you so I won't try except that I want you to know that the door of our home will always be open and anything we ever have, or all of it, is yours for the taking and you mustn't even bother to ask."

She walked on out and closed the door. I waited until I was fairly certain she wouldn't be back for something she might have forgotten and then picked up the gray ledger again. Janet had left her pencil on the table by the bed. I took the ledger, opened it wide and then bent the covers back until they touched. That made the part of the book that connects the two covers stick out. I took the pencil and pushed around down in the hole and a piece of paper which had been rolled into a cylinder and squashed flat, fell out on the bed beside me. I opened it just long enough to tell that the search was at an end, then I struck a match, set fire to it and nursed the flame until every particle of it was destroyed.

I was glad it didn't take a minute longer. There was a great clattering of the elevator door and then a regular procession came into my room.

First, there was the nurse, with curves sticking out in every direction, as usual, and a table which she set up with a flourish. After that came a colored waiter with a big grin and an enormous tray which was simply hopping up and down with delicious smells. Janet brought up the rear with the color back in her cheeks again and her slightly horsey face transfigured by a gorgeous smile.

Janet had already paid for the meal and I let her tip the waiter without a murmur. I didn't know what the future was going to bring but if Janet had her way, I didn't want to start any bad habits.

The waiter and the nurse made a discreet withdrawal to positions prepared in advance and I saw that the table was set for two.

I didn't know what to say so I fell back on inanities and said brightly: "Well, I see you're eating with me."

"Yes," said Janet, "you might as well get used to it."

It was pretty awkward trying to eat sideways from the bed and I thought it would be a lot more convenient if my dinner had been on a tray, but I was beginning to get the idea that Janet was a very determined sort of creature and as long as she was paying for it, I thought it would be better to keep my damn mouth shut.

It was a glorious meal. When it was all gone and I had polished off my third cup of coffee, she said: "Happy?"

"I suppose I will be. Right now there's one thing that's worrying me. You gave me a few bad moments out at Sheely's and I want to know the truth. Either you take an awful long time in the bathroom or else you made a telephone call. If you made a telephone call, it doesn't escape me that about the right time elapsed and then someone was waiting outside and did his best to bend some of my skull bones."

"Well, I'll be damned," said Janet, "so that's the way you figured it."

"Well, all right. Did you or didn't you make a phone call?"

Janet Harper blushed and looked away and then she looked back at me and her eyes had a twinkle in them. "You really want to know?"

"I did a minute or two ago but I don't like the expression on your face and if it's all the same to you, we can skip it."

"You could have skipped it a couple of minutes ago but you have a nasty, suspicious mind and if you don't get an answer, you'll be consumed by the poison of curiosity for the rest of your life, so I'll tell you. I made a phone call but it wasn't the kind of call you thought it was. It made me madder than hell. I called to find out whether you can get a marriage license in the middle of the night and the county clerk's office wouldn't answer. I guess the telephone people are used to that sort of thing because some little bitch in the telephone exchange had the nerve to break in and call me Dearie and tell me I would have to be patient until morning."

ABOUT THE WAR

This is written at a time (March, 1943) when the aggression of the Axis nations seems to have been brought to a halt on every front. The Russians have regained much of the territory lost to Germany in the summer of 1942 and are hammering at Smolensk, although giving ground in the area around Kharkov and Belgorod. The British and Americans have backed Rommel against the sea in Tunisia and appear to be ready to move in. The Australians and the Americans have stopped the Japs in the Solomons and New Guinea. We are between rounds.

History holds the pen as the story of 1943 is written. In this year we will learn whether a weary and exhausted enemy can stalemate the rising might of our United Nations, or whether the hammer blows that are being prepared for him will be enough to crush, to demoralize, to disperse.

At best, we will have our hands full for a long time to come. Many of us who are not yet in uniform will be called into service, and we will be ready. Those of us who are not suitable for military or naval service, or who are required for the farms or production lines at home, will have to be ready, too—ready for more sacrifices, more work, harder work, more sorrow, even, and heartache.

But of this we may all be certain: That the things we love and live for will be preserved for our children, and their children after them; that they will enjoy these things because of us, and because of what we are doing; that the day will come when we can once again take up the instruments of peace, proud in the consciousness that we did not stumble or falter when the job was before us.*

—C. W. Grafton

---

*Unfortunately, the war wore on for more than two years, with tens of millions more dead, wounded, or displaced, not ending finally until Germany's unconditional surrender in May 1945 and Japan's surrender in August.

READING GROUP GUIDE

1. Why do you think Ruth McClure decided to get help from a lawyer from outside Harpersville?

2. Why do you think Gil Henry decided to take the case?

3. How does Gil's behavior with Ruth compare to what you'd expect from someone in the current year?

4. Is Tim McClure praiseworthy for his behavior?

5. What do you think about the behavior of Miss Katie? Nurse Knight?

6. Do you think William Harper's conduct over the years was morally correct? What about John McClure's?

7. How do you think Janet Harper should have behaved in the circumstances of her father's death?

8.   Was Alice Holt Harper blameworthy for what she did over the years? Or did she behave morally?

9.   What's your ultimate assessment of Gil Henry? A commendable guy? Too smart for his own good? Out for himself?

10. Did you deduce who was the murderer? How did you know?

FURTHER READING

Grafton, C. W. *The Rope Began to Hang the Butcher*. New York:
Farrar & Rinehart, 1944.
———. *Beyond a Reasonable Doubt*. New York: Farrar, Straus
& Giroux, 1950.

Baker, Robert A., and Michael T. Nietzel. *Private Eyes: One
Hundred and One Knights, A Survey of American Detective
Fiction, 1922–1984*. Bowling Green, OH: Bowling Green
State University Popular Press, 1985.
Geherin, David. *The American Private Eye: The Image in Fiction*.
New York: Frederick Ungar Publishing Company, 1985.
Klinger, Leslie S. *Classic American Crime Fiction of the 1920s*.
New York: Pegasus Books, 2018.
Madden, David. *Tough Guy Writers of the Thirties*. Carbondale:
Southern Illinois University Press, 1968.
Van Dover, J. K. *Making the Detective Story American: Biggers,
Van Dine and Hammett and the Turning Point of the Genre,
1925–1930*. Jefferson, NC: McFarland & Company, 2010.

ABOUT THE AUTHOR

Cornelius Warren ("Chip") Grafton (June 16, 1909–January 31, 1982) was born and raised in China, where his parents were Presbyterian missionaries. He was educated in Clinton, South Carolina, studying law and journalism at Presbyterian College. In 1932, he married his childhood sweetheart, Vivian Boisseau Harnsberger, and they settled in Louisville, Kentucky, where he became a municipal bond attorney. They had two children, daughters Ann and Sue.

Vivian and Chip were both alcoholics, their daughter Sue recalled. While Chip was serving in the military during World War II (he served as a deception officer, working under Lieutenant-Colonel E. O. Hunter),* Vivian was a responsible mother; when Chip returned home in 1945, she deteriorated rapidly. Sue described her father as "the family's functioning alcoholic." She said he "downed two jiggers of whiskey and went to the office" every day.*

Sue also recalled that as a child, she spent a good deal of time reading mystery novels, an activity encouraged by her father, who kept the house filled with them. Vivian died in 1960, and Grafton

---

*Quoted in Natalie Hevener Kaufman and Carol McGinnis Kay, *"G" Is for Grafton: The World of Kinsey Millhone* (New York: Henry Holt and Company, 1997).

married Lillian Fleischer, who was nine years younger than him.* Lillian survived Chip by seven years, and they are buried together in the Zachary Taylor National Cemetery in Louisville.

C. W. Grafton wrote four books, the present volume (1943); *The Rope Began to Hang the Butcher* (1944), also featuring Gil Henry; a non-mystery novel, *My Name Is Christopher Nagel* (1947); and another work of crime fiction, the highly regarded *Beyond a Reasonable Doubt* (1951). The latter is about a young lawyer who commits a murder and then, using his legal skills, tries to avoid conviction.

In an interview, Sue called her father "probably the greatest influence in my decision to write mystery novels because he was always so passionate about the genre itself... The titles of his projected eight-book series are based on an English nursery rhyme... I have the partial manuscript of the third novel, 'The Butcher Began to Kill the Ox,' which he never finished."[†] In a short memoir of her father,[‡] she recalled that he set aside his writing career when he realized that he couldn't support his family by writing. He planned to take writing up again when he retired at age 75. Sadly, he died at age 72.

William L. DeAndrea, in his monumental *Encyclopedia Mysteriosa*, observes, "Time and Fate have arranged things so that C. W. Grafton's greatest fame in the mystery world will forever be that he is the father of Sue Grafton, but his own contributions to the genre should not be ignored."[§]

---

*There is a "Lillian" mentioned in the dedication to Grafton's second novel as working in Grafton's law office—the same woman?

†Brandy McDonnell, "Sue Grafton sees mystery behind ABCs; Author to visit city," *Daily Oklahoman*, April 15, 2007.

‡Sue Grafton, "Legacy," *Chicken Soup for the Soul: The Wisdom of Dads* (Cos Cob, CT: Chicken Soup for the Soul Publishing, 2008), 218–22.

§William L. DeAndrea, *Encyclopedia Mysteriosa: A Comprehensive Guide to the Art of Detection in Print, Film, Radio, and Television* (New York: Prentice Hall General Reference, 1994), 140. It is ironic that the other major surveys, *Encyclopedia of Mystery and Detection* by Otto Penzler and Chris Steinbrunner, and Rosemary Herbert's *Oxford Companion to Crime and Mystery Writing*, do ignore Grafton. His three books are mentioned kindly, however, in *A Catalogue of Crime* by Jacques Barzun and Wendell Hertig Taylor.

THAT AFFAIR NEXT DOOR

The first book in an exciting new classic mystery series created in partnership with the Library of Congress, *That Affair Next Door* follows Miss Amelia Butterworth, an inquisitive single woman who becomes involved in a murder investigation after the woman next door to her turns up dead.

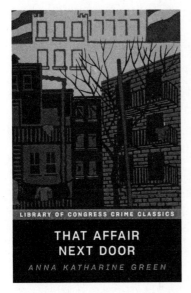

LIBRARY OF CONGRESS CRIME CLASSICS

THAT AFFAIR NEXT DOOR

ANNA KATHARINE GREEN

Miss Amelia Butterworth, an admirable woman in her fifties, is an observer of human nature. Such an observation is made late one evening when Miss Butterworth notices a man and woman enter the supposedly empty house next door. Looking out from her window, she notices the man leave the house some time later, but not the woman. The next morning Miss Butterworth's curiosity gets the better of her, but when her knocking at the door is met with silence, she calls on the police.

When she convinces the officer to enter the house, they are greeted by a shocking scene; they find the woman dead, crushed under a cabinet. Though Detective Ebenezer Gryce leads the murder investigation, Miss Butterworth does her own sleuthing to try to solve the murder.

"Cleverly plotted mystery... This inaugural volume in the Library of Congress Crime Classics series, featuring the first woman sleuth in a series, is a must for genre buffs."

—*Publishers Weekly*, Starred Review

For more Library of Congress Crime Classics, visit:
sourcebooks.com